A GOOD ENOUGH MOTHER

SHEILA NORTON

Sheila Norton

B
Boldwood

First published in Great Britain in 2024 by Boldwood Books Ltd.

Copyright © Sheila Norton, 2024

Cover Design by Colin Thomas

Cover Photography: Colin Thomas

The moral right of Sheila Norton to be identified as the author of this work has been asserted in accordance with the Copyright, Designs and Patents Act 1988.

This book is a work of fiction and, except in the case of historical fact, any resemblance to actual persons, living or dead, is purely coincidental.

Every effort has been made to obtain the necessary permissions with reference to copyright material, both illustrative and quoted. We apologise for any omissions in this respect and will be pleased to make the appropriate acknowledgements in any future edition.

A CIP catalogue record for this book is available from the British Library.

Paperback ISBN 978-1-78513-661-0

Large Print ISBN 978-1-78513-657-3

Hardback ISBN 978-1-78513-656-6

Ebook ISBN 978-1-78513-654-2

Kindle ISBN 978-1-78513-655-9

Audio CD ISBN 978-1-78513-662-7

MP3 CD ISBN 978-1-78513-659-7

Digital audio download ISBN 978-1-78513-653-5

Boldwood Books Ltd
23 Bowerdean Street
London SW6 3TN
www.boldwoodbooks.com

For my husband and family, with thanks as always, for all the love and support.

1

It's bitterly cold, the sort of cold that takes your breath away, and I'm gasping as I run from the bus stop to my daughter's school. I'm not late today – not quite – but it seems that every other reception class parent is already waiting at the classroom door when I arrive. The door opens dead on the dot of three-fifteen and I clutch my side, panting, as the teacher begins to let out one child at a time. For once, Mia doesn't have to be kept back in the classroom because I'm not there. It's difficult to get away from work at exactly at two-forty-five to make it here in time, and the buses aren't reliable. Mia goes to the after-school club two days a week (as well as going to the breakfast club) but I couldn't get a place for her every day, so I've had to drop some of the hours I worked at the shop when she used to be at nursery all day. Fortunately Margaret, my boss, the elderly owner of Chapters Bookshop, is understanding, but part-time jobs are hard to find and I can't afford to let her down.

Mia's always tired when she comes out of school. It's a long day for a four-year-old, even on days like this, when she's not staying for the extra couple of hours. It was different, somehow, at nursery, where the emphasis was just on play, and there was always a rest time.

We're going to the nursery now, to pick up her baby brother. Archie's quite happy to be left there every day – so far. It's still quite a new experience for him. He started there when my maternity leave finished when he was a year old, in November, and we're only in January now.

'When can we go home?' Mia's whining now, dragging her feet as we walk down the main road to the nursery.

'As soon as we've got Archie.'

She sighs and smothers a yawn. She never tells me much about what she's been doing at school, but her teacher says she's fine, that she mixes all right with the other children and does whatever she's asked to do without any apparent problems, so I don't badger Mia for information. She just wants to relax when she's at home.

Archie, on the other hand, is full of beans when we arrive at the nursery. He toddles a couple of steps across the room to me, smiling and shouting some of his few understandable words before tumbling down abruptly on his padded bottom and laughing.

'Mumma!' he calls out, holding out his arms to be lifted up. 'Hup-up!'

I carry him outside and put him in his buggy. Mia's complaining that her legs ache as we start the walk home, and I try to distract her with the promise of a drink and biscuit when we're indoors. It's a short walk from here, and I'm at the bottom of the stairs up to my flat, just starting the process of folding the buggy, holding onto Archie's arm to stop him trying to crawl away, as Mia skips up the stairs, chanting, 'One, two, three, six, seven...' when a voice from behind me calls out breezily:

'Well, hello! You must be our upstairs neighbour. I wondered when I'd bump into you.'

I turn around and nearly drop the buggy, blinking in shock at this woman – who's the same sort of age, somewhere in her early fifties, I guess, and has the same short dark hair, round face and even the same sort of glasses, as my mum. Except that my mum died when she was around that age. It gives me such a jolt that for a moment I can't talk. I let go of Archie's arm and he starts, on all fours, to follow his sister up the stairs.

'Are you all right, love?' the woman asks as I now drop the buggy while rushing to grab hold of Archie. 'Can I help?'

'Sorry, no, I'm fine, sorry,' I gabble. 'Er... hello. It's nice to meet you. I'm Jess. I presume you've moved in at number one?'

The flat downstairs from mine has been empty for a few weeks. It's been a relief, to be honest, not to have to keep reminding the children not to shout, and telling Mia not to thump around on the floor. But it seems I now have a new neighbour.

'Yes, I'm Helen,' she says, and comes over to me, taking hold of the folded buggy. 'Nice to meet you, too, Jess. Go on, you take the baby, I'll carry the pushchair up for you.' She gives me a smile. 'It must be hard, going up and down the stairs with them both.'

'Oh, I've got used to it,' I say. 'But thank you, um – Helen.'

I'm still feeling flummoxed by her likeness to my mum. Perhaps it's just that she took me by surprise, coming up behind me like that, but when I turned around I thought for a minute it *was* Mum standing there. Ridiculous. She passed away when I was only fourteen – eight years ago now – and I'm not in the habit of imagining every middle-aged woman I see is her, come back to help me with the baby's buggy, for God's sake!

By now, Mia is at the top of the stairs, kicking the front door in her impatience to get inside, and Archie, who's still in my arms, miffed at being stopped in his attempt to crawl up, is red in the face and yelling. I jiggle him as we go up, but he's wriggling to get down, shouting in frustration.

'Oh dear,' says Helen, close behind me. 'Are you tired, little one?'

He stops yelling with a surprised hiccup and stares at her. We're at the top of the stairs now and I put him down, searching in my coat pocket for my key, at the same time telling Mia to stop kicking the door. She pouts and – just for something to do in her impatience while I'm getting out the key – pinches Archie's nose.

'Mia, why did you do that?' I demand crossly as he promptly lets out another scream. He'll carry on now, I think grimly, until I've given him something to eat and drink to pacify him. But, just as I finally manage to open the front door, he stops wailing and gives a little chuckle. I look around and see Helen playing peek-a-boo with him behind her hands. He laughs again and Mia looks round too, joining in the laughter.

'Archie likes that,' she informs Helen. 'It always makes him laugh.'

'That's good,' Helen says. She smiles at me. 'It's hard when they're this age, isn't it? They haven't got the words to tell you what's bothering them.'

I feel like saying it's perfectly clear what's bothering Archie – his sister pinched him – but it's nice of her to be so friendly and helpful, so I just agree and thank her.

'No problem at all,' she says. 'Have a nice evening, Jess.'

* * *

I don't see Helen again until the end of the week. Fridays are one of the days that Mia stays for after-school club, so I pick up Archie later from nursery too, and frankly, we've all had enough by the time we get home. Tempers are short, and I don't just mean the kids'. We're probably making more noise than usual – Mia whining that she's tired, Archie grizzling, and me snapping at both of them to give me a minute, I'll have the key in the door in *just one minute* if they would both just *for God's sake, stop crying.*

'Hello?' a voice calls up the stairs. 'Oh – it's you, Jess. Sorry. I heard some commotion outside and thought I'd just better check... No, no, don't apologise, love, I know what it's like, they're tired, aren't they? Go on, yes, get them both inside in the warm. It's so cold out, isn't it? Poor things, you must all be frozen. I won't keep you.'

'Thanks,' I say. And I'm just opening the door when she adds:

'I wondered if you'd like to come and have coffee with me tomorrow morning – unless you work Saturdays? Just to get to know each other a little? With the children, of course – and your other half too, if he's here – my husband will be around.'

'Oh. There's no other half, actually,' I say all in a rush, as if I'm embarrassed about it, which I'm not, actually. 'But, um, thank you, that would be nice but I don't know... I mean, the kids can be really noisy and, well, you know...'

I'm trying, clumsily, to warn her that they'll probably spill their drinks, drop crumbs, break things, make a fuss, cry, and generally cause havoc, but Helen just waves this aside, laughing.

'Oh, I'm not so old that I've forgotten what it's like having little ones around. I love children, Jess. I'll find some crayons and paper for them or something to amuse them, don't worry. It'll be nice to see you all.'

I don't feel particularly reassured by the thought of my two little hooligans being let loose with crayons in someone else's flat. And while, on this second acquaintance, Helen doesn't look quite as much like my mum as I first thought, there's still enough of a resemblance, even in the way she smiles and the things she says, to make me feel a strange yearning to spend time with her. Perhaps I'm being silly; the lack of anyone to act as a grandparent figure to my kids hasn't bothered me up to now, but suddenly the realisation of Mum missing out on being a grandma to Mia and Archie makes me ache inside. I suspect Helen would be offended to know I'm mentally labelling her as grandmother material – she's probably barely old enough. And I haven't even got to know her yet. But even so, I tell her yes, it would be lovely to come for coffee tomorrow morning. I'll just have to bring the kids home if they start causing trouble!

* * *

On Friday evenings I occasionally have a couple of my friends round for a catch-up. It's, frankly, what keeps me sane. I don't really have any 'mum' friends; I haven't had time to get to know any of the other parents at the school – it's always just a quick 'hello' at pick-up and drop-off times, as I'm often the last one there. And I'm conscious of the fact that most of them are probably quite a bit older than me. I'm not saying that's a problem; it's what happens when you have your children very young, but they all seem to know each other or at least be at ease in each other's company. My own friends are like me, in their early twenties, so we have that in common, even if – these days – not a lot else. Oh, we laugh at the same things, we like the same music, watch the same movies, but I'm the odd one out, the one who doesn't go to bars or clubs, doesn't have boyfriends (or sex). Or fun. Or, really, a life – not according to them, although they do say it sympathetically, and they do try to cheer me up. Sometimes I need cheering up, but I don't admit it. I tell them I'm fine; I love my life. And it's true, most of the time. Some of the time. Well, I do love my kids, that's the thing, the only thing that matters.

Do I sound a bit defensive? Probably. Do my friends always manage to cheer me up? Yes, they do! We lark around, laugh a lot, they usually bring a bottle of wine, although I never dare drink much of it in case the kids need me in the night. And we sometimes carpet-dance like idiots, and it reminds me of the days before I met Callum, when I was free, like they are, to do what I wanted, when life was all about having fun. I was the bad girl, then, the one who was eight months pregnant when I left school. I thought I was a rebel. How ironic that feels, now.

I tell the girls, this evening, about my invitation to coffee with Helen tomorrow.

'She's probably lonely,' says Jules.

'No, she's got a husband, apparently. I haven't met him yet. But she says she likes children. She makes Mia and Archie laugh.'

I can't expect them to understand the importance of this.

'She reminds me of my mum,' I add quietly, and then wish I hadn't, as it kills the conversation stone dead. They all look at each other awkwardly – apart from Lucy, who was my best friend at school, and gets me far more than the others do. She looks at me quietly for a minute and then just reaches out and squeezes my hand.

'It'll be nice for you to have a friend here in the flats,' she says with a smile.

'Get her to babysit, if she likes kids so much!' Miranda puts in, laughing. 'Then you can come out with us sometime.'

I shake my head. 'I haven't even got the energy,' I tell her. 'And I don't want anyone else looking after my kids.' She raises her eyebrows at me and I just shrug. 'You wouldn't understand,' I say.

Five minutes later, Archie starts crying. And suddenly, it's time for the girls to leave. The bars in the town centre are calling. And I'm alone in the bedroom with my son, soothing him back to sleep. Of course they can't understand. How could they?

2

I don't work on Saturdays; I'm lucky that Margaret's so understanding. Although she's about seventy, she still works in the shop herself – well, she supervises – and as well as Tariq who's the full-time manager, they have a student, a girl called Emma, who covers weekends. I've only met Emma when I've popped into the shop if I'm shopping in town. She's about two or three years younger than me but our lives are so different, we could be from different planets. She's doing what I thought, at one time, I might do: a degree in English Literature, which is why she likes working in the bookshop. She wants to be a journalist when she graduates, or maybe an English teacher, the sort of jobs my dad wanted for me, until I let him down.

I don't work weekends, and Saturdays are normally my day for having a clean of the flat and then going food shopping, which is never much fun with the two kids. But today, at least, I'm doing something different. The housework is little more than a quick run over with the Hoover, and by ten o'clock I'm ready, with the children clean and as quietly behaved as I can manage, to go for coffee with my new neighbours.

'Come in, love,' says Helen as she opens the door to me, smiling widely. She laughs as Mia walks straight in and immediately begins to tell her the name of the toy elephant she's cuddling – Ellie, her favourite. 'Go through to the living room,' she goes on. 'I've got the kettle on. Tea or coffee?'

'Coffee would be great, thanks,' I say. 'White please, no sugar. Oh!' I add as I almost bump into a tall man with sandy-coloured hair who's come out of the living room to greet us. 'Hello. Er... I'm Jess, and this is—'

'Mia and Archie, I believe?' he says, smiling at us all. 'Helen's told me all about you. Pleased to meet you all! I'm Robert.'

'Nice to meet you, too, Robert,' I say.

He seems as friendly as his wife. I start to relax a little, but I'm still watching the children like a hawk. The carpet looks new and is a lovely shade of cream. There's probably at least a 50 per cent chance of Archie being sick on it or Mia spilling something.

'What can I get the children to drink?' Helen calls from the kitchen just as I'm thinking this.

'Just water for Mia, please,' I call back, before Mia can get the chance to utter the word 'squash'. 'And I've brought Archie some water in his sippy cup.'

'Very sensible; water's much healthier for them than all those sugary drinks, isn't it?' Helen says as she comes in, bearing a tray which she puts down on a coffee table in the middle of the room. 'There are biscuits on the tray – can they have one? And would you like to do some drawing while we talk to Mummy?' she asks Mia. 'I've got crayons—'

'Oh, I brought her Lego with me,' I say, indicating the box I've put down beside me.

'I want to do crayons,' Mia says firmly. 'So does Archie. Can I have a chocolate biscuit, Mummy?' she adds, eyeing them eagerly.

'Um, well, I think a plain one would be—'

'It's fine, I've got wet wipes for their fingers.' Helen seems to have thought of everything. 'And the crayons are those non-staining ones.'

'I hope you didn't buy them specially?' I smile. 'Have you got children yourselves?'

'Grown up,' she says abruptly, in a tone that makes me wary of asking any more questions. Perhaps they don't get on. I wonder if that's how my father answers anyone who asks him the same thing.

Once Mia's had her biscuit, and Archie – held firmly on my lap – has eaten half of one, and had his hands and face thoroughly wiped, Helen lays two giant pads of paper on the floor, scatters the crayons on a tray, and for a little while there's peace, although I'm ready to jump up at any moment if Archie gets up or crawls off with a crayon in his hand. I don't care how non-stain they might be.

'So, who looks after these two while you're at work?' Helen asks.

'Mia's at school; she started in September.' I smile at her surprised expression. 'She's four and a half now. But in a way, it's more difficult than when she used to be at nursery, like Archie is. I mean, it saves me money, of course, but I still have to pay for breakfast club and after-school club, and then there's all the school holidays—'

'Of course. It must be very difficult – on your own.'

She sounds sympathetic, but I can't help it, I always get a bit defensive when people say those words: *on your own*. I know it's because of my dad's attitude, and not everyone is like him, thank God. But nevertheless, to my ears it always sounds critical.

'It's better than being with the wrong person,' I say.

'Oh, definitely!' she says at once.

'I left their father,' I continue. Again, I know it's perhaps perverse of me, but I always like to make this clear. I don't want to be thought of by anyone as a poor abandoned woman. But I also can't spell out, in front of Mia's flapping ears, the reasons why I left Callum. 'It was... the only choice, as far as I was concerned.'

I actually left him when I was pregnant with Archie, and thank God I did. But I can't deny life's been difficult since, for me and for the children. Especially for Mia.

'Good for you,' says Robert.

I look round at him in surprise. He's nodding and smiling at me in approval.

'Thank you,' I say. 'Unfortunately, my dad didn't see it that way. He barely speaks to me now. But then again, he'd already made it clear he was disappointed – no, more like disgusted – with me, for getting pregnant at seventeen.'

'Oh dear,' Helen says. 'That must be very hard for you. But surely your mum—'

'I haven't got a mum any more.'

'Oh dear,' she says again, looking distressed now. 'I'm so sorry.'

I have to take a moment before I can respond.

'Thank you. It was... tough, losing her. I was only fourteen. I kind of went off the rails a bit, afterwards. I should have done well at school. I was, you know, one of the bright ones. In all the top streams. Supposed to be getting good A-levels and going to uni. But instead... well, here I am, a single mum with two kids, working in a shop. No wonder my dad's disappointed, really.'

'No,' Robert says. 'He should be proud of you, if you ask me. Working and bringing up two lovely children on your own.'

'Yes,' agrees Helen. 'It's hard work, and without even having parents to support you.' She shakes her head, pauses, and then goes on. 'What kind of shop do you work in?'

'The bookshop in town. Chapters.'

'I don't know it yet,' she says. 'We've moved here from London, so we've still got to get to know the area. Do you enjoy working there?'

'Yes.' I smile. I could do worse, I know that; it's a nice job, even though the pay isn't that great. But with the extra I get in universal credit, and the bit of child maintenance I've been able to squeeze out of Callum, I just about get by. I sigh, and add, 'Well, I would enjoy it, if I wasn't always on edge, wondering if these two are OK, and whether the bus will be on time for me to get back to Mia's school at three-fifteen. I could only get her a place at the after-school club for Wednesdays and Fridays. I'm hoping next year I'll be able to—'

'I could always help,' Helen says. 'If ever you're running late, or if there's any problem, I'd be happy to mind the children. Look at them, they're no trouble, are they?'

'They're not always like this,' I reply, laughing. They're both still engrossed in their crayoning, Mia having already completed two drawings, one of a house, the other of something with four legs and a head that could possibly be an elephant, and Archie concentrating on scribbling hard, in circles, in every colour crayon, sometimes one in each hand. 'They can be awful. I wouldn't inflict them on you! And anyway, I... sorry, I shouldn't presume, but I guess you go to work yourselves.'

I mean, they're surely not old enough to be retired. And if they were wealthy enough not to have to work, they wouldn't be living here, in one of these flats, would they?

'I'm a delivery driver,' Robert says. 'But I start work very early – when everyone's asleep – and I'm home by ten, most days.'

'And I'm... off work, at the moment,' Helen says, in a tone of voice that – as with the mention of the grown-up children – prevents me from asking any further questions. 'So, really, we have plenty of time to ourselves, and the odd bit of help, if you need it, wouldn't be any trouble at all.'

'That's really kind,' I say, feeling awkward now. I don't even know them properly yet, so there's no way I'd take them up on the offer to babysit for me. 'But honestly, I manage fine.'

'I'm sure you do,' says Robert calmly.

'Thank you.' I look back at the kids now, just in time to see Archie struggle to his feet, a red crayon still clutched in his chubby little fist, and totter his unsteady wide-legged gait towards me. I jump up and just manage to grab him before he overbalances. 'He's still not walking terribly well,' I apologise as I prise the crayon off him. 'He's better off crawling, really, but, well—'

'His ambition exceeds his capability?' Robert suggests, and I laugh.

'Yes, something like that!'

I like him. I like them both. They seem very kind. But I won't outstay my welcome on this first occasion. Archie's getting fidgety anyway, and I suspect from the nasty smell beginning to come from him that he needs changing.

'Come on, Mia,' I say, thanking Helen and Robert for the coffee and biscuits. 'We've got to go shopping. And I promised to take you to the park today, didn't I?'

It's freezing cold out and to be honest, I'd much rather stay indoors with a blanket over us and the TV on. But we're out of bread, vegetables, washing powder and... nearly everything else, too. At least the park will tire them out. And it's free entertainment.

* * *

It's even colder this evening. Archie's already in his cot, fast asleep, tired out from the excitement of the baby swings in the park. Mia's in her pyjamas, pink-skinned from a warm bath, and I've put the gas fire on while I read her a bedtime story. We've got a blanket over us both and her eyes are almost closed as she listens to the familiar lines. These are the times I love most, when she or Archie are snuggled up to me, their soft little bodies close to mine, my face resting on their silky hair. I've always read to both of them – even Archie will fall asleep in my arms as I turn the pages of one of his picture books, making up little stories from the pictures. Mia, too, likes it just as much when I make a story up as she does when I read one. She's caught the habit from me: she loves to concoct little stories of her own – they're often quite scary, too. I've heard that children do this to accustom them-selves to being frightened – to face their own fears. Maybe that's true but I prefer the happy stories she dreams up, about beautiful princesses living in castles. I don't suppose any mother wants to think about their child being scared.

As I finish tonight's story and carry Mia – now on the point of sleep – into her bedroom, I make the promise to myself that I make every evening when both children are tucked safe and secure in their beds: I promise that if I do nothing else in this life, I will make sure that nothing, and nobody, will ever hurt them.

3

January's been a long month, and I'm desperate for my month's wages to be paid into my account. I've been too worried about stretching the budget, paying the bills and feeding the kids to think about much else for the last week or so, and I've only seen Helen or Robert occasionally, as I'm rushing in or out on my way to or from work and school and the nursery. They seem very quiet, considering they're at home nearly all the time.

Today is one of the few occasions that I'll speak to my dad. It's his birthday, and however little he seems to care about me these days, however much he ignores me and has nothing to do with the children, I still feel this weird obligation to call him on his birthday, as well as on Christmas Day (when I'm never invited), and on the anniversary of Mum's passing. I don't really know why I put myself through it: it's always the same, it always makes me cry. And I hardly ever cry; I've worked hard at being as cheerful as possible, squaring my shoulders (as my mum used to say) and getting on with things. But talking to Dad somehow manages to break me.

I wait till both the children are asleep. And even now, I'm

giving myself a stern talking-to. *Why not forget it this year? Why feel any duty towards him? What's the point?* But I can't. Somehow I just can't stop myself from dialling his number.

'Hello,' he says in a bored, resigned tone.

'Happy birthday, Dad. How are you?'

'How do you think I am?' he snaps. 'The same as ever. What's the point of a birthday when there's nothing to celebrate?'

'Oh, come on.' I try to sound cheery. 'You've still got your health, a good job, a nice home.' He's silent, and suddenly I feel so frustrated, I'm almost angry. 'What do you think Mum would say if she could hear you talking like that?'

'Don't you dare bring your mother into this!' he retorts. 'She'd turn in her grave if she knew how *you've* ended up – how you've let me down, let *her* down! Living in squalor with your two brats, when you should have been—'

I end the call, cutting him off.

I'm shaking. At least, for once, I'm not crying – I'm too angry. How dare he call his grandchildren *brats*? He's never even met them! How dare he say I'm living in squalor, just because I'm in a poky little rental flat – which I'm lucky to have, and he's never even seen – and wouldn't you think, if he really thought things were that bad for me, his only child, he'd have done something, anything, *anything*, to help me? He's a bank manager, he lives on his own, in a big detached house, drives a big fancy car, and of course he's lonely, I get that, but that's his own fault. I don't understand him, I really don't. I know he's disappointed in me – he's told me that often enough, together with accusing me of being useless, not fit to raise children, even though he knows nothing whatsoever about what kind of mother I am. But for God's sake, I just cannot imagine turning my back on either of my kids, ever, no matter what they do. It's unnatural. It's unforgiveable.

In fact, that's what I need to do, I decide. From now on, I won't forgive him. I'll stop wondering if he's OK, if he's still depressed, still grieving, *what's wrong with him.* I'll just give up.

* * *

I'm still, internally, steaming with anger the next morning, having had a bad night's sleep, going over and over all the horrible things Dad's said to me during the years since I got pregnant with Mia. I should just put it behind me and get on with my life, but I know his cruel comments have undermined my confidence. If your only close relative tells you you're a failure, stupid, that you've wasted your life and aren't fit to look after your children – however much you try to ignore it, some of it sticks. I didn't have a mum to tell me how to be a mother, I had to follow my instincts. My kids seem happy enough, on the whole, so I try to tell myself I must be doing OK, but what if I'm not? What if my dad's right, and I'm too young, too stupid, not capable of bringing them up properly? How will I ever know?

By the time we're all home again this afternoon I feel a bit better. Mia's in a good mood because she was chosen to sing a little song in class today, and she's such an extrovert, this made her day. She keeps singing it to me, at the top of her voice, and Archie lies on the floor covering his ears, making me laugh. I go out to the kitchen to put some washing on, make myself a cup of tea and get the children a biscuit each – but by the time I've boiled the kettle, the washing machine still hasn't started. I check I've programmed it right, turn it off and on again. Nothing. It's old, but it's always been reliable, never done this before. I feel like kicking it but somehow restrain myself. I've got a whole load of clothes and towels to wash – we won't manage till the weekend unless I can get them clean and dry.

'*Shit*!' I whisper so that Mia can't hear me. 'What the...?'

I'm going to have to take it all to the laundrette. I can't call anyone in to see if it can be fixed, not until I've been paid at the end of the week, anyway. Crossly, I pull out all the dirty laundry and bundle it into a bag.

'Sorry, Mia, finish your biscuit,' I tell her. 'We've got to go out.'

'Oh, but I want to watch TV,' she says, pouting.

'You can when we get back. Bring something to play with.'

'Where are we going?' she demands truculently as I pass her her coat and force a struggling, crying Archie back into his waterproof pram suit.

'The laundrette.'

'*Why*? I don't want to—'

'Mia, it's not always about what you want to do, OK?' I snap. 'Get your coat and boots on *now*.'

She's in a temper now, of course. Throwing her boots across the room, scowling and stamping her feet. I have to close my eyes and try to calm myself, because, as usual when she's behaving like this, I could so easily get hold of her and shake her. But I won't. I'm determined not to be the type of parent my dad obviously thinks I am. Instead, I hold her still, push her feet into her boots and her arms into her coat and finally, with both of them crying, I'm ready to go back out.

I bump into Helen at the bottom of the stairs.

'Oh, hello,' she says, smiling, and then – seeing the red, angry, tear-streaked faces on both of my kids – says, 'Oh dear. What's all this about, then?'

Mia stops crying abruptly and stares at her feet, embarrassed.

'My washing machine's not working,' I tell her, hoping she's not going to hold me up by wanting a chat right now. 'So I've got to go to the laundrette.'

'What a nuisance for you. And with the little ones tired out, after they've just got home,' she says – and then adds, suddenly, 'What am I thinking? You can bring your washing in and put it in my machine. Come on, just shove it in and I'll let you know when it's finished.'

I start to refuse, to be polite, tell her I wouldn't want to put her to the trouble, but before I can get the words out, she's going on:

'It's no trouble, I can put it through the dryer too so it's all ready for you to put away.'

I haven't got a dryer. The thought of having all this laundry returned to me, not only washed but warm and dry, too, instead of having to hang it over the airer, steaming in front of the gas fire, suddenly seems irresistible. It would have been the only benefit of taking it to the laundrette, but Helen's offer obviously has the added bonus of me not having to sit there, waiting for it, with two disgruntled children.

'Are you sure?' I say. 'I mean, it's very kind of you but—'

'Absolutely sure. Come on, come in and choose what programme you want and tell me how long to dry it all for. There, Mia – see? That's a *much* prettier face now you're smiling. I wonder if I've still got some of those chocolate biscuits in my tin?'

'They've just had a—' I begin, but then stop myself and smile. She's being kind. I'm grateful. 'Thank you,' I say instead, and we troop into her flat behind her.

'Them's my knickers,' Mia announces to Helen as I'm throwing clothes into her machine. 'That's Archie's jumper, he was sick down it. That's Mummy's bra and Mummy's knickers.'

'All right, Mia, we don't need a running commentary,' I say, laughing. I feel almost giddy with relief now that the prospect of the walk in the rain and the wait in the laundrette has faded away. 'Sit down with that biscuit, please, and keep an eye on Archie. Crumbs!'

'Now then,' Helen says as she slams the door of the washing

machine shut and presses the start button, 'would you like me to ask Robert to come and have a look at your machine? He's no expert but he's quite handy with mechanical things. He might be able to sort it out.'

'Oh, I don't want him to go to any trouble,' I say. But inside, I'm thinking, *Yes! I might not have to pay a repair man! I might not have to go without a washing machine until I can somehow find the money for a new one!*

'Don't be silly, he won't mind at all. Robert!' she calls into their living room. 'Jess's washing machine's not working. Go back with her and have a look at it for her, would you?'

I hear the TV being turned off and Robert comes out, saying hello to us all and agreeing that of course, he'll see if he can help; it might only be something minor. He actually seems almost eager at the prospect of being able to offer me some assistance.

As he follows me back up the stairs, holding Mia's hand while I carry Archie, I find myself feeling weak with some emotion I can't even identify, and the sudden thought that comes into my head: *I've got friends. Nice friends who seem to care about me, who want to help me.* It gives me this really odd sense of relief, as if I can imagine the load of my anxieties suddenly feeling lighter. A woman who reminds me of my mum. A man who seems absolutely nothing like my dad. Has my luck finally changed, just a little bit?

4

The bus is late again today. It always seems to happen on the days that Mia isn't at after-school club. I jump off at my stop and hurtle down the road to the school, panting, my scarf flying behind me in the wind. Mia's been held back to wait for me in the classroom with her teacher. She gives me a filthy look – Mia, not the teacher, Mrs Green, who's reasonably understanding as long as I'm not ridiculously late.

'I'm *so* sorry!' I gasp, hanging onto the classroom door while I try to get my breath back. 'The bus—'

'You're always late, Mummy,' Mia accuses me.

'Well, at least Mummy's here now,' Mrs Green tells her. 'Off you go, I'll see you tomorrow. Don't forget your reading book, will you?'

'*I* don't forget, Mummy forgets!' she says, making me feel even worse.

'Well, Mia, I think you could try to remember it yourself, couldn't you, to help Mummy?' Mrs Green says gently.

Thank you, dear teacher! But I still feel guilty.

We collect Archie from the nursery and we're halfway home

when I see Helen walking towards us on the other side of the road. I call out hello to her, and she crosses the road to talk to us.

'Aren't you a bit later than usual?' she says, making me wonder if she sits at her window watching us coming and going.

'A little bit. The bus was late,' I say. 'They're so unreliable.'

'It must be stressful for you, waiting for it and then having to rush to pick up the children,' she says, looking at me sympathetically. 'Honestly, I don't know why you don't take my phone number. If the bus is late, you can just call me and I'll pop down to the school for you. And the nursery,' she adds, smiling down at both the children. 'You wouldn't mind me meeting you from school occasionally, would you, Mia? If Mummy's held up?'

Mia looks thoughtful. 'Would we come back to your flat? Would you give us chocolate biscuits and crayons?'

'Mia!' I exclaim. 'It's rude to ask for things.'

But Helen's laughing. 'I expect I'd be able to provide those! But it would probably only be for a little while, till Mummy gets home. What do you think?' she adds, to me. 'It would save you all this worry.'

She's already offered this several times – and I know it makes sense to accept, but I've held back so far, not wanting to take advantage of how kind she and Robert have been. Fixing my washing machine was just the first of the little jobs he's done for me during the last couple of weeks: he fixed the handle on my front door that kept jamming, mended one of Mia's toys that I'd thought was beyond repair, and has helped me up the stairs with the buggy on several occasions. I'm used to doing it myself, obviously, it isn't that heavy, but it's just the kindness of it that I appreciate.

'The thing is,' I tell Helen now, 'I'd have to give the school and the nursery your name and phone number if you were going to pick the kids up, even if it's occasionally, even if it's just once. And the nursery even insists on a photo of you, to make sure they recognise you—'

'And that's absolutely right and proper, of course,' she says firmly. 'Why don't I walk down there with you tomorrow morning, so you can show me where I have to meet them – which door, which classroom – and you can introduce me, if you like, and give them my details?'

'Are you really sure you don't mind? It would only be very occasionally, in an emergency, but—'

'Of course I don't mind. It will save you all that anxiety and rushing. I'll see you in the morning, then. I'm just off to the shop – I forgot a couple of things this morning. Anything I can get you?'

'No, we're fine, thanks.' I smile at her. 'Thanks, Helen. I do appreciate it.'

* * *

The weather's so awful over the weekend that Helen knocks and offers me the use of her tumble dryer again. I must admit, her timing's perfect, as I've just finished the biggest wash-load of the week, including all our bed linen. I've stopped trying so hard now to refuse her offers of kindness, as I'm starting to think she and Robert are probably a bit lonely as well as being bored, and it seems to give them pleasure to help me out.

'Why don't you bring the children in and have a coffee and a chat while it's all drying?' she suggests.

I'd been planning to do some housework, but Archie's cutting some back teeth and has been fractious after a bad night, and Mia's been difficult too because she's fed up, so the thought of sitting down, for an hour or so, and just relaxing, is too tempting to refuse.

'Can we have the crayons again?' Mia asks as soon as we've got through Helen's front door. She glances at me and I can sense the effort with which she stops herself also asking about biscuits.

Robert's gone into town this morning, apparently, to do some shopping, and once we're settled with our coffee – and once Archie's finally stopped grizzling and I've persuaded him not to chew on the crayons – it's quiet in Helen's lovely warm lounge. I'm worried that I might actually doze off, after the sleepless night with Archie, so I sit up straight and make an effort at conversation.

'Whereabouts do your grown-up children live?' I ask, and when Helen hesitates for a moment I wonder again if – as I suspected when she first mentioned them – there's been some kind of falling out in the family.

'Our daughter lives in Scotland,' she says eventually. 'So we don't see her too often. And our son is at college. In America.'

'Oh, I see. You must miss them both a lot.'

'Yes,' she says flatly. Her customary smile has dropped and she's staring ahead, looking quite desolate.

'It must be difficult,' I say, feeling a little awkward now as she hasn't expanded on this brief response. No mention of the daughter's job, or what the son's studying, no indication of whether there's a partner or son-in-law. I go on, quickly, to talk about my own situation instead, telling her that I'm an only child, without any family apart from my children... and my dad.

'And you said you're not on speaking terms with him?' she remembers. 'That's very sad. Does he at least see the children sometimes?'

'No. He's never seen them, and he never sees me. And that's his decision, not mine,' I say, slightly more harshly than I mean to. 'I called him the other day because it was his birthday, but he just started insulting me again, and calling the children *brats*, so I'm not going to bother again.'

'How could he not want to see his own grandchildren? What a silly man; he's the one losing out. And to call them brats! That's just awful. They're lovely children, you should be proud of them.'

'Oh... thank you, Helen.' I have to swallow a lump in my throat. I can't remember anyone ever saying that to me before. 'You've no idea what that means to me.' I look away, feeling a little bit silly for what I'm about to say, but I turn back to say it anyway: 'I haven't told you this, but you... you remind me so much of my mum.'

There's a few seconds' pause, where we're both just sitting looking at each other, and then she suddenly reaches out her arms and gives me a hug. And I know this is silly but... I kind of feel like I've come home.

5

It's not long before the first occasion occurs when I need to call Helen to pick up the children for me. Today the bus I normally catch isn't just late, it's failed to turn up at all, and there's such a crowd of frustrated people waiting for it, or the next one, that I realise I might not be able to get on, even when it does arrive.

Helen answers my call straight away, as if she's been sitting in her living room just waiting for the phone to ring. Perhaps she has.

'I'm so sorry,' I tell her, 'but there's a problem with the buses. I don't know how long I'm going to be. Would you mind—'

'Of course I wouldn't mind!' she says immediately. 'I'll set off right away. I'm looking forward to having the children. So don't you worry at all, they'll be fine, just get yourself home whenever you can.'

'Thank you so much.' The relief I feel is instant. I can feel my breathing slowing, my heartbeat settling down, and my shoulders relaxing – I hadn't even realised I'd been stressed until the instant Helen said it would be fine. 'I'll see you soon, I hope.'

I don't even mind so much now if I don't get on the bus. One comes along about fifteen minutes later, already half full, and everyone at my stop surges forwards. What happened to queue-ing? I can remember my gran, years ago, saying how everyone used to queue patiently outside shops in the 1950s when there was food rationing. I can't imagine it happening now. There'd be a riot. I get bowled along with the crowd and I do, at least, get on the bus, even though it's standing room only.

Up till now, when the journey has been like this, I've arrived at the school anxious and cross, giving the afternoon a sour taste before I've even got the children home. Today, I go straight back to the flats and knock at Helen's door. Mia runs out to greet me and hugs me around my waist, telling me she's on a new reading book, the teacher has given her a 'super reader' sticker, and she's playing a really, *really* funny game with 'Auntie Helen', who's given her a *chocolate suggestion biscuit* – as she's always called them – and an apple.

'A chocolate digestive *and* an apple?' I say, laughing and hugging her back. 'Wow!'

'Come and see the funny game what we're playing,' she goes on, dragging me into the living room. 'It's called Buckaroo and you hang things on the donkey and it kicks them off. Archie can't play, he's too young,' she says with satisfaction. 'So he's playing with a phone.'

My smile drops at the idea of my baby boy getting his hands on someone's smartphone – but when I go into the living room, he's sitting on the carpet with an old-fashioned toy phone, playing with the dial and lifting the receiver, which plays a tune.

'Oh, Helen, I hope you didn't buy these toys specially?' I ask as she watches Robert hang a basket onto the Buckaroo donkey. 'Hello, Robert. Careful with that!' I add as his hands wobble.

'Charity shop,' Helen says, smiling. 'Ah, they were only a couple of quid. My treat. We can keep them here for whenever the children come. Now then, how about a cup of tea or coffee before you rush off home? The children have both been very good,' she adds. 'We sang "If You're Happy and You Know It" all the way home – didn't we, Mia?'

'*If you're happy and you know it, shout yippee!*' Mia sings, at ear-shattering volume, and Archie drops the toy phone's receiver in fright.

'Well, OK, thank you – a quick one would be nice,' I agree.

I can't believe how relaxed I feel. Normally when we get in from the school pick-up I'm feeling rattled, tired, and irritable, however hard I try not to show it. If only I could afford a car, my life would be so different! Of course, I'd have to learn to drive first – I've never even had lessons.

I sip my tea, eat my *chocolate suggestion* biscuit and laugh as Mia hangs a shovel on the Buckaroo donkey and it bucks, making her shriek and Archie fall over with surprise.

'One more game?' Mia pleads. 'Come on, Mummy, you play this time!'

'Well, we really should be getting back...' I begin, but Helen stops me.

'There's no rush. Unless you've got something urgent to get back for?'

Anything urgent? I suppose not, really – only to prepare the kids' tea, and to be fair, sausages and baked beans don't take long.

'No, nothing really urgent.' I smile at her. 'OK, Mia, I'll join in for just one quick game – but then we must go, all right? Otherwise Auntie Helen and Uncle Robert won't want to have you again.'

'Can you pick us up again tomorrow?' Mia asks Helen when the game is over and we're getting ready to leave.

'Only if Mummy asks me to,' Helen says.

'No, Mia, only in emergencies,' I tell her firmly.

'Well, can it be an urgency tomorrow?' she suggests. 'You're always late, Mummy, but Auntie Helen wasn't late, she was there when the door opened.'

'The thing with emergencies,' Helen tells her calmly, 'is that we don't know when they're going to happen. So when they do, it's a surprise – see?'

'I like surprises,' Mia says, nodding happily. 'Hurry up and have an urgency, Mummy.'

I have to laugh. I know it's just because today has been different for her, a novelty. But it's such a relief to know there's someone here who can take over if necessary – someone Mia actually seems to *like* picking her up from school!

* * *

The next day, just as I'm getting my packed lunch out of the fridge in our little staff room at the back of the shop, Tariq comes in and closes the door behind him.

'Jess,' he begins, sounding a little awkward. 'Have you got a minute? I need to talk to you about something.'

'Oh, yes, of course.' I put my lunch box down on the table. 'What is it?'

'Well, it's about your hours,' he begins.

My heart sinks. 'Tariq, I'm so sorry about the way I have to rush off on the days Mia isn't at after-school club. Margaret's been so good about it, but I realise it's—'

'I didn't say anything about your timekeeping,' he says, more gently. 'I know you have to leave promptly; Margaret and I both understand that. It's just that Margaret's wanting to take more of a back seat these days. We can't blame her – she should be enjoying her retirement now, really, instead of still coming in to supervise and lend a hand here! And, well, frankly – to get to the point, Jess

– we're going to need someone here, other than me, who can work longer hours. Preferably full-time.'

My heart gives a lurch. I really didn't see this coming.

'Are you getting rid of me?' I blurt out.

'No, of course we don't want to do that. You're a good worker, you're a valuable member of our team. Margaret is very keen to keep you on, but we'd really need more hours from you, Jess. Can you possibly see your way to doing more?'

'I... I don't know. I mean, yes, if I can get Mia into after-school club on the other three days, but that might not happen until the next school year.'

And she's only four, I think to myself, feeling a pang at the thought of her tired little face on Wednesdays and Fridays. But then I think about the alternative: am I going to be losing my job? I feel an involuntary shudder.

'And then there are the school holidays,' Tariq goes on, looking at me solemnly.

'Oh, I've already told Margaret, I've got Mia into the holiday club at her school. Um, they don't do it for half-terms, but she's booked in for a week at Easter and two weeks in summer. It's mornings only for her age group, but at least it means—'

'—you can be here until lunchtime. But not in the half-terms,' he says, quietly, nodding. 'The school holidays are our busiest times, though, Jess.'

'But I thought Emma was going to work in the school holidays now, anyway?' I say, struggling to keep the pleading tone from my voice. 'That was the whole point – she'll be an extra pair of hands when we're busy—'

'Except that Margaret won't be here now. Or not so often. Don't get me wrong, Jess, I know she wants to keep you on – and so do I, obviously. But we'll have to see how it goes. I just thought it was only fair to warn you, we are all looking at our hours now, and what we can do to make it easier for Margaret to take a well-deserved break.'

I want to scream. I want to say, *No, we're not* all *'looking at our hours'*. You're *looking at* my *hours*. I want to say, *Please don't fire me. Please understand! I can't afford a childminder. I need this job. I can't lose it*. But I know it won't help to plead and beg. I need to sound professional, to offer to meet him at least halfway.

'I'll see what I can do,' I say, looking away from him, down at my cheese and pickle sandwich, which I now feel too sick to eat.

'Thank you, Jess. We'll have another chat next week, then, and see what we've been able to work out between us.'

It must be something that managers like Tariq learn on a course somewhere. How to sound as if you're working *with* your employee on a problem, when really you've just given them the problem and left them to find a way to solve it.

* * *

I worry about it all afternoon, and I'm so distracted that I direct someone to the wrong shelf for Young Adult fiction. Luckily Tariq doesn't witness my mistake, as he's with a customer himself. The worst thing I can do now would be to really mess up, and give him a good excuse to replace me with a full-timer. I think about it on the bus back to the school. Would it be worth me having a quiet word with Margaret? Perhaps she doesn't even know what Tariq's planning. She's always been good to me, and it's her shop, at the end of the day – but on the other hand, I get that she deserves to take a step back from it now. And it would be seen as undermining Tariq's authority, not a good look.

'*Mummy!*' says Mia crossly as we're walking back to the nursery to pick up Archie. 'You're walking *much* too fast and my legs don't like it, they can't keep up with me. And you didn't even look at my painting, you just putted it in your bag, and I'm *very* hungry.'

'Sorry, sweetheart.' I smile down at her. 'I promise I'll look at your painting properly when we get home. And you can have your favourite biscuit. I bought pink wafers.'

They were on special offer in Asda when I popped in this morning.

'Pink wafers!' she shouts, instantly cheering up. 'My absolute very best super favourite!'

Laughing now, and her legs apparently having forgiven her, she skips ahead of me to the nursery gates, saying she's going to tell Archie about the pink wafers. I watch her, my heart feeling heavy with foreboding. What the hell is going to happen to us if I can't keep my job?

6

'There just aren't jobs around that fit with school hours,' I try to explain to Lucy when I call her tonight. It's always Lucy, of all my friends, that I talk to when I'm worried.

'What about working in a school?' she says. 'Teaching assistant – you don't have to be qualified, Jess. That would be perfect!'

'Yes, and everybody in the world with young children wants one of those jobs. The people who get them, hang on to them. Not that they pay very well,' I add gloomily.

'So could you maybe look for opportunities where you can work from home?'

'Doing what, though?' I feel like crying. 'I'm not *trained* in anything. I'm not *qualified* for anything. Who's going to take me on with my handful of mediocre GCSEs? I know it's my own fault, but... well, I'm not even any good with computers. I haven't even got a laptop.'

'Well,' she says, 'I hate to say it, Jess, but the answer is staring you in the face. If you want to keep the job at the bookshop, you need to have a talk with Mrs *I Love Kids and I Don't Go to Work* downstairs.'

'I've only known Helen for a few weeks, though, and she's only looked after the children once, for less than an hour!'

'But you like her. And so does Mia.'

'Yes, I do like her, and him – Robert. They've been lovely. But what if it turns out to be too much for her, having them as often as I'd need? And even if she does agree to have them, I'd *definitely* have to pay her.'

'But surely not as much as you'd have to pay a registered childminder?' Lucy says. 'And you'd be working full-time. You could afford to give her something. OK, you might end up no better off, but you'd still have your job.'

'And I'd hardly see the kids at all,' I say quietly. But I know – I know perfectly well, really, that Lucy's right.

Could I ask Helen? Would it be right, when we're still so new to each other, even if we do seem to get on well? Can I trust her with my children? And would she even want to do it, if I paid her? Would she be offended? Or would she jump at it? I suppose I'll never know unless I ask her.

* * *

Over the weekend I'm still so worried about the situation that I find it hard to give the kids my full attention. Mia's sitting on the side of the bath while I'm cleaning the bathroom, trying to tell me one of her made-up stories – about a fairy who lives with an elephant (elephants feature in most of Mia's stories) – and she gets upset because she realises I haven't been listening properly. I have to promise to sit down with her and hear the whole story again from the beginning. Archie's still teething and is miserable, red in the face, dribbling and whining. I've given him some

Calpol and put him down for his nap, but he's still half-awake, grizzling quietly to himself.

After lunch I take them both with me to do the shopping, and try my best to make it a fun occasion instead of the chore it really is – a worrying chore at that, with the prices of everything going up nearly every week. I get Mia to look on the shelves for the various things on my list and have her call out their prices to me. And I give Archie things to hold as he sits in the trolley seat – he seems particularly pleased with the packet of cereal with a picture of a tiger on the front – while I encourage him to try to say the name of each item before he drops it into the trolley. It does mean we'll have broken biscuits and bruised apples but it's worth it to keep him from screaming all the way round the shop.

He *is* screaming, though, by the time we get home.

'What's the matter with him now?' Mia says irritably.

'His mouth is sore, Mia. You used to cry like that too, when you had new teeth coming through.'

'He's getting on my nerves,' she says with heartfelt emphasis.

'Oh, poor Archie!' says a familiar voice from behind me. It's Helen, following us down the access road to our flats. 'He can't help it, Mia. He just needs something nice to take his mind off how much it hurts.'

'Like what?' Mia asks, sounding genuinely interested. 'A biscuit?'

'Mia!' I admonish her, but she turns to me, her eyes wide with feigned innocence.

'I'm not asking for me, Mummy, I'm asking for Archie, to take his mind off his hurty mouth.'

Helen's laughing. 'Bring them in with me for a little while, Jess – at least while you unpack all that shopping. Wait there – I'll call Robert to help you up the steps with all those heavy bags.'

'Oh, I'm fine, honestly, Helen, it won't take me long—'

'You're tired already,' she insists. 'I bet you're not getting much sleep while Archie's teething.'

She's already opened her front door, and I wait, giving in, because she's right – I'm exhausted. She calls Robert, who comes straight out and heaves three of my bags at a time up to my own door. I'm almost overcome, again, by their kindness. It wasn't so much Archie's teething that kept me awake last night, as my anxiety. And seeing Helen shepherding my daughter into her flat while she lifts Archie out of his buggy, holding him close and murmuring endearments to him, I know suddenly, and with certainty, what I need to do. If I don't at least ask, I'll still be worrying about the ifs and the buts and the whethers, when it's all too late and I've lost my job.

'Helen,' I begin tentatively, my voice shaking slightly – not with nerves but with sadness, with resignation, because this is something I never thought I'd have to do. 'I need to ask you something. It's a huge thing to ask, but if you can do it – if you *want* to do it – I'll pay you.'

She nods, looking at me with such understanding in her eyes that I suspect she already knows what I'm going to say.

'Pack away your shopping,' she repeats, 'and then come in for a cup of tea. Once the children are settled we can talk about it. OK? Whatever it is, we'll help if we can – won't we, Robert?'

Robert's coming back down the stairs after putting the last couple of bags on my doorstep.

'Of course we will,' he agrees, touching my arm and giving me a sympathetic smile. 'Whatever it is, Jess.'

I manage to get inside my flat before the tears come. I don't even know yet if they *will* agree when I spell it out to them, but I'm so indebted to them already – just for their simple kindness.

* * *

The children are busy with the crayons again by the time I return to the downstairs flat. Helen leaves Robert in charge and takes me into the kitchen, pouring me out a mug of tea and then closing the door behind us. She indicates a stool at the kitchen counter.

'Now, sit yourself down and tell me what's happened,' she says. 'It's obvious something has.'

I spell out the conversation with Tariq, the situation with Margaret wanting to retire, the need for a full-time member of staff, the fact that I need to give him an answer quickly.

'So, basically, you need the children to be picked up and cared for on Mondays, Tuesdays and Thursdays,' she says with a nod of understanding.

'Well, Mia, at least. I might be able to get Archie some extra hours at nursery for those days,' I say quickly.

'But surely it would be better to have them both brought home together on those days,' she says. 'No point going back again for Archie a couple of hours later, is there?'

'Well, whatever you... I mean *if* you...' I stammer.

'Of course we'll do it,' she interrupts me, smiling. 'We'd love to. I know Robert will agree. We can't have you worrying about losing your job, and we wouldn't want paying for it, either, before you start saying anything.'

'Oh, but I'd have to! This is more than just a favour, it's three days a week, every week—'

'For just a couple of hours! Honestly, Jess, it'll be our absolute pleasure. We love having your children. Now then,' she adds, looking at me over her glasses. 'What about the school holidays?'

I look away, sighing. 'I've put off thinking about that. It's the half-terms I need to think about first. Mia's booked into holiday club at school for a week at Easter, and I'm off myself for the other week. But the holiday club is for mornings only.' I feel a jolt of panic, remembering Tariq's comment about school holidays being the busiest time. 'And I think they're going to ask me to work all day then too.'

'Well, look on the bright side!' Helen says cheerfully. 'More money for you, Jess. That'll help, won't it?'

'Yes, so I'll definitely pay you—'

'Shall we debate that a little later? Let's see how it goes, first? When is half-term?'

'Two weeks' time.'

'So, look, why don't we see how we get on with the extra hours over the next couple of weeks, and perhaps we'll do this first half-term holiday as a kind of trial, before we discuss payment. You might not like the way we look after them!'

'I'm sure I will,' I insist, gratitude almost choking the words out of me. 'They love coming here. I wouldn't have asked you, otherwise.'

'That's settled, then.' She gives me a beaming smile, and, seeing how relieved I must look, she comes over and hugs me. 'You poor thing, having all this worry and keeping it to yourself – you should have told me right away. You've got enough on your plate, bless you, without being frightened of losing your job. Now, let's go and see what they're up to in the other room, shall we – or would you rather just go home and put your feet up while the kids are happy?'

'No. Thank you, Helen. Thank you so, so much – for everything. But I'll take them home now. You're doing more than enough for me already.'

I feel almost light-headed with relief as I take the children back upstairs. It's all going to be OK. I'm going to be earning more money. The kids are going to be looked after, they'll be safe, they'll be happy, and I'll just have to get used to not being with them as often as I'd like. Thank God for Helen and Robert.

The new regime goes even better than I'd hoped. Neither of the children have seemed the least bit upset by going to Helen and Robert's for a couple of hours, three days of each week after school. In fact, I'd say Mia seems positively happy about it, but of course, I realise it's early days and the novelty might wear off after a while. Am I thinking this because I *want* her to say she's fed up with it? Because I'm hurt that she's not missing me? Hurt that even my baby boy doesn't seem to care who picks him up from nursery or how little time I spend with him? I hope I'm not that shallow. I hope I can rise above my own insecurities and try to be happy that the children are happy, but I have to admit it isn't easy, because *I* miss *them*. In some strange way, I even miss the rush to get to the school gate in time to meet Mia – but that's just being perverse, isn't it? I've still picked her up from after-school club on Wednesdays and Fridays and collected Archie from nursery, but today – the final Friday before the half-term holiday – Mia actually pouts when she sees me waiting outside the school. She says she forgot it's not an *Auntie Helen day.*

'Well,' I say, 'how would you like to go to Auntie Helen and Uncle Robert every day next week?'

She looks at me in surprise. 'But it's the holidays!'

'I know, sweetie. But I've got to work.'

'Oh.' She looks crestfallen for a moment. 'Poor Mummy. But me and Archie can go to Auntie Helen's?' she adds, brightening up.

'*Archie and I*, Mia.' I know she's only four, and her vocabulary is really very good for her age, but I do try to teach her correct grammar – just as my mum did for me – even though I realise it's expecting too much for her to always remember it. I so badly want to prove to everyone that I can be a good mum. 'Yes, Auntie Helen says she'd be happy for you to go to them.'

'Yay!' she exclaims, giving a little skip. 'Every day? All day? All the week? Yay!'

'You don't mind?' I persist. Not that there's much I can do about it now anyway, but I suppose I was hoping for a flicker of disappointment that she wouldn't be spending the holiday with me.

'No. It'll be fun. Auntie Helen and Uncle Robert play games with us and read us stories, and we do drawings and paintings.'

'Well, that's nice, then.'

I smile down at her. She can't possibly realise how insecure it makes me feel to hear about all the lovely things Helen and Robert do, while I'm all too conscious that I sit them in front of the TV more than I should, and never seem to have time to play a game with them. But of course, I do realise how lucky I am, how well it's all worked out, solving my problems so easily and conveniently. Tariq's pleased, Margaret's pleased, Helen and Robert appear to be over the moon and are insisting that the only payment they'll take from me is a small amount to cover the children's lunch and snacks. And I get the impression they've only agreed to this to pacify me because I insisted on paying something.

So I've given them packs of nappies, the children's favourite cups and plates, and I'll be sending them in with a couple of their favourite toys, as well as Archie's blanket and dummy for his nap. Helen's going to put him in the middle of their bed, with pillows on the floor in case he rolls off in his sleep. But I'm also giving them my spare key, so that they can go and find anything I haven't thought of, anything Mia might suddenly wish she'd taken with her and start asking for. Despite her excited reaction today, she's the one I've been a little bit concerned about. Archie, being used to nursery now, doesn't seem to be the type of child to have any qualms about being looked after by someone else, doesn't cling to me and cry, and I know I should be grateful for this too, even if it gives me such a pang inside, such a selfish urge to smother him with my maternal love and insist on somehow keeping him with me all the time: *my baby – mine!* No. I have to work. I have to let them go. I have to be grateful.

* * *

The first Monday of the holiday goes quickly. It's busy in the shop, with lots of parents bringing their children in for our special holiday reading sessions, so it's good that Emma and I are both working. It's nice to spend some time with her, getting to know her better, hearing how her university course is going.

'I'd have loved to do something like that,' I say, trying not to sound envious. 'I was always good at English, especially literature.'

'Well, I'm sure you could still do it as a mature student,' she says, with such wide-eyed innocence that I can't help smiling.

'Maybe one day,' I say, rather than disillusion her with any stark and unpleasant facts of economic reality.

* * *

When I get back to the flats, before I've even knocked at Helen's door to collect the children, I stop short at the sight of Callum, my ex, at the top of the stairs, leaning against the door of my flat. It's not a pleasant sight.

'What are you doing here?' I say. I can't remember when I last saw him.

'Waiting for you,' he says abruptly. 'Where have you been?'

'At work, not that it's anything to do with you. How did you get into the building?'

He shrugs. 'Some bloke was coming in, he held the door open for me so I thought I'd wait in the warm. Where are the kids? It's the school holidays. You haven't left them on their own, have you?'

I feel a tightness in my chest, conscious that my hands are clenched into fists and my heart's racing. I don't want this. I don't want a confrontation with him – not anywhere, but definitely not here, above Helen's door, with the children just the other side of it.

'Of course I haven't. And it's none of your business where they are,' I say, trying to sound firm. 'You agreed to me having sole custody. You weren't interested.'

'I'm still their father. I pay you maintenance—'

'Only because you have to.'

'Where are they?' he insists, more loudly.

'With a childminder. So if you'll just let me go inside and put this shopping bag down, I'll be going to collect them. Bye, Callum.'

'I'll come with you.'

'No, you won't. Please go.'

'I want to see what kind of childminder this is. I don't like the idea of it. You should be at home with them.' He raises his voice even further, beginning to sound aggressive. 'What sort of mother abandons her kids with a childminder?'

'Most mothers have to, Callum,' I retort. 'That's the reality now.'

It's as much as I can do not to ask him what kind of father wants nothing whatsoever to do with his children. What kind of father turns up eighteen months after the relationship ended and starts demanding his non-existent rights? But I don't want a fight. I don't even want to talk to him. I just want him to go.

'If you'll excuse me,' I go on, as calmly as I can manage, 'I need to get inside. I need you to go.'

'I'll wait,' he shouts back at me. 'I want to see who—'

The door behind me opens – the door to Helen and Robert's flat. Just what I *didn't* want to happen. I hold my breath. Callum mustn't see the kids. I don't want him to know where they are. Also, I don't want any trouble for Helen and Robert.

It's Robert who comes outside, pulling the door to behind him.

'Is everything all right, Jess?' he asks, staring up at Callum. 'I heard raised voices – is there a problem?'

Callum's expression, and his tone of voice, his whole attitude, change in an instant. He was always good at this.

'Oh, sorry, mate,' he says, starting to walk down the stairs. 'Nothing to worry about. Jess and I were just sorting a couple of things out between us.' He smiles at Robert now. 'I'm Callum, Jess's ex. Just discussing the children, you know how it is.'

Robert continues to stare at him, stony-faced. I wonder how much he heard.

'Would you like me to call the police, Jess?' he asks. He's got his phone in his hand, his finger hovering over the call button.

'No need for that,' Callum says, with a little apologetic laugh. He won't want the police involved, that's for sure. He's already got a record. 'But I'm glad Jess has got a good neighbour, someone looking out for her. I worry about her, here on her own with the kids. Really sorry if we disturbed you. We're fine now, aren't we, Jess? See you again soon.'

I don't bother answering. He saunters off, hands in pockets, whistling.

'So that's the children's father,' Robert says, watching Callum's retreating back.

'Yes, unfortunately.'

I'm furious. How dare he? He's never once turned up at my flat before – I don't even know how he found out where I live. And of all the times for it to happen, it had to be now, the first time I've ever left the children all day with someone else.

'I'm so sorry, Robert,' I add. 'But I really didn't want him to know the children were in your flat. He... can get difficult. He couldn't really care less whether I've got *someone looking out for me*. And anyway, it's none of his business. He agreed to me having sole custody of the children – he's never been interested in them.'

'Don't apologise, Jess,' he says, putting a gentle hand on my shoulder. 'I hope I wasn't being too interfering, but when Helen and I heard a disturbance out here, we agreed she'd keep the children inside while I checked if you were OK.'

'Thank you. But if he ever turns up here again – if he ever finds out the children are with you – I *will* want you to call the police.'

'OK. I'll make sure Helen knows that too.'

'Thank you.' I take a deep breath and force a smile. 'How have the kids been today?'

'As good as gold!' he says, smiling. 'Come on inside, they'll be glad to see you. Helen was putting the kettle on.'

* * *

I'm so relieved to see that Mia and Archie do seem to be perfectly happy that I force myself to stop thinking about Callum for a moment. Mia can't wait to tell me about the story Helen's been reading them, and the one she's made up on her own, about a witch and a princess. She's also drawn a picture of her two characters – the princess, as always, wearing a golden crown and a beautiful long dress, while the witch (who doesn't seem to have any arms, but I don't mention this, of course) is completely green, including her face and her hair.

'It's very good, sweetie.' I hold her close and shower her with kisses. 'I'm glad you've been having a good time. I've missed you so much today.'

'I missed you a little bit,' she replies with the heart-breaking honesty of childhood, 'but not very much.'

I laugh. 'And what about you, young man?' I ask Archie, picking him up and spinning him around, making him giggle. 'Did you miss me?'

'Miss,' he repeats obediently, squirming to get down.

Helen brings me in a mug of hot tea, and while the children go back to building the Lego house that Robert's helping them with, I try to recover from the shock of finding Callum at my door. I'm uneasy at the thought that he's going to come back again, that he might eventually work out where the children are and demand to see them.

'I'm sorry to have to ask you this,' I say quietly to Helen while the kids are occupied, 'but if by any chance my ex finds out that the children are with you, please could you *not* let him see them?'

'Is he banned from having any access to them?' Helen asks quietly, looking concerned.

'Well, not exactly,' I admit. 'But I have sole custody, and he's never asked for any visitation rights – in fact, he said he didn't care if he never sees them again. And he can be... very unpleasant. They're doing fine without him.'

'Fair enough,' she says, nodding.

'Don't worry, Jess,' Robert puts in, looking up from the Lego. 'We get the picture. He won't be allowed in, even if he works out that they're here.'

'Who's here?' Mia chirps. 'Who's not allowed in?'

I really should know better than to underestimate how much she takes in, even when I don't think she's listening.

'The big bad wolf!' I tease her, and I drop to my hands and knees and crawl across the carpet to grab her and pretend to start eating her. 'Yummy, yummy, little girls taste *so* good!'

She squeals with excitement and rolls over, away from me, almost demolishing the Lego house.

'Sorry,' I apologise to Robert, but he's laughing. 'I think I'd better take them home now. They must be tired. Thank you both *so* much for today. Do you think... do you still think, after today, that you'll be OK to have them again tomorrow? And—'

'And for the rest of the week,' Helen says at once. 'Of course we will. We're having a whale of a time, aren't we, children?'

'What whale?' Mia says, looking puzzled, and we all laugh.

How did I get to be so lucky with these neighbours? Despite the contretemps with Callum, I feel such a wave of relief wash over me that I can't even speak. I give Helen a big thank-you hug and start packing the kids' bag ready to go home.

8

We're at the end of the half-term week, and thank God I haven't seen or heard any more from Callum. Yesterday, Helen asked me if it would be OK if they took the children out to the park today, now that the weather's improved. I must admit I felt a frisson of anxiety at first. Should I spell out to them the fact that Archie can only use the baby swings and the baby slide, or should I presume they'd know that? After all, they have had children of their own, even if they are grown up now. Although maybe I should warn them that Mia has a tendency to beg and plead to climb up to the top of the big slide and then become too scared to slide down it? In the end I told them everything, deciding it was better to be thought of as a fussy mother than to risk problems or accidents.

I must admit, though, I've felt anxious at work all day today, imagining all sorts of things going wrong. My precious babies have never been taken out by anyone else in their lives – while Callum and I were still living together, Mia was hardly ever even looked after by her own father. Have I really known Helen and Robert for long enough to trust them with the care of the only two human beings I truly love and adore? Am I making a terrible mistake? I can't wait to get home this evening to see if they're all right; but of course, everything is absolutely fine. Mia still looks rosy-cheeked from the fresh air and is bursting to tell me all about the fun she had on the climbing frame and the fact that Robert caught her at the bottom of the big slide and she's not scared of it any more.

'And we had hot chocolate in the café!' she yells, jumping up and down on the spot with excitement. 'And cake! Archie got chocolate all down his jumper!'

'Sorry. I put it in the wash; it's clean and dry now,' Helen says. 'I went into your flat to find him a clean one, I hope that was all right. Mia came with me to show me where to look.'

'Of course it's all right,' I say, relief and gratitude flooding me. 'I should have thought to leave you some spare clothes for Archie. Honestly, it's been so good of you both – I can't thank you enough—'

'We should be thanking you,' Helen insists. 'We've had so much fun, haven't we, Robert?' Her smile drops for a moment as she adds quietly, 'It's been a long time since we've had little children to take to the park.'

'Perhaps you'll have grandchildren of your own one day,' I say gently. I don't like to say any more, as she still doesn't talk to me about her children and, to be honest, I find it quite strange. I'm sure there must be some kind of problem there.

'Perhaps,' she says vaguely, and then changes the subject abruptly. 'Now then, Mia, how about we tidy away these toys before you go home, so that they're all ready for you in the toy box next time you come?'

'Don't want to,' Mia says, flopping down on the sofa. 'I'm tired.'

'Mia,' I warn her. 'Come on, do as Auntie Helen's asked you, please. I'll help you.'

'Make Archie help,' she says with a scowl. 'He played with the toys too.'

Archie pulls himself to his feet, picks up a toy car and staggers towards me with it.

'That's new, isn't it?' I say to Helen, nodding at the car. 'I hope you haven't been spending more money on toys – you must let me pay for them.'

'Oh, it was just another little bargain from the charity shop,' she says breezily, but she's looking away from me and I can tell it's a fib. I bet she paid full whack for it – and the new doll I can see lying in a corner, too. 'We enjoy getting them a little treat occasionally.'

Still scowling, Mia goes to pick up the doll, and drops it carelessly into the toy box, along with the car and a couple of books I haven't seen before. I know she's tired, but I'm still cross and embarrassed that she's acting up, after Helen and Robert have given them both such a lovely time today.

'Sorry,' I say quietly to Helen. 'I think this one needs to go to bed early tonight.'

'Ah, don't worry,' she says, smiling. 'Too much excitement; she's overtired, bless her. Archie had a good long nap after we came back from the park, and I tried to get Mia to lie down on the sofa and rest for a little while, but she wasn't having it!'

* * *

'I hope you're not rude to Auntie Helen when she asks you to do something,' I say to Mia when we're back in our own flat.

'No, *she's* rude to me,' she retorts. 'She tells me off.'

I stare at her. I'm not one of those parents who think their children are always perfect little angels – I know Mia can be difficult at times, especially when she's tired. But up till now she's been so besotted with Helen and Robert that it's quite a shock to hear her talking like this.

'Mia, if Auntie Helen's had to tell you off, I'm sure you must have deserved it. It's no different from when I tell you off, or your teacher tells children off, at school.'

Even as I'm saying this, I'm hoping fervently that Helen *hasn't* had to tell her off. Surely she'd have let me know if there'd been a problem. Should I say anything – ask her about it? No, I don't want to make a fuss. I look at Mia now, flopping on the sofa, tired out. She's probably still just a bit sore about being asked to tidy the toys away. Mia's quite capable of making things up, too – like most little kids. I suppose, there's a fine line between truth and her overactive imagination. I decide to ignore it for this evening, and concentrate on giving them both an early dinner and early bedtime. To be honest I'm glad it's the weekend now. I'm tired too, still getting used to working the longer hours. The extra money I'm earning will make it all worthwhile, I know, but if Helen and Robert still refuse to let me give them any more, I'll have to, at the very least, buy them something as a thank-you gift.

9

The first few days back at school pass without any problems. Mia seems happy enough with Helen taking her home, but she's making up more stories than usual, mostly about princesses or various animals, but also some tall tales about things she claims she and Archie are, or aren't, apparently allowed to do in Helen and Robert's flat. These stories are so outlandish – for instance, that Helen makes Archie change his own nappies, and won't let Mia go to the toilet – that I just laugh and tell her not to make things up. But even though the claims are so ridiculous, I can't help feeling unnerved by the fact that she finds it necessary to make up stories about Helen at all, and wondering yet again whether I ought to discuss Friday's outburst with Helen. The idea of her having to tell Mia off is still playing on my mind, however hard I try to dismiss it. I just hope it isn't true, and that the incident – whatever it might have been – has led to Mia inventing these ridiculously far-fetched stories. But she seems happy enough to go back there, so once again I decide to ignore her storytelling for now.

* * *

Despite being tired, I'm actually enjoying the extra time at work. Without the stress of the rush to get away on those three days, I'm more relaxed, free to serve customers without trying to sneak a look at my watch. So everything seems to be going well. That is, until I pick Mia up from the after-school club on Wednesday.

As soon as she comes out, she looks upset. She scowls and shrugs crossly when I ask her what's wrong. I wait until I've collected Archie, we've arrived home and she's had her drink and biscuit before pulling her onto my lap for a cuddle and trying again to find out what's bothering her.

'You know you can tell me, don't you?' I say gently. 'It doesn't matter what it is; if you're unhappy I need to know so that I can try to help.'

'You can't help, if you're not there,' she says, her lower lip wobbling.

'Not where, Mia?' I pull her closer, stroke her hair. 'At school? At the after-school club?'

'Yes. That.'

'So what's gone wrong there today? Normally you have fun there.'

She shakes her head. 'No, not always. Not when Reggie's there.'

'So what's wrong with Reggie?' My inner tigress is on alert, making my voice sharper than I intend, and I try to rein it in. I want to ask if he's done anything to hurt her. But I take a breath and instead just ask, 'Don't you like him?'

'No,' she says vehemently. 'He's horrible. He pulled my hair and called me names.'

'Did you tell the teacher?' I ask her.

'No.'

I don't know this Reggie. At the after-school club the children are mixed with some from other classes, of course. But already I don't like the hair-pulling, name-calling little bully, whoever he is.

'You need to let the teacher know, if someone's being mean to you, Mia,' I tell her.

'I cried, and Reggie called me a cry-baby,' she says. She's starting to cry now. 'If I tell the teacher, he'll call me a tell-tale.'

'Has this happened before, sweetheart?' I tighten my arms around her, as if I can protect her soft little body from all the dangers in the world. If only.

'It always happens.'

Always? Why am I only just hearing about this?

'Well, I'd better have a word with the teacher,' I say.

'No!' She pulls away from me, sitting up straight, a horrified look on her face. 'I don't want to get told off.'

'But, baby, you won't be told off; it's not your fault if someone's being nasty to you.'

'I *will* be told off,' she insists. 'I always be told off.'

'OK, don't cry, Mia.' I'm not going to argue the point, as she's too upset, but I'm definitely not going to let this rest. She's never mentioned being told off before, not in class and not in the after-school club. I'm pretty sure she's just scared at the thought of getting the teacher involved, but that's what I'm going to have to do, regardless. If there's bullying going on at after-school club, which is supposed to be fun, supposed to be a safe haven for my child while I'm working – a safe haven I *pay* for! – then what the hell is the teacher doing about it?

* * *

I think about it constantly while I'm at work the next day. I feel a white-hot rage in my heart every time I imagine my little girl having her hair pulled and being called names while I'm innocently imagining her being kept happy and entertained. Her class teacher isn't one of those who works at the after-school sessions, but Mrs Harper, the other reception class teacher, is in charge of the youngest kids on both of the days that Mia's there, and I've already sent her a message on the school's system, saying I'd like to speak to her when I next pick up Mia.

When I arrive on the Friday, she ushers me into an adjoining room before Mia has a chance to see me, leaving one of the teaching assistants to supervise the other kids' departure.

'You said you had some concerns?' she asks me pleasantly.

'Yes.' I get straight to the point. 'Mia's told me she's been bullied by a boy called Reggie.'

Mrs Harper raises her eyebrows. 'Really? I'm very surprised to hear that. Reggie's a quiet little boy—'

'Well, I don't need to tell you that even quiet little boys can turn spiteful and—'

'Of course,' she soothes me. 'I'm not saying it's impossible, just that it would be out of character. When was this, and what exactly did Mia say happened?'

I repeat the story Mia told me, and Mrs Harper nods at me knowingly.

'I see. Well, yes, there was an incident on Wednesday—'

'So has it been dealt with? Mia said she was too frightened to tell you about it.'

'I'm sorry, Miss Andrews, but I'm afraid it was Mia that I had to deal with. She was unkind to Reggie about a painting he'd done. He got very upset about it, and unfortunately before I could reach him, Mia had called him a cry-baby and pulled his hair.'

I can feel my mouth opening and closing in shock as I struggle to find any words. *My sweet little girl*? Being unkind to someone, pulling his hair – and then *lying* to me about it? So was she only upset because the teacher had told her off? I'm blinking at Mrs Harper like an idiot.

'I'm... so sorry,' I manage to stutter.

'Ah, these things happen,' she replies. 'I should apologise – I should have told you about it when you collected Mia on Wednesday. I was explaining about the hair-pulling to Reggie's mum, and you and Mia had already left when I looked for you. It is the sort of thing we normally like to tell parents about, in case something's said at home. It's so easy to misinterpret a four-year-old's explanation, isn't it?'

'Yes,' I murmur. Especially when they deliberately lie about something! 'But... have you had to tell Mia off more than once? Does she seem to have an ongoing problem with Reggie?'

'No, I haven't noticed any issues before. Why?'

I shake my head. 'She's told me he's been mean to her before but she's the one that always gets told off,' I admit.

'I think you'll find that's just... her imagination,' Mrs Harper says tactfully. 'Is everything all right at home?' she adds gently. 'Mia's not... unhappy in any way?'

'No, she's fine.' I stare at her. 'Why do you ask?' I can't help feeling like I'm being criticised in some oblique way. Do all single parents feel like this? Like everything that happens must be our fault?

'I only ask because it *is* the first time Mia's done something like this. It's really not like her at all to be unkind. But don't worry, I'm sure it was just an isolated incident. She's been perfectly well-behaved today. Rather quiet, if anything.'

* * *

Mia's giving me an anxious look as I go back into the other room
– where she's now the only child waiting with the teaching
assistant. She must realise I've been talking to Mrs Harper, but
she doesn't say anything; in fact, she stays unusually quiet all the
way home, holding my hand and walking with her head down. I
don't want to say too much to her about the incident with Reggie;
I'm worried that if I do, she won't want to confide in me again. It's
been dealt with by the teacher, and she was obviously upset by
the telling-off. But is that enough?

I worry about it for the rest of the evening, wondering if – in
view of her silly stories about Helen, too – Mia's going through a
phase of telling lies. How am I supposed to know how to deal
with things like this? What would my mum have done, if I'd been
in trouble at school, at such a young age? Perhaps I *should* rein-
force the teacher's ticking-off by giving Mia a stern talking-to
myself? I don't want her to grow up thinking it's OK to pull a little
boy's hair and then lie about it, turning the whole incident
around to get my sympathy. Eventually, I decide I do need to
address the lie now, but I tackle it gently, after I've read her a
bedtime story.

'Mia, I know what really happened with Reggie,' I tell her,
pulling her close to reassure her I'm not going to get angry. 'I
know you didn't tell me the truth about it. We all do things we
shouldn't do, sometimes, sweetie, and Mrs Harper did have to tell
you off about it; you were very unkind to poor Reggie. That's not
like you.'

'He's annoying. He can't even paint a house, and when I said it
was a silly painting he cried like a baby.'

'That was really mean, though, Mia. Not everyone can paint
nice pictures. And you shouldn't have made up a story about
it, OK?'

'But I *like* making up stories,' she says with a shrug.

'I know you do. But not about things that really happen. You need to tell the truth about them, otherwise I might not know whether to believe you if something horrible really does happen to you.'

'But it did!' she insists. 'It *was* horrible that I got told off.'

I could go on trying, but I'm struggling to know how to make her understand. She'll be five in the summer – should she have a clearer grasp by now of right and wrong, truth and lies, or am I expecting too much? How am I supposed to know? How am I going to cope with all the problems I'm going to face as my children grow up, if I don't even know how to deal with this?

I tuck her into bed and kiss her goodnight, but I feel too upset and sad to concentrate on the TV this evening. Perhaps I should have been firmer with Mia about the lying, or should I just laugh it off and accept that all kids probably do it? I need someone older to talk to, someone who understands, someone who's brought up their own kids and can help me make the right decisions. I need my mum.

I want her back, I think, childishly, fighting back tears of self-pity as I get myself ready for bed later. *Why did you have to leave me, Mum?*

Then I think about Helen and Robert. I look on them as real friends now – not just kind neighbours who do quite a lot of childminding for me, but people I like and respect. But we haven't quite achieved the level of closeness I'd need to be able to confide this sort of anxiety to them. What's holding me back, I wonder? Is it the fact that they don't seem to want to talk to me about their own families? Or is it, really, because I feel too vulnerable? I don't want them to see how useless I feel at times, how uncertain I am as a mother, how unsure I always seem to be about whether I'm doing the right thing. I remember how struck I was, at first, by the likeness between Helen and my mum. And yes, she has the same quiet, gentle manner, the same kind smile, that reassuring way about her. I think I'll talk to her about this. Perhaps she'll have some good advice. Yes: I'll have a chat with her tomorrow.

10

It's Saturday, the sun's shining, and I feel a bit more cheerful. Helen's coming in for a coffee later; I thought it would make a change for her to come here, and Mia's ridiculously excited about showing her everything in her bedroom – so much so, that she's tidying up the toy cupboard, not being helped much by Archie, who's sitting on the floor beside her, playing with all the toys as she rearranges them on the shelves.

'Well, *what* a tidy cupboard!' Helen exclaims when – as soon as she walks through the door – Mia drags her by the hand into her room and shows off her work. 'You are a lucky girl, having your own little cupboard and all these toys.'

'Mummy says it's Archie's cupboard too because he hasn't got his own bedroom. The babyish toys are his ones,' Mia says.

'Well, they all look very nice.'

'Not as nice as the shop though,' Mia says.

'Shop?' I ask. 'What shop?'

Helen laughs. 'Oh, we played shop when they came in on Thursday, didn't we, Mia?'

'Not like we do with you, Mummy, with old teabag boxes and things,' Mia says dismissively. 'With a proper shop, like a real one, with real money—'

'*Play* money, Mia,' Helen corrects her. 'It's plastic!' She smiles at me. 'It's just a cardboard counter, with miniature tins and packets. I found that in the charity shop, too. It all folds away into a box.'

'Helen, you really mustn't buy any more toys for them,' I say. 'I'm grateful, obviously, but—'

'Oh, it was a bargain, I couldn't resist it,' she says, waving aside my protest. 'It brought back such memories, playing shop with...'

She breaks off, looking away, shaking her head.

'With your own children?' I prompt, but she just nods and changes the subject, suggesting Mia brings one of her toys into the living room to show her, while we have our coffee.

I wait until we've got our coffee in front of us, and both the children are settled, playing fairly quietly in the corner of the room, to raise my worries about Mia's behaviour.

'When your own children were little, like Mia,' I say carefully, 'did you used to worry about them?'

'Of course,' she says. 'All parents do, Jess. Why? What is it you're worried about?'

'Mia,' I say, lowering my voice to practically a whisper. 'She's been telling lies.'

'Making things up?'

'Worse, really: inventing her own version of something that happened.'

'Oh, I see. Well, I'd say this is the age for it. She's got the vocabulary now to invent things, hasn't she? Twist things around to her advantage. And I have noticed she's got a pretty good imagination!'

'I hope she hasn't been telling *you* any fibs,' I say quickly.

'No, not at all. She just likes to make up little stories. She probably still doesn't understand the difference.'

'But she needs to! I've told her, if she doesn't tell me the truth I might not believe her if something bad happens to her.'

'That's all you can do, really. Just keep reinforcing how important it is and show her you're not pleased if she *does* lie to you. Maybe tell her the story about the boy who cried wolf?'

'That's a good idea. Thank you, Helen.' I pause, and then go on quickly: 'I... sometimes feel... kind of alone, with these issues. My friends are lovely but they don't understand.'

'You must miss your mum.'

I sigh and close my eyes, and she gives me a hug. 'I'm always here for you, love, if you want to talk things over.'

'Thank you. I'll take you up on that. Honestly, I sometimes think I'm such a useless mother. I just never know whether I'm doing the right thing.'

'You're doing just fine. Look at them both – healthy and happy. You've got nothing to worry about.'

* * *

I keep repeating this to myself afterwards. *Nothing to worry about.* Perhaps Helen's right, and I just needed some reassurance. But I love my kids so much, I don't want them to grow up into the sort of people who tell lies, let alone say nasty things to other kids and pull their hair. I didn't even mention the hair-pulling to Helen, I felt too embarrassed about it. Perhaps I should have done, though – she was so understanding and sensible. I wonder if her own children did things like that when they were little. I wonder if *I* did? There's nobody I can ask. Not even my dad, now.

* * *

In the afternoon, after we get back from shopping, I tell Mia the story of the boy who cried wolf. She listens carefully and at the end, says the boy was very silly, but I'm not sure that she's made the connection I wanted her to.

'So what did the little boy do wrong?' I ask her.

'He saw the wolf!' she sings out happily, then adds thought-fully, 'Have you ever seed a wolf, Mummy?'

'*Seen*,' I say automatically. 'No. Well, perhaps, in a zoo, but—'

'Can *we* go to a zoo? I want to see a wolf. Are they scary? Like a monster?' She jumps down and runs around the room, pretending to be a monster, or a wolf – it's hard to tell – roaring at Archie, who's getting to his feet to try to toddle after her.

'But the point of the story is—' I start to explain, but she's now far more interested in trying to frighten the life out of Archie than in listening to me. I give up. I doubt she even understands that there was a moral to the story. Perhaps it's asking too much. Perhaps she's still too young. I'll try again another day.

* * *

On Monday afternoon, after I've collected the children from Helen's, I'm preparing their dinner when Mia wanders into the kitchen and tells me calmly, as if it's a perfectly normal and natural occurrence, that she saw her daddy earlier.

I nearly drop the saucepan I'm holding.

'*What*?'

'We saw Daddy. When we was going to get Archie from nursery.'

'Are you *sure*, Mia?' For once, I don't even correct her gram-mar. I'm too shocked; shocked that she's even mentioned him (she never does), let alone saying she's seen him. To be honest, I'm amazed she could even recognise him now. 'It wasn't just a man who looked a bit like Daddy?'

'No. It *was* Daddy. He said hello. He said, "Hello, Mia."'

My heart's racing. First he comes to my flat, then he turns up at pick-up time? What does it mean? What's going on?

'What did Auntie Helen do? What did she say?'

'She said hello, but then she said we had to hurry up, to get Archie. I wanted to stay and talk to Daddy.' She pouts. 'What's for dinner, Mummy? Can it be beef burglars?'

I stare at her for a minute, too distracted to even answer. No, surely this didn't really happen. Helen doesn't know Callum; she wouldn't have said hello to him. She'd have asked Mia who he was, and more to the point, she'd have told me about it!

'Mia,' I say, 'do you remember what we talked about the other day? About telling lies?'

'Making up stories,' she says. 'Like the boy who saw the wolf.'

'Yes. You mustn't—'

'I want to see one, Mummy! Can we go to the zoo? Can we go at the weekend? Please, Mummy, can we, please. Archie would like to see a wolf, he's never seed a wolf too!'

I'm seriously bothered about this. Of course, the idea of Callum being anywhere near the children bothers me the most, but I'm also really worried if it's *not* true – if Mia's making it up. I'm not sure which worries me the most about that: the fact that she's lying, or the fact that she would even want to see her father.

'Mia, listen to me, please,' I say. 'What I'm trying to tell you is, you mustn't make up stories and pretend they're true. Do you understand?'

'Isn't the story true? Wasn't there really a wolf?'

'Yes! No! I mean, that's just a story, but listen: you didn't really see Daddy, did you? I'm not going to be cross, Mia, but you need to tell me the truth. It's important.'

'You *sound* cross,' she says doubtfully.

'Well, I'm not, I'm just... trying to find out why you're saying you saw Daddy. OK?'

'I did see Daddy. I told you I seed Daddy.' She pouts at me. 'I want to go and watch TV.'

I sigh. I'm still not getting anywhere. I follow her into the living room and turn the TV on for the children's programmes. Archie crawls away from the toy he's been playing with and plonks himself down in front of the screen next to her, and I just leave them to it and go back to the kitchen. I'm trying to stop myself from trembling as I start peeling potatoes, horrible images coming into my head of Callum hanging around near the school, near the nursery, looking out for Mia and Archie, planning – what? I don't even want him talking to them. I don't want him anywhere near them! I can't believe I'm actually hoping Mia *is* lying, this time. Well, at least there's an obvious way to find out.

* * *

I wait until both children are asleep before I call Helen.

'Did you see Callum – my ex – while you and Mia were walking from school to the nursery today?'

'What?' She sounds confused. 'No! Sorry, Jess, but I wouldn't even know what he looks like – it was Robert who saw him the other week when he was outside the flats here, wasn't it? Not me.'

'I know. I didn't think it was likely. But Mia's insisting she saw him while she was with you. She says he said hello to her, and—'

'Oh, dear, is she still telling porky pies?' Helen says. 'Honestly, Jess, if anything like that had happened I'd have told you as soon as you came to pick them up this evening.'

'I know, I was pretty sure she must have made it up.' I sigh. 'But I thought I'd better ask, you know, in case you forgot to say—'

'I wouldn't forget!' She sounds hurt now, and I feel bad. 'Of course I'd tell you.'

'Sorry, Helen. I... just felt like I had to check, before I got really angry with Mia about it.'

'Ah, don't be too angry with her. She's only four and I'm sure it's just a phase she's going through. Perhaps it might be better, after all, if you try to ignore the fibs for a little while instead of making too much of a thing about it? You can never tell with children; sometimes the more you make of something, the more they're going to do it.'

'Maybe,' I say, doubtfully. 'The story of the boy and the wolf didn't help, anyway. She's now obsessed with the idea of seeing wolves.'

Helen laughs, and then we're both silent for a minute and I feel awkward.

'I'm sorry,' I say again. 'But I just... thought I'd better check.'

'Absolutely,' Helen says. 'Of course you had to. Don't worry, Jess. I love your children, I won't let anything happen to harm them, I promise you.'

'Thank you. I can't tell you how much I appreciate it.'

I hang up, feeling relieved and reassured, until I start to wonder what on earth I should do about Mia. Just ignore it, as Helen suggested? Perhaps she's right. After all, Mia seems to have forgotten already about the whole thing. And the last thing I want to do, is encourage her to talk about Callum, or even to think about him. Even to explain why the hell, after all this time, she's suddenly inventing stories about seeing the father she's barely mentioned since we walked away from him. Because I hope, I really hope above all else that she isn't suddenly showing signs of missing him.

* * *

The next day, to my surprise, Mia announces that she doesn't want to go to Helen and Robert's after school.

'Why not?' I ask her gently. 'You always have such a lovely time there.'

'Well, I don't want to go there ever again. I don't like going there any more,' she says, glaring at me. 'I *hate* it there, Auntie Helen is horrible, and I want to stay with you.'

'But you need to tell me *why* you don't want to go downstairs any more, Mia. Has something happened?'

'What I already said before. Auntie Helen's rude to me. She tells me off.'

'Mia, I'm sure she'd have told me if she'd had to tell you off. Are you telling stories again?'

'Yes, I'm telling you the story about Auntie Helen. About when she tells me off. She goes red in the face and shouts at me. Very loudly, like this...'

Mia opens her mouth and screams at the top of her voice, making Archie, who's sitting on the floor next to us, jump with fright and start crying. I pick him up to calm him, at the same time telling Mia that that's enough. But I'm worried now. I'm sure, as sure as I can be, that she's just telling stories again. There's no way Helen would be shouting, or screaming, at her like that, even if she had been naughty and needed to be told off. But why would Mia even *say* a thing like that? What if it's true? People say there's no smoke without fire, but perhaps there's something Mia's misinterpreting; perhaps Helen's tone of voice or change of expression, I don't know. I'll have to find an opportunity over the weekend. I mean, what if Mia really has been so naughty that Helen actually did have to scream at her – and then she couldn't face telling me! It's no good, I'm not going to feel happy about the children going back to Helen and Robert until I've broached the subject and reassured myself that this didn't happen.

11

Saturday. I've just put Archie into his buggy for the weekly supermarket trip, and closed the outside door to the flats behind me when I notice Robert just ahead of us, looking at something on the grass. He turns at the sound of the children's voices and puts his finger to his lips.

'Shh. Come and have a look,' he says. 'It's a baby bird – a blackbird, I think. Fallen out of its nest. Come quietly, Mia, don't frighten it. It doesn't know how to fly yet.'

'Where's its nest?' Mia asks, her voice raised in excitement as she stands with Robert, staring down at the baby bird.

'Shh, Mia!' I remind her.

'I don't know where the nest is, Mia, but probably in that tree.' He points up at the branches of the oak tree spreading above us. I was told when I moved here that it's a protected tree, so the green space where it's situated was preserved when the flats were built.

Archie's trying to pull himself up out of his buggy to see what's going on, but he's being restrained by the straps. I take him out and we all watch quietly as Robert steps a bit closer to the little bird and then bends down to pick it up and put it into a cardboard shoebox that he's placed on the ground.

'Why are you putting him in a box?' Mia squawks.

'To keep him safe until we can either find his nest, or...' he hesitates, then goes on, 'until he's learned to fly. He doesn't seem to have hurt himself.'

'Couldn't he just stay sitting on the grass till he learns to fly?' Mia says. 'I don't think he'll like it much in the box.'

'No, because a cat could get him,' Robert explains.

'And eat him?' she says with horrified excitement. 'Eat him all up?'

'Well, yes, that's the danger.' Robert smiles at her. 'He's quite all right in my box. What do you think we should give him to eat? And how are we going to find the nest?'

Mia's loving this whole Save the Baby Bird mission. This gives me a good opportunity to speak to Helen about what Mia's been saying – much as I'm dreading it. I ask Robert quietly whether Helen's at home, and whether he'd mind if I leave Mia with him just for a couple of minutes. Archie's already lost interest and is showing signs of wanting to sit down and pull up handfuls of grass, so I take him with me and go to knock on Helen's door.

'Hello, Jess,' she says warmly. 'I was just thinking of giving you a knock. I said to Robert, wouldn't the children like to see the baby bird.'

'Yes, Mia's completely taken up with it. Robert might have to stop her from climbing up the tree to look for the nest!' I take a deep breath. 'I'm actually about to go shopping, Helen, but I wondered if I could have a quick word?'

'Of course. Come in.'

'Well, I'll just step inside – I don't want Mia to know I'm talking to you about this.'

'What is it, love? You look worried.'

I sigh. 'Not so much worried as embarrassed, really. I hate to ask you this; I don't want it to come across as... well, as criticism or anything, because it's not. But look, if Mia's naughty when you look after her – if she's rude to you, or doesn't do what you ask her to, you'd be absolutely right to tell her off, OK? But you'd tell me about it, wouldn't you?'

'What?' Helen's staring at me. 'Tell her off? I've never had to, Jess. She's always been perfectly behaved. Oh, she might not always feel like clearing away her toys, but that's just normal, isn't it? I don't tell her off, I just say I'll help her, give her a bit of encouragement, that's all. Is that what you meant?'

'No. Well, I don't know. She just said you've told her off – and the thing is, as you know, she's been telling lies lately but I didn't want to accuse her of doing that again without making sure it's not true.'

Helen's response came a little too quickly, and I wonder if she's just brushing my concern aside. I don't suppose Mia has full-blown tantrums with Helen, like she sometimes has at home, but even so: *always perfectly behaved*? No grumpiness or talking back, even when she's tired after school? Perhaps Helen's just trying to be polite about her – but I'd rather know the truth.

'Of course I'd mention it, Jess, if I ever *had* to tell her off,' she goes on now, 'but I presume she's on her best behaviour when she's with us.' She pauses, seeming to think about it for a moment. 'I wonder...' She shakes her head. 'No, that wasn't a *telling-off*, at all... but I did talk to her, the other day, about the story she made up about seeing her daddy. I wasn't cross, not at all, I just talked it over with her and said it would upset *you* if she made up things like that. I'm sorry, Jess. Perhaps that was wrong of me – I probably shouldn't have got involved, really. But I knew it had worried you and I thought perhaps I could impress on Mia that it was important not to invent stories like that.'

'Oh. I see. Well, I'm sorry, if that's all it was, but...'

I hesitate. To be honest, I'm not sure whether I believe this *is* all it was. I can't see why Mia would have got so upset over such an apparently gentle discussion about inventing stories – let alone claiming that Helen actually screamed at her. Perhaps Helen worded it a little more strongly than she thinks. But I don't want to offend her by keeping on about it if it really was that innocent.

'It's all right,' Helen's saying. 'I'm not offended, Jess – they're your children and of course, you must follow up on anything that worries you. But I promise you, if I ever have to tell Mia off, I will let you know.'

'Thank you.' I give her a hug. 'Actually I'm glad you did talk to Mia about pretending she'd seen her dad, because now that she knows you're not pleased about it, any more than I am, hopefully she won't do it again. I just hope she didn't invent it because she'd *like* to see him. She's never asked to, and, well – I certainly don't want him involved in our lives, ever, if I can help it.'

'Ah, Jess, I doubt it was anything other than Mia's overactive imagination,' Helen says. 'Now, do you want to leave the children here while you go and do your shopping? If Mia's enjoying herself with Robert and the baby bird, you can just leave Archie here with me. Mia can come indoors if she gets bored.'

I hesitate for just a second, remembering what Mia said about not wanting to stay with Helen any more. But I can't have her interpreting any gentle reprimand or discussion with Helen as a telling-off; I need to get her over this.

'You'll get the shopping done much more quickly on your own, I'm sure.' Helen's encouraging me, and I smile.

'Yes... well, it is tempting. Thank you, then.' I take Archie's pram suit off him. 'I'll tell Mia as I'm leaving.'

Mia's squatting on the grass outside, next to the shoebox

where the baby bird is cheeping loudly, probably in fright. I watch her for a moment, loving the way she balances like that, her little bottom only inches from the ground, her head bowed in concentration, a finger hovering over the box.

'Careful, he might bite your finger!' Robert warns her. 'Shall we leave him alone for a little while now so he can eat that worm we've given him? I'll pop the lid on his box. I've made little holes in it – see? So he can breathe.'

Mia stands up. 'Can we look for his nest while he eats his worm?' she says, taking hold of Robert's hand so trustingly, it makes my heart ache.

'Well, we could have a walk around the tree, looking up in the branches, couldn't we?' Robert says. And then: 'Oh, look, your mummy's here now. I think you're supposed to be going shopping.'

'Actually, Robert, Helen's kindly suggested the children can stay here with you both,' I say. 'I've left Archie with her. Would you mind hanging on to Mia? I promise not to be long.'

'Yay! Please let me stay with you, Uncle Robert, I want to find the nest and find more wiggly worms for Beaky. That's what we're calling him, Mummy,' she explains. 'The box is his hospital and I'm his nurse.'

'That's a very important job, Mia.' I smile at her. 'But only if—'

'Of course she can stay,' Robert says at once. 'If it gets too cold, we'll go inside, OK, Mia?'

'OK,' she agrees happily.

I feel a rush of relief as I thank Robert and hurry off down the road to the shop. It would make everything so awkward if Mia starts being difficult about being left with Helen, so it's lovely to see her looking happy about it. And it makes me feel even more convinced she must be lying about the 'telling off'.

* * *

I'm nearly home afterwards with my heavy shopping bags when I catch sight of someone hanging around outside the flats. My heart starts racing. *Callum.* Not again!

I slow down, wishing there was some way I could detour to avoid him, but at the same time, he turns round and sees me.

'Where have you been?' he demands.

'Well, hello to you, too.' I'm struggling to keep my voice level, to stop it from shaking. 'I'd have thought it was obvious where I've been.' I indicate the full bags of shopping. 'What's it got to do with you?'

'I suppose you've dumped the kids again?'

'No. I never *dump* them. They're with someone who cares about them, which is more than you ever did.' My eyes stray to the shoebox which has been left on the path next to the wall of the building, with its lid on. Thank goodness, Robert and Mia must have gone inside.

'So already, you're fed up with looking after them,' he says, sneering. 'I knew this would happen. You're useless. You haven't got a clue. I don't know why the courts let you keep them.'

This was how it always used to go. He'd start by insulting me, making me feel as rubbish as he obviously thought I was, and it would gradually escalate. It's been over a year and a half since I walked out, during which time I've been able to put his abuse to the back of my mind, try to forget about it – or at least, pretend to myself that I'm forgetting about it – and get on with my life, but now it all comes back to me with horrible clarity. How it felt to be so demeaned, to feel so worthless that I lost all respect for myself. *Why now?* Why, after so long of apparently not giving a damn what the children and I are doing, or whether he ever sees any of us again, is he suddenly turning up, starting all this again?

I straighten up, look him in the eyes. The difference, now, is that I've grown up. I've moved on, made a life for myself and the kids. I don't have to care what he says.

'I'm going home,' I tell him firmly. 'Please get out of my way.'

He shrugs and steps aside, but I feel his eyes on me, following me all the way to the outside door of the flats.

'I'm warning you, Jess,' he calls after me. 'If you carry on neglecting those kids, don't think I won't report you. You might have custody now, but that doesn't mean it can't be taken away from you.'

'I am *not* neglecting them!' I retort – but he's already strolling away. He kicks the cardboard box as he passes it, laughing to himself as if he actually knows what's inside it.

As soon as he's out of sight round the corner, I go to pick up the box and check the baby bird's OK, and thank goodness, he's sitting up and cheeps at me as if in recognition. I put the lid back on and leave the box closer to the wall.

I don't want to go straight into Helen and Robert's flat until I've calmed down. I go upstairs first to unpack the shopping, but I'm shaking as I do it. What the hell is he *doing*, suddenly turning up like this – twice, now – trying to intimidate me, talking about the custody arrangements as if he even cares about them?

I suddenly stop, thinking again of Mia's story about seeing her daddy the other day; was she telling the truth after all? Perhaps Helen didn't even see him, didn't even hear him saying hello to Mia, so she's ignorant of the whole thing? Mia might have just *thought* Helen said hello to Callum, or imagined it, but the rest of it is beginning to feel ominously like it could really have happened.

I can't have this. I can't have him turning up like this, making threats – it'll only be a matter of time before he finds out where I'm leaving the children, and then what? I can't let Helen and

Robert be terrorised by him hanging around their flat. I'll have to stop sending the kids there. I'll have to move.

I'm close to tears now, but I do my best to compose myself before going downstairs. I can't let the children see I'm upset. As it is, Mia rushes to meet me as soon as Helen opens the door to me.

'We couldn't find Beaky's nest!' she says. 'So Uncle Robert says we'll leave him in his hospital box till he can fly. Please can we bring him into our flat, Mummy, please, please, please? He'll be cold outside all night.'

'No, Mia!' I lift her up and hug her. 'He's not going to be any colder in the box than he'd be in his nest.'

'Warmer, probably – that's what I've been telling you, isn't it, Mia?' says Robert. 'We've made him up a little bed in that box, with lots of dead leaves to lie on. He'll be fine. Anyway, taking him indoors would frighten him.'

Mia sighs but gives in gracefully. 'I love Beaky,' she says. 'I'm glad we rescued him.'

I try to ignore the mental picture I have in my head of Callum's size-twelve boot kicking the box where she lovingly settled the baby bird on his bed of leaves. Did he look inside it before I arrived? Or, even worse, had he been watching while Robert and Mia were tending to the bird earlier? I don't think I want to let my thoughts go down that route.

* * *

The next day, under pressure from Mia, we're downstairs and outside before we've even had breakfast. But as soon as I catch sight of Beaky's 'hospital' box, I know he's gone. The lid is off, the box is empty.

Mia stops, staring at it, her lower lip quivering.

'Where's he gone?' she says, looking around her on the grass. 'How did he get out?'

'He must have jumped about and knocked the lid off,' I say.

'Why didn't Uncle Robert stick the lid on with Sellotape?' she asks crossly. 'Poor Beaky. Has he got eated by a cat?'

'*Eaten*, Mia. But no, I don't think a cat would have got him. He's probably learned to fly, sweetie.'

'But we should look for him, in case he's just hopped off. I'm supposed to be his nurse.' She gives me a furious look. 'I *told* you we should take him indoors.'

'He'd have been very unhappy indoors, Mia. If he's managed to fly, he'll be much happier now – flying up in the sky, like he should be doing. Hopefully he's found his nest.'

'And found his mummy?' she asks, tearfully.

'Yes. Let's hope so.'

'But I wanted to keep him!' Mia starts to cry properly now. 'I wanted him to be my pet bird. I want him to come back.'

'He's a wild bird; he'd never be a pet,' I say. 'It would be cruel to keep him. He needed you yesterday, but now he's feeling better and he needed to... be a wild bird again.'

While we've been staring at the empty box and having this conversation, Robert must have seen us as he's now come to join us.

'Mummy's right, Mia,' he says gently. 'Beaky probably felt so much better because you nursed him so well yesterday, that his wings grew stronger and he learnt to fly really quickly. You can feel very proud of that.'

'Thank you,' I whisper to him as Mia bends down to pick up the empty shoe box, staring into it wistfully.

'Please can I keep the box?' she asks in a pitiful voice. 'So I can show my teacher when I take my drawing of Beaky to school?'

She drew a picture of Beaky – with a worm in his mouth – while I was shopping yesterday.

'Of course you can,' he says, smiling. 'Your teacher will be very interested to hear all about Beaky, and how you looked after him.'

She's stopped crying now, although she still looks mournful. I'm glad we've managed to convince her that the baby bird freed himself and flew away. But I can't help wondering whether someone who was hanging around out here yesterday, who kicked the box as he was leaving – might have come back later. I tell myself not to be silly. Why would Callum want to do that? I'm probably just still feeling stressed about the encounter with him yesterday afternoon; it's ridiculous to imagine him doing such a petty thing, for no obvious reason.

But then again, what did Callum ever do that wasn't petty, spiteful, and unreasonable?

12

The sun's shining, I can smell spring in the air, the children seem settled, and most importantly, Callum hasn't turned up again. I think, now, that I was overreacting. Yes, he's always been a nasty piece of work so it wouldn't surprise me that he hasn't changed, but as for 'Beaky', why would he even bother with that? I think it's more likely another kid in the flats here found the shoebox and opened it out of curiosity. They probably got a fright when the bird hopped out! But Mia seems happy enough with the story I told her about him finding his nest and his mummy. Every black-bird we see now she decides is probably Beaky 'all grown up', and she always says hello to them.

I like to think she learnt quite a lot from the experience. Not just about birds – Robert has told her loads of stuff that even I didn't know, about how to recognise a blackbird's eggs, and their distinctive song, and about how fast they mature and get their proper black feathers – but also about disappointment and loss and accepting that what she wants isn't always the best thing for others. I hope so, anyway. I'm not always very good at that sort of stuff so it's been lovely to have back-up from a nice father – or grandad? – figure like Robert.

She got a lot of praise from her teacher, too, for providing such an interesting topic for the class at Show and Tell. Her drawing of Beaky was put up on the wall and the children were all asked to draw pictures of their favourite birds or animals. Ever since, Mia has been making up stories about Beaky and his supposed adventures back in the wild, alternating these with her stories about elephants and wolves.

There's only one problem: she now never stops pestering me about having a pet or going to the zoo – or both. Robert found her a picture of a wolf on his laptop, and printed it out for her, and Mia asked me to stick the picture on her bedroom wall. She likes to look at it with a deprived expression on her face, reminding me that it's *not fair* that she can't see a wolf 'in real life' or even have a dog or a cat or anything as a pet.

'Perhaps she'll want to be a vet when she grows up,' Helen says to me when I go to collect Mia and Archie after work. 'Animals and birds seem to be her obsession at the moment.'

'Well, I think her teacher made her feel important over the whole episode with Beaky. And I suppose most kids go through a phase of begging for a pet. I've told her, I love animals too but we can't have a dog or a cat. Besides it being another mouth to feed, we're in an upstairs flat.'

'Yes, it's difficult enough, isn't it, feeding two children when you're on a budget,' she says sympathetically. 'Don't worry, if Mia talks to me about having a pet I'll make sure I remind her about what you've told her.'

* * *

'Once upon a time,' says Mia the next day, as she's bouncing up and down on my bed while I'm trying to put clean sheets on it, 'there was a big bad wolf who lived in a zoo. His name was Wolfie.'

I smile at her. Her stories seem to have the same characters in them for several weeks until she gets bored, but Wolfie has survived for quite a while now, having all sorts of adventures in his zoo.

'And what did Wolfie do?' I ask her. 'Mia, please get off the bed while I'm trying to make it.'

She bounces off, landing with a thud on the rug and nearly knocking over her brother, who's toddled into the room to join us.

'Wolfie was very bored,' she says. 'Because there weren't any children coming to see him at the zoo. Their mummies said it was too expensive.' She gives me a meaningful look. 'So he moved in with the elephant.'

'Why would he do that?'

She sighs, as if I'm being deliberately obtuse.

'Because the elephant was his friend and Wolfie liked him.'

'OK. And what happened then?'

'They made too much noise,' she says sadly. 'So they got told off.'

I laugh. 'I bet a wolf and an elephant *would* make a lot of noise together.'

'Yes, like little girls and boys make too much noise and get told off,' she says.

'I expect your teacher has to tell some of the children in your class off for that,' I say with a smile.

'Sometimes. And at Auntie Helen's, me and Archie got told off and we had to sit on the naughty step and be still and quiet and behave ourselves.'

I stop midway through changing a pillow case, and turn to

look at her. She doesn't seem particularly bothered – she said it in a completely neutral tone as if she was just describing being asked to wash her hands or take off her shoes. But it's ringing alarm bells with me, especially as Helen so recently assured me she'd always tell me if there was a problem.

'Auntie Helen didn't say anything to me about this, Mia,' I say, sitting down on the bed and pulling her towards me. 'What happened?'

'What I just said. We had to sit on the naughty step—'

'What's the naughty step?' I interrupt her. There aren't any stairs in our flats, of course, so it can only be a concept, if anything.

'It's that little step in the bathroom, like what we've got in ours, Mummy,' she says with a sigh implying I'm being deliberately difficult. 'What I climb on to go to the toilet.'

'I see. But did Auntie Helen say why you had to sit on it?'

'She said we was too noisy.'

I take a breath. Being too noisy? Wouldn't she have dealt with any noisy exuberance by just asking them to keep it down? A *naughty step*? Really?

'What – were you shouting?' I ask Mia.

'It was mostly Archie. He was screaming; it was when his tooth was coming through.' She pauses, shrugs, and adds, 'He was getting on my nerves so I screamed too, to try and make him stop.'

'I see.'

Again, I wonder how much of this I can believe. Helen has *promised* me she'd tell me if she has to tell Mia off, hasn't she? And as for Archie – obviously, a one-year-old who's in pain from teething isn't being naughty. I took pain-relieving gel in to Helen's for her to use when he was cutting those last couple of teeth, and I'm sure she wouldn't have got cross about him crying, even if Mia did. No, I don't believe it, it's just Mia's overactive imagination again.

'Well, it's not a good idea to scream back at Archie, Mia,' I tell her. 'He can't help crying if he's in pain. He's still a baby.'

'He can walk now. Babies don't walk.'

Sometimes my daughter's logic is too much for me. I smile at her and turn back to making the bed, but I'm still feeling uneasy. Mia doesn't seem upset enough for any of this to really ring true. But where would she have got hold of the idea of the naughty step, if Helen hadn't used the expression? I'm sure neither the nursery nor the school use such an old-fashioned concept. I'm going to have to ask her, for my own peace of mind.

'So what happened to Wolfie?' I ask, to change the subject.

'He slid down the elephant's trunk,' she says, quoting the words of one of her favourite children's songs. She jumps up from the rug. 'I'm bored with that story now, Mummy. Can I have a biscuit?'

* * *

I don't waste any time in bringing up the subject of the 'naughty step' with Helen the next time I'm collecting the children.

'I presume this is just Mia's overactive imagination again,' I say, watching Helen's face carefully. 'But she's been telling me she and Archie had to sit on the *naughty step* because they were so noisy.'

Before I can even go on to express my surprise at Mia having any concept of a naughty step, Helen starts to smile.

'Oh, bless her – that's my fault; it was just a game,' she says. 'I was telling her, the other day when she was shouting at poor Archie – you know, the day his tooth was coming through and he was really grizzly – that some strict parents in the past used to make their children sit on the bottom stair when they were being noisy or difficult, and they called it the naughty step. She thought it was so funny, she took Archie with her and went to sit on the little step we've got her for the toilet. She treated it as a game; sat there for a minute, with Archie sitting on the floor next to her, then ran back into the living room, shouted loudly again and sent herself back to the step! I had to distract them both with something else in the end!'

I can't help smiling – it sounds so plausible, and in fact so like Mia to make a game out of something like this. And Helen's response was so immediate, she surely couldn't have made it up on the spot if it wasn't completely true.

'I would have told you if I'd really had to reprimand her,' she goes on. 'I did promise you I would.'

'I know. I was just curious about how Mia had got hold of the idea of a naughty step,' I say quickly. 'And I should pay you for the toilet step. And anything else you've had to buy for the children – you must tell me what you need so that I can sort it out for you. You shouldn't have to—'

'Oh, you'd be surprised what Robert and I find in charity shops,' she says, smiling. 'Don't begrudge us having the pleasure of spending a few pence here and there.'

It's odd how I've ended up feeling less concerned now about the whole naughty step story than I am about this business of them spending their money. It doesn't seem right, and I shouldn't be letting it happen. I can't seem to get through to Helen that it's silly them buying things for just the few hours they're having the children. Anyone would think they were going to be caring for them full-time.

* * *

When I pick Mia up from the after-school club the next afternoon, she rushes out, telling me excitedly:

'Faiza in my class isn't going to get any Easter eggs because her family don't have an Easter.'

'No. That's because they're a different religion.'

'I know. Mrs Green told us. *And* Ben isn't getting Easter eggs either. He's getting a puppy.'

I groan. I know exactly what's coming!

'Please can me and Archie have a puppy or a kitten instead of Easter eggs, Mummy? *Please.* I know you said we can't have one in our flat so why can't we go and live somewhere else and have a puppy? It can share my dinner, I won't mind. It can have the veggiebles.'

'Mia, you know what the answer is. We can't live somewhere else. We can't have a pet, and that's all there is to it.'

'It's *so* unfair,' she says, pouting.

'Well, I'm sorry, but lots of things are unfair. We just have to put up with them. Come on, don't be grumpy about it.'

'*Daddy's* got a puppy,' she shoots back.

I stop midway out of the school gate, dropping her hand in shock.

'No, he hasn't. What makes you think he has?' I ask her.

'I sawed him. He was taking his puppy for a walk. It was little, and black.'

'Mia, I don't think that's true, is it. You haven't seen Daddy.'

'Yes, I have. And he had a puppy, its name was... um... its name was Beaky.'

I laugh with relief. She's making up a story again. She couldn't think of a name, so she came up with the name she gave that baby blackbird. I *knew* these stories about seeing Callum have been made up – this makes me even more certain!

'Puppies aren't called *Beaky*, Mia. That's a name for a bird. Birds have beaks, puppies don't!'

She shrugs moodily. 'Well all right, I don't know what its name was but it was Daddy's puppy, 'cos Daddy had him on a lead and he brought the puppy over the road so that I could see it. But Auntie Helen said I wasn't allowed to stroke it and we had to hurry up.'

I stare at her. 'Are you *sure* this is really what happened, Mia? You really think it was Daddy, not just another man? When did it happen?'

'The other day,' she says crossly. 'You *never* believe me, Mummy. I *did* see it, and it *was* Daddy. I'm not making up stories. Ask Auntie Helen!'

I feel a cold sense of dread coming over me. Suddenly, I doubt everything I thought I was sure about. I look at Mia's indignant little face. She might be mistaken – it might be that it wasn't really Callum, but I definitely don't now think she's making the episode up. And there's something about the idea of Callum having a puppy, just to get Mia to talk to him, that rings so horribly true, so horribly likely, that I shiver from head to toe. Of course, I can ask Helen about it, but the chances are she just thought he was an innocent man with a puppy who was being friendly. Callum would be good at that – at pretending to be an innocent, friendly man. I know that only too well, to my cost.

All I know is… I'm going to have to pay more attention to Mia's stories from now on, if they include any mention of Callum. And the nice spring sunshine has suddenly turned cold.

13

As I expected, Helen immediately tries to reassure me when I ask her about the man with the puppy.

'Oh, it was just one of the other parents at the school gate,' she says, laughing. 'Mia wanted to stroke the puppy but I said we needed to hurry to pick up Archie.'

'She's so sure it was her dad,' I say. 'And what worries me is, you wouldn't know, Helen, would you?'

'Well, look, I wouldn't hang around, with the children, where *any* strange man was concerned, obviously,' she begins, but I just shake my head. I can't expect Helen to understand, but I have a bad feeling about this particular episode, and it's making me doubt whether any of Mia's previous stories were lies.

'OK, well I'd prefer it if you'd tell me about any *strange men* who try to talk to the kids, please,' I say. I feel rattled, annoyed. Why *didn't* she tell me? 'Come on, children – we need to get home. Let's try and decide what you're both going to have for dinner.'

'That's always a chore, isn't it,' Helen sympathises. 'Especially if they're fussy eaters.'

I feel myself flinch. Fussy eaters? Why would Helen mention fussy eaters? Of course, that's exactly what Mia is – and Archie, too, I suppose, but he's still a baby and hasn't even had time to develop his own tastes yet! But I'm on the defensive straight away. Is this a thinly-veiled criticism? Why else bring it up?

'What do you mean?' I ask her. 'I hope they're not too difficult with you when you give them their snack after school?'

'Ah, no, they're fine. As long as it's biscuits or crisps!' she says, smiling. 'But I gather Mia mostly has things like burgers and fish fingers and baked beans for her dinners at home. She pulled such a face when I asked her if she didn't like nice healthy things like chicken or fish, and fresh vegetables, you'd have thought I'd suggested eating a plate of worms!'

I feel myself going red.

'Well, yes, I suppose she's a bit fussy with vegetables,' I admit, 'like most kids, I think. And to be honest, I just... well, I suppose I feel so tired in the evenings, I normally give them something easy – things I know they'll eat without making a fuss. But I do sometimes buy chicken, and mince, and, well, she'll eat carrots, or peas,' I finish, realising how defensive I must sound.

'Oh, I'm not criticising, love, really I'm not. I know how difficult it can be,' Helen soothes me. 'And of course you're tired, after working all day every day, on your feet. But I just wonder if some of those convenience foods are more expensive for you than the healthy options.'

I can feel my face turning to a *sulky teenager* expression now. She might say she's not criticising me, but I certainly feel suddenly as if my parenting is being questioned. I'm not feeding my kids the healthiest food, or even the cheapest food? What kind of mother am I? The trouble is, I'm sure she's right.

'Well, now I'm earning a bit more money it's not such a big deal,' I say a little brusquely – for all the world as if I'm a multimillionaire, chucking money away on luxuries, rather than just buying value packs of fish fingers and reduced-price chicken nuggets. 'It's worth it, if it means I can spend more quality time with the kids.'

'Of course,' Helen says calmly. 'I understand.'

I think about it all evening. I feel stupid now – a fraud, as well as inadequate. Who did I think I was, talking about *spending quality time with the kids*? What quality time? They mostly sit in front of the TV, apart from when I'm reading to them. I never seem to have any time. What's wrong with me? How do other parents manage?

I suppose Helen's only trying to be helpful. She's just thinking about the children's health, as well as my budget. She's right, isn't she: I should be buying better food, making them eat it whether they want it or not. But isn't that a bit... *draconian*? Surely most children are fussy eaters at Mia's age?

Was *I* fussy? Did my mum have this sort of problem with me? What did she do about it? What would she say, if she were here now, being Mia's and Archie's grandma, helping me with them, giving me her advice?

I watch Mia shovelling up her burger and oven chips with gusto, while I cut Archie's dinner up for him and help him to feed himself. Surely the most important thing is that they're fed and happy? In fact, why the hell am I taking any notice of what Helen thinks about it? Much as I'm grateful for what she's doing to help me, I didn't ask for her advice. I'm sure she means well, but she's just being old-fashioned and frankly, it's not her place to comment on what I feed my kids.

* * *

'My mum used to force me to eat Brussels sprouts,' Lucy says, when she calls me this evening and I can't help bringing the subject up. 'And now I hate them so much, I feel sick even at the sight of them.'

'Exactly,' I agree. 'They'll grow out of it, won't they? I must admit I was a bit worried when Helen came out with it; you know how I am, always lacking confidence. But to be honest I just think some of her ideas are a bit old-fashioned. Perhaps she brought her own kids up really strictly – or maybe her kids weren't fussy at all, so she just doesn't understand.'

'Whatever,' says Lucy. 'The point is, she should keep her opinion of your parenting to herself, really.'

'I know. But... I know it's silly, but I don't like the thought of her disapproving of me. Apart from the fact that she's looking after my kids regularly, I... well, I think of her as...' I falter, and come to a stop. 'As a friend,' I add eventually.

But I'm sure Lucy knows exactly what I really want to say. I don't *just* think of Helen as a friend, but... sort of... as a mum, too. Not that anyone could ever replace my own mum, but she's so similar, I can't help relating to her in that way, and any suggestion that she's criticising me makes me feel like a little child being chastised by Mummy. I want her to approve of me, to like me, to help me feel good about myself – and if she doesn't, it makes me feel resentful and sulky. Whether she's right or not!

14

My work has been exhausting recently. Tariq seems to be taking over more and more from Margaret, and making changes. He has his own ideas about how the shop should be run.

'*Events* are the way forward,' he tells me, just as I'm getting my coat on to go home. Unfortunately, I haven't really got an excuse to rush off urgently because today is one of the days Helen picks up the children, and she never minds if I'm a bit late getting back. 'We need to welcome people into the shop without making them feel under obligation to buy anything,' he goes on.

'But surely that's the whole point—' I begin, but he's shaking his head at me.

'People are hard up these days, Jess, and they're wary of coming into the shop to browse in case we jump on them and try to persuade them to part with their money. If they know they're being welcomed in without any pressure to buy, they're more relaxed, and, in a roundabout way, more likely to buy.'

I'm not convinced by his argument, but I smile and nod.

'So what are you suggesting?'

'We need to hold special events, and promote them. Like a

storytelling day for little kids, for instance, and perhaps a day where we feature a certain genre in particular and decorate the shop appropriately.'

'We did that for Valentine's Day,' I point out. 'We showcased lots of romance books, and we put hearts everywhere—'

'Exactly. That's the kind of thing,' he says enthusiastically. 'So give it some thought, will you? In your spare time?'

'Me?' I squawk. What I'm actually thinking is: *spare time? What the hell is that?* But I force another smile, say goodnight to him before he can think of anything else to detain me with – and rush out to catch the bus.

It's bugging me while I'm doing the kids' dinner – trying to think of some kind of book event I can suggest to Tariq to show I'm doing my bit, without making too much extra work for myself – and I'm not really listening to Mia prattling on about what games they played with Helen and Robert after school. Not until she suddenly gives a huge sigh, as if she's so exasperated by my inattention that she can hardly be bothered with me, before saying, slowly and at top volume:

'I *said*, Mummy, why don't we live with Daddy any more?'

I'm so surprised, I nearly drop the fork I'm turning sausages with. She never asks about this; well, perhaps once or twice she might have done, back when we actually left Callum. But ever since then, she always seems to have just accepted it.

I turn to look at her.

'You know why, poppet. I explained it to you at the time. Sometimes mummies and daddies stop loving each other and don't get along very well any more so they don't want to keep living together.'

'But the mummies and the daddies still love their children?'

I put the fork down, squat to her level and put my arms around her.

'Of course, sweetie. I love you and Archie more than the whole world. You know that, don't you? I won't ever, ever, ever stop loving *you*.'

'And the daddies still love their children too?' she says, giving me a pointed look.

Ah. I should have anticipated this.

'Well,' I say. 'Of course, all mums and dads love their children, but—'

Why am I telling her this? It's an outright lie. Callum never loved her or Archie. He didn't even want them. He never bothered with them, they irritated him and got in the way of his selfish, spoilt-brat life.

'But, well, sometimes, it's best for everyone if the children just live with one parent,' I finish awkwardly.

'The one who loves them the most?' she asks hopefully.

'Absolutely!' I laugh and hug her again, squeezing her tight, and she giggles and squeals. 'And nobody could love you more than I do!'

She seems satisfied with this – for the moment. She walks away, singing to herself, but it's as if I can see her little brain ticking over, thinking this through, turning it over, getting ready for the next question. I suppose it was naïve of me to think she was never going to want to know more about the situation. I just wonder what triggered it right now. I think about the stories she's told me about seeing Callum and I try to stifle the feeling I have, the little lurch of unease, the little voice in my head again asking whether they were true. I don't want her thinking about him, not at all, not in any shape or form. I realise I'll have to explain a few things to her eventually, when she's a bit older: unpalatable truths about her father that I don't even want to talk about, myself. If I don't tell her what he was really like, she might grow up with a different version of him based on her imagination, a much more favourable and undeserved impression. It would be awful if she thought of him as a sad, mysterious, lonely figure who could be longing to have a relationship with her. If she did, the truth would come as more than a rude awakening, it would break her heart. But I can't tell her yet. She wouldn't understand, it'd frighten her and upset her, and I wouldn't be able to bear it.

I go back to cooking the sausages, and try to focus my mind again on ideas for book events, but unsurprisingly, I've lost my concentration.

* * *

'What about something for Easter?' Helen suggests when I talk to her about it the next day. 'Or perhaps just spring, in case Easter might not be suitable for people of other faiths.'

'Yes, but what?' I counter moodily. 'It's all right for kids – during the Easter holiday we can have pictures of fluffy chickens and read stories from Beatrix Potter about Peter Rabbit and so on, but how can we turn that into a subject for adults?'

She ponders on this for a moment, while I sigh with frustration at my own inability to *think outside the box*, as Tariq described it this afternoon when he was asking if I'd come up with anything yet. I felt like asking him if *he'd* had any ideas, since he's paid a lot more than me to come up with them.

'I know!' says Robert suddenly from across the room, where he's been doing a puzzle on the floor with Mia. I didn't realise he'd been listening. 'A display of books about nature. And gardening! Everyone with a garden starts getting interested in it in spring. And perhaps guidebooks – books about the footpaths and countryside around here. Anything outdoorsy. Could you invite people from a rambling club, or camera club? That sort of thing?'

I'm nodding, slowly. I don't know how many books it would sell, but it'd be *something*, wouldn't it? It might get people into the shop, as Tariq seems to want, even if they're not spending their money.

'Thanks, Robert. Those are good ideas,' I say, smiling at him. 'At least it gives me a suggestion to put forward. I've been racking my brain all day, but since I've been a mum I think most of my brain cells have withered and died.'

'No they haven't,' Helen says stoutly. 'It's just that you've got too much on your mind.'

'I suppose so.' I turn my head away from the direction of the children and add in a whisper: 'Has Mia been asking any questions about Callum while she's with you?'

She frowns. 'No, why?'

'Oh, no reason. I just... had to field a question yesterday, and it's unusual. That's all.'

'Well, I suppose it has to happen, love. Curiosity.'

'Yes. I realise that.' I sigh. 'It... will be difficult to explain.'

'Honesty usually works best with kids, doesn't it?'

I just nod, but I can't tell her how impossible it would be, to be completely honest with a child about someone like Callum.

15

'That's a very good idea, Jess,' Tariq says when I report back to him with my – or, I should say, Helen and Robert's – suggestions for a spring book fair in the shop. 'Right, while Margaret's here today, we can spare you for an hour or so. Would you like to get on the computer and see if you can track down any local societies with a gardening or hiking interest, or anything similar? Make a note of contact details for their chairperson or leader or whatever. I'll talk to Margaret about an appropriate date for the event – it'll be a Saturday of course, but I presume you'll be able to work?'

'Oh.' I blink at him stupidly. 'Well, it's—'

'I know it's normally your day off but you'll be paid overtime, obviously. We'll have Emma here, but we'll need all hands on deck as it should be a busy day. I presume you can book your childminder.'

He walks off without waiting for me to answer.

I go into the office at the back of the shop and log onto the computer, feeling miffed. I don't like the way he presumes. I can't even *presume* anything myself, until I've spoken to Helen. But I do at least manage to find details of a local rambling club, a horticultural society, an allotment holders' group and a birdwatching club. I've just finished listing all their contact details when Tariq comes to see how I'm getting on. He seems pleased.

'Great, well done! Margaret and I have agreed this event will run on the Saturday at the start of the Easter holidays. Now, I'd like you to do a search for any new books being published on any of those subjects. Ideally I'd like to invite one or two authors to come and talk about their books. And I want to get invitations out to all of these groups as soon as I can, start advertising the event on social media and get some posters printed. You can help.'

He bustles off again to confer with Margaret, looking chuffed with his own self-importance. I wonder why I used to like Tariq. He's now irritating the life out of me.

* * *

I hate having to ask Helen and Robert for another favour, but my apologies are waved aside, both of them beaming with pleasure at the thought of having my kids for a whole Saturday.

'That's no problem, Jess. And we're having them every afternoon of the following week, aren't we?' she goes on, smiling. 'We're looking forward to it.'

'Aw, thanks, Helen. I'm a bit cross about this whole thing with the spring event, to be honest,' I add. 'Margaret never used to ask me to take on extra stuff like this, when she was in charge. I hope Tariq's not going to make a habit of it.'

'Perhaps he'll give you a pay rise.'

'Huh. I don't think so. The shop's struggling, that's why he's trying to get people in, by holding this event.' I give an involuntary shudder. 'I hope sales do pick up.'

I don't need to spell out my worst fears. Independent bookshops are closing down every day, we all know that.

'So I guess you do need to support him,' Robert points out, 'if he's trying new ideas to get customers in. And we *never* mind having your children, Jess. It's an absolute pleasure for us.'

'Thank you so much. And I'm on annual leave for the second week of the holidays. I can't wait. It'll be my first break since Christmas and it'll be so lovely to spend a whole week with the children.' I drop my voice, checking neither of the children are listening. 'I'm planning a special treat for them – a day at the zoo. I've been looking online for ticket prices. But it's a secret – I'm not mentioning it yet.'

'Oh, Mia will love that, won't she!' Helen says, smiling. 'She's always on about going to the zoo.'

'Yes, exactly.'

* * *

The next Friday evening my friends come round. We're celebrating Miranda's birthday and they're going on for an Italian meal afterwards. We've clubbed together for a bottle of fizz to toast Miranda with, and we all scream with the usual kind of excitement as the bottle opens with a pop and the cork flies across the room, prompting us into fits of giggles before we've even sung 'Happy Birthday' at the top of our voices.

These days I usually stick to one glass of wine, if I have a drink at all, but as this evening is a special celebration, I allow myself a small second glass. But the other girls are soon on their second bottle, and they're all singing along at the tops of their voices to one of our favourite songs, while I try my best to shush them a bit – when Mia suddenly appears in the room in her pyjamas, clutching Ellie Elephant under her arm and staring at me.

'Mummy!' she says accusingly. 'You woked me up. And Archie's crying.'

'Oh f... flip! Sorry, sweetie.' I jump up. 'Can you turn the volume down, please?' I add to my friends as I run out of the room.

Archie's standing up in his cot, his dummy having been spat out onto the floor, holding onto the rail and red in the face with distress.

'Mumma! Mumma!' he howls at the top of his voice. I lift him into my arms and wipe his tears, shushing him gently as he gradually hiccups himself into silence. My precious baby – how could I have been so thoughtless, making so much noise with my friends that I didn't hear him crying? I can't put him straight back down to sleep now when he's been so upset. He might have been having a bad dream, and when he cried for his mummy, I didn't come, I didn't hear him, I was too busy enjoying myself. I feel terrible.

I carry him through to the living room, where the music's now playing more quietly. Everyone looks a little subdued. Mia's still standing in the middle of the room, holding court, telling everyone that she'll soon be five and she wants a kitten for her birthday (which in fact isn't until June) and she likes singing 'Happy Birthday' and would my friends like to hear her singing it? The girls all smile at her kindly enough as she trills her way through the song but I'm sure they're now thinking it's time they made a move – which is what they do straight after the final line.

I sit with Archie on my lap and Mia sulking beside me as they all kiss me goodbye and tell me they wish I could go with them. And then they're gone, and I'm alone with a grizzly baby and a cross daughter who's been deprived of her audience. And I've got to get them both back to sleep. I find myself wondering, just for a second, what it would be like to go with them all to an Italian restaurant. To sit round the table, to order something from a menu, to laugh and chat and eat together for the rest of the night.

And then I look down at Archie's tearstained little face, and Mia's funny grumpy one, and I'm filled with such an overwhelming love that nothing, nothing, let alone a pizza or a risotto, could possibly ever come close.

'How about another story?' I suggest. 'A really late, bedtime one?'

'Can we have it with us all snuggled together in your bed?' says Mia.

'We definitely can!' I agree.

And that's what we do.

* * *

I've got a headache when I wake up in the morning. Archie's sitting up in his cot, sucking on his dummy, cuddling his teddy bear, and I can hear Mia singing to herself as she runs around the living room. *She's running around the living room.* Mia's up, running around, doing God knows what, while I'm still... urgh! I groan. OK, I shouldn't have had that second glass of fizz – I'm not used to it these days. But more than anything, I'm just so tired. It took me ages to get off to sleep, with Mia and Archie both fidgeting next to me. In the end I lifted Archie back into his cot once I knew he was definitely sound asleep, but it was the early hours of the morning by then.

I need to get up! I leave Archie in his cot for the moment, push open the living room door, and find Mia, now sitting cross-legged on the floor, cuddling Ellie Elephant and singing along to some inane kids' breakfast show on the TV.

I stand for a moment, staring at her.

'Who turned the TV on?'

Mia swings round, looking at me in surprise. 'I did. You was still asleep so I didn't wake you up. You look funny, Mummy.'

I don't know which of these statements to address first. Yes I do: the TV.

'Since when did you turn on the TV by yourself?'

'I've seed you do it, Mummy. It isn't hard. It's just this button on the thingie.'

She waves the TV remote at me. I try to remember what was on TV last night. Surely she doesn't already know how to change channels too? No, I didn't watch any TV, not after the kids were in bed, because of my friends being here. But at least the TV was tuned to a kids' programme – imagine if Mia had turned it on and there'd been something unsuitable, something scary, or worse, showing?

'Mia, you mustn't do that, OK? If you want the TV on, you must ask me first.'

She pouts. 'But you was asleep. I didn't want to wake you up.'

'That was nice of you,' I concede. 'But in future, I'd rather you did, OK? Now, I'm just going to get Archie up, then we'll have some breakfast.'

Yawning, I head into the kitchen to put the kettle on, but recoil at the sight of the empty bottles, the unwashed glasses. I can't face clearing up yet. Instead I go back into the bedroom and lift Archie from his cot and get him changed and dressed, before returning to make breakfast. To be honest, I'd love to just go back to bed, but I'm a mum, I can't. I've got to wake up and pull myself together. I put Archie in his highchair and call Mia in to sit at the table while I put bread in the toaster.

'Are you all right, Mummy?' Mia asks. 'You still look funny.'

And just at that moment, there's a ring at the front doorbell. And it's Helen.

* * *

'Oh dear,' she says when I open the door. 'You don't look very well, Jess.'

'I'm fine,' I say, immediately on the defensive. 'I'm just tired. I... overslept.'

'A late night last night?'

'Not really, but I didn't get much sleep.' I suddenly stop short, remembering the noise. The music, the shrieking, the singing. 'Oh, Helen, I do hope we weren't too noisy.'

She smiles, but it's the sort of smile a teacher gives a naughty child, and for a moment I feel a bit resentful. But then I remind myself: they live downstairs from me. I'm not being fair. I should have warned them.

'It was one of my friends' birthdays. Sorry.'

'How nice. Well, I thought perhaps I should check to see if you're all right this morning. We did wonder if you might be a little bit... tired.'

I think she's implying that I might be hungover. I'm not, really, but I feel myself turning red anyway.

'Oh. Thank you, but I'm fine.'

'Well, perhaps you could do with a rest? I was going to suggest we take the children to the park. If you'd like us to.'

Mia's appeared behind me in the hallway.

'Mummy, the toast popped out of the toaster.' She looks up at Helen and down at her feet again.

'All right, Mia. I'm just coming.'

'Mia,' says Helen, 'how would you and Archie like to go to the park this morning? It's a nice day—'

'Will Mummy come too?' she says, looking round at me.

'Why don't we leave Mummy here and let her have a nice rest? She's very tired this morning.'

'Mummy didn't wake up. I putted the TV on, all by myself.'

'I *was* awake, Mia, I was just a bit tired—'

'Poor Mummy,' says Helen. 'She works very hard, Mia, and she needs a little rest sometimes.'

I suddenly stop feeling resentful and decide to feel grateful instead.

'It *would* be nice to go to the park, wouldn't it, Mia? After you've had your toast.'

'Will Uncle Robert come?' she asks Helen.

'Yes, I'm sure he'd like to.'

'OK.' She nods. 'I'll go and tell Archie. I'll get dressed after I've had my toast. I can try to get Archie ready too,' she adds importantly. 'So Mummy can have a rest.'

'You're such a helpful girl,' Helen tells her. 'I'll come back for you in a little while, then.'

'Thank you, Helen,' I say as Mia runs back to the kitchen. 'And... I'm so sorry – I should have warned you we might have been noisy.'

'Well, we'd always be happy to have the children overnight in future, if you want to have... a little celebration with your friends.'

'Thanks, but it won't be necessary.'

* * *

I can't deny it's absolute bliss to be able to lie down on the sofa and doze off peacefully for a couple of hours while the children are gone. By the time they come back, I'm feeling better, but feeling even more determined not to drink in future. Not that I drank much, but obviously my tolerance is low. When I check my phone, there's a whole stream of WhatsApp messages from my friends, saying what a great evening they had at the Italian restaurant, but I don't feel envious, especially as they're all now complaining of hangovers, obviously feeling far worse than I do.

'Thank you so much,' I tell Helen when she delivers Mia and

Archie back to me. 'I did need that rest. The children kept me awake last night.'

She gives me a knowing look. 'It doesn't hurt to let your hair down now and again,' she says. 'But next time, please remember we'll have the children overnight.'

'There won't be a next time!' I insist. And there's no way I'd ask them to have my children all night!

* * *

After we've had lunch, while Archie's having his nap and Mia's watching some TV, I gather all the bottles and crisp packets and other detritus from last night together and – leaving the door open and warning Mia to stay put, take it down to the recycling bins just outside the main door of the flats. As I open the lid of the bottles-and-jars bin and begin to drop the bottles in, a cough behind me makes me jump almost out of my skin. I wheel around to find Callum leaning against the wall, watching me.

'What are you doing here?' I demand shakily.

'I was just wondering what *you* were doing. Getting rid of the evidence, eh?'

'Evidence? What are you talking about?'

He nods at the bottles in my hands, which I quickly drop into the bin with the others and close the lid.

'Bit of a boozy night, was it?'

'None of your business,' I snap, turning away.

'No, but it might be the business of Social Services,' he retorts, 'if you're getting off your face while you're supposed to be in sole charge of my kids.'

'*Your kids*! Don't make me laugh.' I feel a tremor of fear run through me. I don't like the way he mentioned Social Services. I know how good Callum can be at convincing people with his lies.

Would anyone believe me over him, if it ever came to it? Would they believe me if I told them I'm normally a perfectly good mother? I'm beginning to even doubt that myself, especially after the criticism from Helen about how I feed the children and appear to have drunken parties. 'You never wanted anything to do with the kids,' I remind Callum. 'And I wasn't *off my face*, at all, not that it's anything to do with you.'

But my hands are shaking, I can hear the tremor in my voice, and I'm guessing he can, too, because I can hear him laughing as I head back inside.

'Piss off, Callum,' I say, looking back at him and trying to keep my voice steady. 'If you keep coming round here, harassing me, I'll call the police, I mean it.'

'Really?' he drawls. 'Well, I think they might be quite interested in what I have to tell them. A mother who drinks at night while her kids are crying for her—'

'I wasn't! They weren't!' I shout back at him, trembling with anger now – but he turns and saunters away, still laughing his horrible mocking laugh as he goes.

I have to stand outside my door for a few minutes just to try to compose myself before I go inside to Mia. *Why* did Callum have to turn up now, today of all days, while I'm piling wine bottles into the recycling? And why do I even care about his stupid threats, why do I still let him get to me? There's no way he'd want to fight for custody of the children. And he isn't going to go to the police; they'd only have to look at his record, to treat anything he says with a dose of scepticism.

But still.

It's Callum, and I know how evil he can be, how much damage he can cause if he wants to. If he wants to find a way to hurt me, even now, I know he'll do it. That's what really scares me.

* * *

The next day, Helen invites us in for a cup of tea in the afternoon while Robert's out somewhere. Archie toddles into her living room and heads straight for the toy box in the corner. He pulls out the little car he always likes playing with – and then a little plane, which he proceeds to lift into the air, making what he must think are appropriate noises but that really sound more like a cow mooing. By the time I've sat down, he's put both of these down and got out a purple plastic dinosaur that sings a song, a shape-sorting puzzle toy, and a police car with flashing lights and sirens. Meanwhile Mia has gone straight for a pink toy camera, which she's pretending to use to take photos of Archie, telling him to sit still. I turn to Helen, feeling suddenly very anxious.

'More new toys?' I ask her. 'You *must* let me pay you for these, Helen, even if they are from the charity shop.'

As usual, she waves this aside.

'Robert's been getting most of them for nothing – one of the other drivers at the depot gives him things his kids have grown out of.'

'But you're going to get overcrowded with toys soon!' I'd already noticed the toy box was overflowing.

'Oh, don't worry,' she says, laughing. 'I've got a cupboard in the spare bedroom. I keep a lot of the things we've acquired in there, and rotate them every now and then so the children don't get bored with them.'

'Oh. Well, that's all very nice, but...' I begin, but then I stop, shaking my head, not wanting to say what I really think about this because Helen would think me ungrateful. The truth is, I don't like it. It's just too much. I don't like this spoiling of my kids with so many new toys. It feels like Helen and Robert are *bribing* them to spend time here. I don't want Mia to start asking why I can't provide the same sort of things she's getting at Helen and Robert's. I suppose I'm jealous; I'd love to be able to buy her and Archie more toys but they only get new ones for birthdays and Christmas. I'd like to think they appreciate them more because of that. They won't, if they get too used to this continual feed of new things every week.

'Are you feeling less tired today?' Helen asks me, smiling, completely unaware of the annoyance I'm fighting against.

'I'm fine,' I say, a bit snappily. Is she going to keep harping on about the birthday party forever now?

'We was all tired yesterday, wasn't we,' Mia puts in, 'because of Mummy's noisy friends.'

'We *were*, Mia.'

My annoyance is increasing. At no point have I referred to *mummy's noisy friends* – she can only have got that from Helen! Has she been talking about me, listing my faults to my kids? But before I can protest, Mia continues:

'But it was nice, 'cos me and Archie had a late-night bedtime story in Mummy's bed.'

'In Mummy's bed?' Helen repeats, looking surprised. 'Aren't you a bit too big for that?'

Mia looks puzzled.

'No, I'm not too big,' she says. 'I still fit in Mummy's bed. Me and Archie always get in bed with her if we wake up in the night.'

'Really?' Helen gives me a look. She quite obviously disapproves, but she's not going to say any more because Mia's listening, still looking puzzled. I hate the fact that she's now going to wonder whether it's strange, not normal, to come into bed with me when she's upset. Again, I wonder why Helen seems to have such old-fashioned ideas. Did she have a strict mother herself, who then lectured her about her parenting of her own kids? Well, whatever, I wish Helen would just keep her opinions to herself!

16

As the weekend goes on, I start to regret overreacting. OK, so Helen might think I'm doing the wrong thing by taking the kids into my bed, but perhaps she just never did that with her own children so she finds it strange. Being on my own, it seems the most natural thing in the world to me. Mia only really wants to come in with me these days if she doesn't feel well, or she's woken up scared from a dream or something like that. But I often take Archie in with me, that's why his cot is next to my bed. If he's unsettled because of teething or illness or just having a run of restless nights, it's so much easier to just lift him out and bring him in next to me. If his cot was in Mia's room he'd be keeping her awake too. I've never felt bad about it or questioned whether it was a good idea – until now. But I've got to do what I think is right for my kids, and for me, haven't I?

I suppose it's because I can't help associating Helen with my mum, that I feel hurt – and resentful – if I think she's criticising me. It feels like being told off by Mum. I wonder if Mum *would* be saying things like that, if she was here now; telling me off, making me feel like I was doing things wrong. I somehow don't think she would. I'm pretty sure my dad would, but I'm not likely to find that out, any time soon.

* * *

I'm busy at work all this week. Tariq has me working on plans for the spring event whenever I'm not actively serving customers. To be honest, I'm quite pleased about how it's all coming together. Margaret comes in on Wednesday and looks over everything I've done so far. She congratulates me on getting agreement from two authors to come along and talk to people here: Andrew Waters who's written *Nature in Your Garden*, and Debbie McFarlene whose latest in a series of children's books about British wildlife, is called *What to Look for in Spring.* The morning talk will be by Debbie, for children, and the afternoon one by Andrew, for adults.

Using the shop computer in the back office, I've designed posters for the event, too: a couple of different ones. I asked both the authors to send me photos of themselves, and I put those on one of the posters together with pictures of their book covers. On the other design, I used copyright-free pictures of spring flowers and baby birds and rabbits on a bright yellow background with 'SPRING BOOK EVENT!' printed at the top. I have to say, I'm really pleased with these – considering I've never had any training in design.

* * *

Being busy, working on something different, makes the days pass faster.

'You seem happy, love!' Helen comments when I pick up the children on one of the last days of term.

'Yes – I'm enjoying all this extra stuff at work,' I admit. 'I didn't think I would.'

'So are you looking forward to Saturday now?'

'Yes.' I smile. 'We've decorated the shop now and I think everything's nearly ready.'

'I hope your manager appreciates you, for all the extra work you've been putting in.'

'I think he does, actually.'

'Well, hopefully he realises what you're worth. You *are* worth more, you know, Jess. You could easily get a much better-paid job—'

My smile drops. 'No, I couldn't. I'm not qualified for anything, and anyway, I have to work around the children. They're my priority.'

'Of course they are,' she soothes. 'But *we're* here now. If an opportunity ever arose, for a better job, you wouldn't have to worry about childcare. We're here.'

I nod and thank her. I know she means well. I know they seem to love looking after my kids. But I don't like the way it makes me feel – almost as if she's saying Mia and Archie don't really need me. I look at them now. Mia's kneeling on a cushion at Helen's coffee table, drawing an Easter egg, frowning in concentration, her hair falling over her eyes. Archie's playing with the singing purple dinosaur, running it backwards and forwards on the carpet and toddling after it. They both seem perfectly happy. Perhaps they *don't* really need me. The thought gives me a spasm of pain in my heart.

'Come on, Mia, Archie. Let's go,' I call. 'Chicken nuggets for tea.'

'You don't need to rush off,' Helen says. 'Or you can leave them here while you cook?'

'It's OK, thanks.' I nod at Mia as she asks if she can bring her drawing home to finish. 'You've got them both all day on Saturday. We'll leave you in peace for now.'

* * *

I sit down with the children while they're eating.

'You know you're going to Helen and Robert for the whole day on Saturday, don't you.'

'Yes. Is it Saturday tomorrow?' Mia asks.

'No. Friday. Your last day at school before the holidays.'

'Easter holidays!' She grins. 'Can we have Easter eggs?'

'Perhaps, if you're good.' I smile back at her, stroking back that stray lock of shiny blonde hair that always tends to fall over her eyes. 'And you're going to Helen and Robert's in the first week of the holiday, too. Are you looking forward to it?'

'The whole week?' she says. 'Every day?'

'Every afternoon. You'll be at the holiday club in the mornings – remember?'

She falls silent. 'Will the holiday club be fun?' she asks eventually, as she toys with her food. 'Will I like it?'

'I'm sure you will. Some of your friends will be there. You'll play games and do craft – drawing and making things.'

'I want to go there,' she says, nodding enthusiastically. 'I like doing crarf.'

'*Craft.*' I smile. 'Good.'

'I want to go there instead of Auntie Helen's.'

My smile drops. Is she upset about something that's happened at Helen and Robert's? I hope she's not about to make up another of her stories about Helen. 'You can do both, sweetie. Holiday club in the morning, Auntie Helen's in the afternoon.'

'I don't want to go to Auntie Helen's. Nor does Archie,' she adds, as she often does, as if by annexing her baby brother's supposed opinion she can gain more ammunition.

I sigh. 'Archie will be at nursery in the mornings and he's going to Auntie Helen's in the afternoons, like you.'

Mia gives me a hostile look. 'Well, I *don't* want to go there.' She sticks out her lower lip and puts down her fork, folding her arms defiantly. 'Auntie Helen doesn't like me, she tells me off. She says I make up stories, but I *like* making up stories, don't I, Mummy?'

I stare at her. I'm completely thrown by this. Mia has seemed perfectly happy being left with Helen and Robert recently, but here we are again with the complaints about Helen telling her off. Why would Helen be saying anything to Mia about her *making up stories* – which I presume refers to her lying? I wish I'd never confided in her about Mia's fibs and asked for her advice; she shouldn't be talking to Mia about it. Unless, of course, Mia's just making this up again? I've been a mum for long enough to have worked out that children can be completely contrary and unpredictable; they can play you for a fool and play havoc with your emotions. But right now, I feel like I don't know where I am with Mia – whether she really loves being with my neighbours, or just goes there under sufferance. Is she really telling lies again, or should I be worried? Is Helen really 'telling her off' or is there a perfectly good explanation, something Mia's misunderstood? I know I've got proof now from the incident at the after-school club, that she invents her versions of the truth, so I'm not sure when to believe her any more. And it's too late now, anyway, to do anything about it. I've got no other childcare options and I've got to work on Saturday, and next week, whatever happens.

17

The bookshop's spring event is today; I want to get in to work early, but Mia's still being difficult about going to Helen and Robert's.

'Me and Archie don't like going to Auntie Helen's,' she says, her lower lip trembling and tears welling up in her big blue eyes. 'And I've got a tummy ache.'

I'm not fooled by the tummy ache. I reckon every child – including me when I wanted to bunk off school on the days when I had a double maths lesson – can give themselves a tummy ache if it's convenient to their case. But I am worried about her not wanting to go.

'But you've always had such fun with them, Mia,' I say. I crouch down to her level, turning her face gently to mine so that she has to look at me. 'Why don't you want to go today? What is it that you don't like about going there, all of a sudden?'

I'm waiting anxiously for her response, wondering whether she's going to repeat what she told me the other day – that Helen doesn't like her because she *makes up stories*. I'm pretty sure it's just that she'd prefer to be at home. But I'm pressing her, like you press on a bruise to see if it hurts, even though you know you'll regret doing it. Because I need to know! I need to see if she'll say it again.

But she just shrugs and mutters, ''Cos I don't. Nor does Archie.'

'Actually Archie looks quite happy about it.'

Archie is sitting by the door, pulling his shoes onto the wrong feet.

'Go?' he says, standing up.

'Come on, Mia,' I encourage her. 'You'll have a lovely time. Auntie Helen's going to give you lunch today, too.'

'Yuck. I hope it's not broccli,' she says, pulling a face. 'Auntie Helen says I should eat broccli.'

'No, I'm sure it'll be something nice.' I hope so, anyway. I wonder if I should have prepared something the kids like, and given it to her this morning instead of giving her the money. I look at my watch. 'I'm sorry, sweetie, but I need to go to work now. You're going to have fun – you've got all those lovely toys at Auntie Helen's now.'

'I want to come with you,' she says, starting to cry, grabbing hold of my hand. 'I don't want to go to Auntie Helen's. She's like the witch.' She sits down on the floor, folding her arms across her chest. 'I don't want the witch to put me in a cage, Mummy! Nor does Archie! Don't make us go to the witch!'

I wish, not for the first time, that I'd never read *Hansel and Gretel* to her. But at least I know now that we've gone from the realms of possibly true, totally into the realms of fantasy.

'Mia, you know Auntie Helen isn't a witch, she's nothing like one, and she hasn't got a cage. Whatever this is all about, we'll talk about it again later but for now I'm sorry, we need to go.' I feel really mean, of course, but I've got no choice. 'Come on, pick up Ellie Elephant, we're going right now.'

* * *

Helen opens her door before I've even rung the bell, a look of surprise on her face.

'What on earth is all that noise?' she says, winking at me. 'I thought I heard some cats fighting out here! Surely it isn't my big girl Mia *crying*? No, surely it must be Archie?'

'I want to go with you, Mummy!' Mia's sobs increase in volume as she clings to me and adopts the dramatic pose of someone going through unbearable trauma.

'Oh, is *that* what all the fuss is about?' says Helen.

'And I've got a *tummy ache*!' Mia cries pitifully, stamping her foot.

'Well now, that *is* a shame. And I'd bought hot cross buns for lunch, too. And a chocolate cake. Well, never mind, I'm sure Uncle Robert and I will be able to eat your share, and maybe Archie can have some extra—'

'Hot cross buns?' Mia's stopped crying, as if by magic, and her eyes open wide.

Archie's already through the front door, muttering, '*Take!*' He can't pronounce *cake* properly yet but he knows what it means.

'Yes, cake for lunch, Archie, but not yet!' Helen laughs. 'Well, I'm sorry you don't want to join us, Mia—'

'I do,' she retorts. 'But I still might cry.' She turns back to me. 'Bye bye, Mummy.'

I bend down to hug and kiss her. My instinct is to ask if she's better now, and to check with Helen that she can cope if Mia has another meltdown – but I know that won't be helpful. Instead, I murmur my thanks to Helen and rush off to catch the bus, while I can.

Once I'm on the bus, I close my eyes for a moment and take a deep breath. I was so worried about Mia this morning, wondering if she was lying again or if something had really happened with Helen to upset her. But after the abrupt change of mood at the mention of hot cross buns, I think today's histrionics were just a straightforward case of not wanting me to leave her. After all, I've never had to work on a Saturday before, and I should have anticipated that she wouldn't like it. In a contrary sort of way, I'm even slightly, selfishly, relieved that she *might* occasionally get upset about me leaving her now. She didn't seem the least bit bothered at one time!

* * *

The event goes really well, especially our morning session, when the shop is packed out with parents and kids. Debbie McFarlene's lovely, and she has a really nice way with the children. She's brought along lots of things to show them, too, to illustrate her talk: a bunch of wild spring flowers, including snowdrops, primroses, daffodils and wood anemones; feathers from various birds, and leaves from different species of trees. She imitates the call of the cuckoo and encourages the kids to copy her. She hops around the floor like a rabbit, and asks everyone if they know the difference between rabbits and hares. It's great. Mia would have loved it, and I feel really bad now for not bringing her – but she'd have been bored as soon as Debbie's talk finished.

The afternoon goes well too. Andrew Waters talks to a smaller, but receptive audience, about how to make a wildlife garden to attract butterflies and bees, and thanks us profusely for the fact that we sell five signed copies of his book. Emma and I stay behind late to help Tariq put away all the chairs and have a tidy up, and Margaret thanks all of us for the extra work we've been putting in over the last few weeks. By the time I'm on the bus home, I'm feeling tired but happy and satisfied. Helping with this event has stretched me and tested me but I'm proud of how I've coped with it all, pleased with the extra cash I'll have in this month's pay packet.

* * *

The children both look tired when I go to collect them from Helen's. Archie's rubbing his eyes, grizzling, and Mia's very quiet.

'Have they been all right?' I ask Helen anxiously.

'Absolutely fine,' she insists. 'Archie didn't nap for long, though – that's why he's tired. And I think we wore Mia out at the park this afternoon!'

'Oh, I didn't realise you were taking them out. Thank you!'

'We enjoyed it,' Robert says, looking up and smiling.

'Well, I'd better get these two home right away, I think,' I say. 'They look worn out. Say thank you to Auntie Helen and Uncle Robert for having you all day.'

'Thank you,' Mia says carelessly.

'Ankoo,' repeats Archie, waving his chubby little hand. He looks tired enough to go straight to sleep, but I don't want him to do that until he's had his dinner.

* * *

As soon as we get home, Mia complains that she's hungry. She mopes about in the kitchen while I'm trying to cook sausages with Archie holding onto my legs, whining with tiredness.

'Archie, for goodness' sake, let go of my legs,' I say eventually, 'or I'm going to fall over! Why didn't you have a proper nap today?'

'He didn't have his dummy,' Mia says. 'He cried and wouldn't go to sleep.'

I turn to look at her in surprise. 'He did have his dummy. I gave it to Auntie Helen this morning. Perhaps she couldn't find where she'd put it?'

I'll check in the bag, but I'm absolutely certain I packed it. And surely, if Helen couldn't find it she could have let herself into our flat and picked up another one – Mia knows where they are.

'Auntie Helen says Archie doesn't need a dummy,' Mia says with a shrug.

I'm turning the sausages and I nearly drop one, I'm so taken aback by this. I can't believe I'm hearing it. I've told Helen several times that Archie always has his dummy to sleep with. He always has one with him when he goes to nursery, in case he gets upset and wants it, and has it for his nap when he stays at Helen's all day. It's always in his bag – Helen knows that. I'm sure she'd have given it to him. Why would Helen say he didn't need it? Does she think I'm doing the wrong thing? *Am* I doing the wrong thing? I didn't have anybody to ask, when Mia was born, but she was such a fussy baby during the first few months, always crying, and giving her a dummy was the only thing that calmed her so that Callum wouldn't yell at us for disturbing him. Archie only has his for sleeping and if he's miserable when he's teething, but I can't see any harm in it. Mia hasn't made this up – I'm sure, this time. Apart from anything else, she's too tired tonight! Surely Helen's not deliberately refusing Archie his dummy? Doesn't she understand that he always needs it to sleep with? Well, I'll have to have a word with her – again.

* * *

I wait until the children are both fast asleep – which doesn't take long, tonight – and then call her.

'Helen, I'm really sorry to trouble you, but I just wanted to remind you about Archie's dummy. He won't fall asleep without it, and, well – it's always in his nursery bag, and I think I left one with you? Only... well, Mia says he didn't have it today and he couldn't sleep.'

'Oh.' There's a silence. She doesn't try to deny it. 'I'm sorry, Jess. I thought I was doing you a favour. I thought you'd probably want to break him out of the habit.'

'Break him...?' I stammer. 'Um... *why*?'

'Well, you know. It's not a very good habit; you won't want him to be running around with a dummy in his mouth when he goes to school, or—'

I laugh. 'But he's still a baby! He's not quite eighteen months yet! And he only has the dummy to sleep with, or if he's upset.' I pause, suddenly flooded with doubts. I know some people disapprove of dummies. 'Do you think it's a really bad thing to do, then?'

Helen's fallen silent. Then she says, gently, 'If you'd prefer me to let him have it, Jess, then of course, I will. You're his mum, it's for you to make these decisions. I don't suppose it hurts, if he only has it to help him sleep. I'm sorry, I honestly thought I was helping.'

I feel myself getting taut with irritation. Helen might have *thought* she was helping, and OK, perhaps I *am* doing the wrong thing. But surely she should have talked to me about it first? She shouldn't really be making those sorts of decisions for my kids, however much of a favour she's doing me.

'Well, thank you, Helen,' I manage to say. 'But yes – I'd prefer him to have it, please. It does help him sleep, and, well, Mia gave hers up perfectly easily when she was about two and a half.'

I'm glad I called her, glad I managed, I think, to sound firm and assertive but still be polite. I wish, though, it hadn't left me wondering if she really thinks I'm doing such a bad thing for my baby by giving him that little bit of comfort. Am I? Am I, after all, a rubbish mum who just takes the easy way out? If only I had joined some kind of parent and baby group, when I was off on parental leave, so that I had friends around my own age who had kids, friends I could discuss this kind of stuff with. Perhaps Helen's ideas are a bit outdated. But she and Robert are undoubtedly the best option I could possibly have found. And already, I don't know how I could manage without them.

18

It's my last day at work and I'm really looking forward to my week off now. It'll be Easter this weekend so at lunchtime I go to the supermarket and buy Easter eggs for Mia and Archie, and I start wondering, while I'm arranging stock in the contemporary fiction section, whether I can afford to take the kids out for a day somewhere during the holiday. Mia's still going on about the zoo, complaining that *everyone* except her has been to the zoo and *everyone* except her has seen a wolf.

I find myself smiling as I hurry home from the bus stop. I'll have to run upstairs to hide the Easter eggs at the back of a cupboard, before going to Helen's. As I'm waiting to cross the road to the entrance to our flats, my eyes are drawn to the back view of someone on the other side of the road, walking away from me in the opposite direction. He's tall and thickset, like Callum, with scruffy, longish dirty blond hair – like Callum's – and is walking fast, with long strides, the way Callum does. And... he's got a little black dog on a lead. Just as Mia said he had when I thought she'd made up a story about seeing him. I freeze at the kerb, tempted for a moment to run after him – but to do what, exactly? Accuse him – if it really is Callum at all – of borrowing someone's dog to try to tempt my children into talking to him? It would make me sound ridiculous – especially if it isn't Callum, which I'm already beginning to doubt, even before he turns a corner at the end of the road and disappears from view.

I stand like an idiot at the kerb for several minutes, trying to collect myself. No, I'm being ridiculous. It could have been anybody. Perhaps there's a Callum lookalike around here some-where who has a little black dog – it would explain Mia's convic-tion that she saw him, wouldn't it? Still, it leaves me feeling a bit shaken and I don't calm down completely until I've picked up the children and settled down at home with them, ready to enjoy the long weekend – and the holiday week ahead.

* * *

'Can we have *The Tiger Who Came to Tea* tonight?' Mia asks, looking through her books to choose a bedtime story.

'Of course we can. Is it still your favourite?' I ask her as she pulls her duvet over herself and cuddles Ellie Elephant.

'Yes. Because I *really, really* want to see a tiger in real life. I wish one would knock at our door and come to tea.'

'You wouldn't like that really,' I say, laughing. 'They're very fierce. But beautiful. Anyway, I thought it was wolves you wanted to see most of all? And elephants!' I point to her favourite toy.

'I want to see them *all*, Mummy. I never seed any of them yet. I want to see a wolf and see if there's a boy who cried. And I want to see an elephant like Ellie. And a tiger like the one who comes for tea. And a lion. And...' She stops, trying to remember what else she's desperate to see. 'And a dragon.'

'Dragons aren't real, sweetie!' I remind her.

'I still would like to see one. *Please* Mummy can we go to a zoo one day? Everyone's been to a zoo except me. *Please*, I promise to be really, really good and not do anything naughty and eat my dinner proply and—'

'Even if I give you broccoli?' I tease her – and her smile drops.

'But you don't give me broccli 'cos you know me and Archie don't like it. Not like Auntie Helen.'

Suddenly I'm not smiling any more either.

'Auntie Helen doesn't give you broccoli, Mia. She's never given you dinner, only nice lunches like sandwiches and cheese on toast and—'

'I know, but she told me off about broccli. She says if you give me broccli I should eat it all up because it's good for me, but I wouldn't, Mummy, because it's *horrible*. Not as horrible as Bussel spouts but almost.'

'Mia, that's not *telling you off.*' Although I have to say, I'm not too pleased to hear Helen's giving Mia unwanted advice about her diet now – having already implied to me that I'm not feeding her properly. 'It's just... Auntie Helen's opinion, OK? People all have different opinions, even grown-ups; it's just her saying what she thinks. You surely can tell the difference between that, and being told off? You know what it's like when *I* tell you off!'

'Yes, your face goes all cross and red and you shout.'

'Exactly!' I cringe a bit inside to hear myself described like this, but... well, I guess it's occasionally all too true. 'And when your teacher told you off?'

She looks down at the floor and shakes her head. I don't think we're going to have a conversation about that.

She shrugs. 'Well, I don't like it when she tells me off.'

I don't think I'm getting through to her. But before I can say any more, she picks up her book again and thrusts it into my hands.

'I thought you was going to read me the tiger story, Mummy. And we didn't finish talking about if we can go to the zoo!'

'Well, I don't know about that,' I say, taking hold of her for a cuddle and a tickle. 'Why do I need to go to the zoo when I've got two little *monkeys* right here?'

But in fact, my mind's made up. I've already been looking at ticket prices and I think I can afford it. I'm going to take them to the zoo this week. I can't wait to see Mia's face when I tell her!

* * *

On Good Friday morning we have hot cross buns for breakfast and as it's cold and rainy outside, we spend a leisurely day indoors, watching silly cartoons on TV and playing games. Halfway through the afternoon, Mia suddenly remembers she left one of her current favourite teddies in Helen's flat yesterday.

'Can we go and get him, Mummy?' she says.

'Yes, but we'll have to wait till Archie wakes up from his nap.'

She pouts. 'Oh, but, I really need him *now*.' She pauses, and then adds: 'Anyway, Auntie Helen says now I'm a big girl I should be able to go downstairs on my own.'

I bristle. Another thing I'm doing wrong? Not letting my *big girl* have a little bit of independence? But she's still only four! I think about it for a moment.

'Well, all right, let me check she's there first. Then I'll come out and watch you walk down the stairs, and wait till I see Auntie Helen open her door. OK?'

'I'll be all right, Mummy,' she insists once I've made the phone call. 'You don't have to watch me.' But I do anyway.

'I'll send her back up when she's ready,' Helen calls up. 'We've got something to show her while she's here.'

Mia's actually down there for quite a while, and eventually I realise it's getting on for tea-time. Archie's still asleep; I quickly check on him, then take my key with me and nip down the stairs to knock on Helen's door.

'Sorry,' I begin. 'I didn't realise the time! I hope she hasn't been a nuisance—'

'Of course not,' Helen laughs. 'We've been having a lovely time! Robert's been reading to her – a book about animals he got from the library.'

'Ah, I bet she's enjoyed that.'

'Where's our little Archie this afternoon?' she goes on.

'Oh, he's having his nap. He's been asleep for ages – I'd better wake him up now, in fact, or he'll never go to sleep tonight.'

Helen looks at me in surprise. 'You've left him upstairs on his own?'

'Oh – well, he's fast asleep and I knew I'd only be a minute... I just came to get Mia back.' Surely I've only been down here for a minute or two, haven't I? Archie's in his cot, he's perfectly OK, but now, of course, I'm worried. 'Well, I'd better get back anyway. Mia!' I call her. And then there's a wail from upstairs and a series of horrendous loud cries.

I turn and fly up the stairs, my heart hammering in my chest.

'Archie!' I yell as I unlock the door and tear inside the flat. 'It's all right, baby, I'm here, Mummy's here – Oh my God – Archie, what have you done?'

He's sitting in his cot, still wailing loudly, and there's a red bump on his forehead, just above his eye. He holds out his arms to be picked up and I hold him to me, soothing him, rocking him, trying to inspect the bump at the same time as shushing him and telling him it's OK. But it quite obviously isn't. I left him – and he's somehow managed to do this to himself.

'It looks like he's banged his head against the cot bars,' says a voice behind me.

Helen has followed me upstairs. I know she's trying to be helpful but I feel like telling her to go away. I feel ridiculously like cursing her for somehow jinxing the whole episode by sounding so critical about me leaving him in his cot. For God's sake, I was only downstairs, and it was only for a minute, two at the most!

But perhaps she was right. Perhaps even that minute or two was too long to leave him. Why didn't I wake him up and take him downstairs with me? What was he doing – banging his head against the bars in frustration because I wasn't there, couldn't hear him?

'Perhaps he tried to climb out of the cot,' Helen's saying quietly. 'They sometimes start trying to do that sort of thing around this age – boys especially, they love climbing. Let me have a look. Should we take him to the hospital, get it checked? Shall I call an ambulance?'

'No!' I say, a bit snappily. 'Of course we don't need an ambulance, he doesn't need to be checked, it's just a little bump, it'll go down, he'll be fine. You'll be fine, won't you, Archie? Look, he's stopped crying already. I'll put a—'

'Put a cold compress on it, then. Perhaps you should—'

'I know what to do, thanks, Helen. We'll be all right. Could you send Mia up to me, please?' I take a breath and add in a calmer voice, 'Thank you for having her this afternoon.'

'You're welcome, love.' She sounds hurt, but I can't bring myself to apologise. I feel got-at, *again*. A bad mother who does everything wrong, who leaves her baby on his own in his cot and lets him hurt himself. Surely it was just an accident – it could have happened if I was standing right next to the cot. Little children hurt themselves all the time. I've got no reason to reproach myself, I've done nothing wrong.

I get the cold compress and sit down in the living room with Archie on my lap, cuddling him and holding the cold cloth against his forehead until he starts to wriggle impatiently to get down. He's laughing and chattering to himself now; he's completely forgotten what all the fuss was about. He'll have a bruise but he'll be absolutely fine. I'll never leave him on his own again and I'll always wonder if it was my fault.

But I don't need Helen to make me feel even worse about it than I already do.

19

Archie's forehead already looks a bit better by Easter Sunday. The kids have started on their Easter eggs but we're going down to Helen and Robert's now, to give them the box of chocolates I've got them as an Easter present. I still feel a bit cross about the way Helen made me feel on Friday, despite trying to tell myself that perhaps she was just flustered and worried about Archie. It still felt like just another little dig at my ineptitude.

Helen hugs us all, spending a while looking sympathetically at Archie's forehead, and gives all three of us an Easter egg in return. So when she asks me to stay for a coffee I feel like I have to accept. Perhaps it's her way of apologising for yesterday. I follow her into the kitchen while she makes it.

'While the children aren't listening,' she says quietly, pulling the door closed behind us, 'I wanted to tell you something, Jess. We've got a special treat for them – a present, an Easter present if you like.'

'You got them an Easter egg each,' I protest.

'Yes, but look – Robert found an advert online for tickets to the zoo during the Easter holiday: a special offer on a family ticket. Each adult can take one child free. And I know how much Mia wants to go to the zoo, she's desperate to see wolves! So we hope you don't mind, but we've bought a family ticket – we've checked, the adults don't have to be the parents, or grandparents – and we'll take them one day during the week, to give you a day to yourself.'

'Oh.' I'm conscious that my face isn't doing what she's expecting it to do. I try, quickly, to take the disappointed look off it, but I don't know if I'm succeeding. 'Well, that's really nice of you. You really shouldn't have spent any more money on them, though.'

'Jess, we *love* having Mia and Archie. We're really excited to be taking them out for the day, and it's a special offer, so...' She pauses, presumably clocking the look on my face now. 'Is that OK? Oh, I'm sorry – perhaps we should have asked you first, but we wanted it to be a surprise. We can use the ticket any day this week, so... unless you've already made plans for them for every day...?'

'Well,' I say, conscious of the tone to my voice now, 'it's just... well, as you know, I'd planned to take them myself, that's all. I haven't told the kids and – I didn't know about the special offer, but I was going to look into it tomorrow and decide which day... but well, I'm not saying no, obviously, I'll just... um, maybe I'll take them somewhere else myself instead—'

I'm gabbling, I know I am. I feel embarrassed because I know I must sound like a spoilt child, and I don't want to appear ungrateful, but yes – I'm disappointed. I was so looking forward to telling Mia we were going to the zoo and that she'd finally be seeing wolves, and to watching the excitement on both of their faces when I showed them the monkeys and the elephants and the tigers... And I'd *told* Helen I was planning this trip. Has she forgotten?

'Oh, Jess!' Helen sounds distressed now. 'Oh, for goodness' sake, of course you must take them yourself – I'm so sorry, I should have asked you first. We just presumed you'd prefer a day to yourself, a bit of peace and quiet—'

'But you've bought the family ticket now.' I hope I don't look, or sound, as sulky as Mia.

'It doesn't matter. You take it – it's a present. You can take one of the children free with it, and Archie might get in free anyway; under-twos sometimes get in free to things like this, don't they? So—'

'No. I can't do that. It wouldn't be fair. You paid for it, and I know you're looking forward to it.' I'm struggling to keep the hurt out of my voice, but I feel completely left out, now, at the thought of the children going to enjoy this new experience with Helen and Robert instead of with me. I can't help wondering if Helen actually wanted to get one up on me – to be the one who made Mia's dream come true, instead of me. 'It doesn't matter,' I force myself to say. 'I'll take them another time.'

'No you won't. I'll tell you what we'll do: you can come with us. We'll just get another adult ticket! There! Problem solved – why didn't I think of that in the first place?'

'Well, in that case,' I go on, 'I'd buy my own ticket, obviously.'

'It'll be a lovely family day out,' Helen says – almost to herself, making me wonder if she's trying to convince herself. It still sounds to me like they'd have preferred to take the kids on their own. 'And *you* must be the one to tell them about it,' she insists. 'Not us. We'll get all the pleasure we need just from coming along on the day.'

'OK, thank you.'

We agree that Thursday would be a good day for the outing, and I tell her I'm looking forward to it already. But inside, I'm still feeling disappointed, feeling like *my* treat for the kids has been hijacked.

I carry the tray of coffees and biscuits and children's drinks back into the living room and listen to Mia prattling about Easter eggs.

'Take a biscuit from the plate, sweetheart,' Helen encourages her. 'And one for Archie, of course. Sit down to eat it, Archie, there's a good boy.'

Archie obliges happily, plonking himself down on his bottom with his Bourbon cream in his podgy little fingers. Mia lingers over the biscuit plate, taking her time to choose the most choco-latey one before starting to nibble it around the edges like a little mouse, dropping crumbs on the carpet.

'Mia!' I warn her, pointing to the crumbs, and she looks quickly at Helen, who I think is pretending not to have noticed. 'Be careful, please.'

I feel strangely on edge until I finish my coffee and get up to take the kids home. I don't think it's anything to do with the way Mia's been acting; it's just a lingering feeling about the trip to the zoo, a feeling of having *almost* been left out of something that I'd planned all along to do with my own children. Perhaps it's me, not Mia, who's behaving badly – because the truth is, I don't really want Helen and Robert to come to the zoo with us at all. I wanted to take my children for a day out on our own – and Helen knew that, didn't she?

20

It's the day of the zoo trip; I didn't tell the kids about it until this morning as I knew Mia wouldn't be able to sleep for the excitement. And of course, when I did tell her, she was so overcome she couldn't even speak for a few seconds, just staring at me with her mouth open. But once she'd caught her breath, she went a little crazy, doing a dance around the room singing about all the animals she wanted to see! We caught an early bus into town together and we're now on the train, heading to the zoo. Mia wanted to sit next to Robert, so I'm sitting with Helen, with Archie on my lap. I'm thinking more and more that Mia prefers Robert's company to Helen's. She's mentioned several times how she likes it when he's there with Helen, and when he goes with them to the park; she often checks first whether Robert's going to be there before she'll agree to spend time with them. Perhaps it's just the usual little-girl thing of having a favourite 'uncle'. But I don't mind: Robert's good with her, and like any favourite uncle, he's full of bits of information that fascinate her.

'Did you know,' he says, 'the zoo has been open for a hundred years this year?'

'A *hundred*?' Mia says, looking suitably impressed. 'So are all the animals very, very old?'

'No,' he says, smiling. 'No, it's just the zoo itself – it was opened a hundred years ago, see? But with different animals then. We must make sure we see all the animals you want to see today, mustn't we? Tell me again your most important ones.'

'He's in his element,' Helen comments quietly to me, nodding at Robert as he listens to Mia's list of animals and proceeds to tell her some facts about them all. 'He was a natural as a teacher. He's very patient, and very good at explaining things.'

'I didn't know he used to be a teacher! Why did he change jobs?'

'It became too stressful,' she says. She looks out of the window for a moment before adding: 'We were both teachers. Primary school, both of us. That's how we met.'

'Oh!'

I don't know why I'm so surprised. Why have I never asked her what work she used to do? She's never mentioned it before, other than to say she wasn't currently working – and I suppose over time I've just assumed she's taken early retirement – *very* early – for some reason she doesn't talk about. And Robert's now a delivery driver. Perhaps they both found teaching too stressful. Perhaps they just wanted to wind down. Fair enough. But at least it explains why they're so good with kids – and perhaps why Helen's a bit strict with them And of course, they've got kids of their own, too – who she still never talks about.

* * *

The morning passes in a whirl of excitement: Mia is loving every minute of it, and even Archie, who's being pushed around the different enclosures in his buggy, is wide-eyed in amazement as he gazes upwards at the giraffe and giggles at the antics of the monkeys. I listen to Helen as she talks to Mia about the various animals, telling her which country they come from and what they like to eat, and I think some more about what she told me earlier.

'Do you miss teaching?' I ask her as we walk from one enclosure to the next. 'I mean, you're obviously good with kids.'

'Not really,' she says, a little abruptly. Then she glances at me, softens her tone and adds: 'I did enjoy it, of course. You're right, I do love children. But it's a stressful career.'

'Yes, I'm sure it must be.' I pause, then add lightly, 'I always wanted to be a teacher myself when I was growing up – although of course, I didn't realise then what hard work kids can be! But I suppose it was the perfect career for you both, while your children were young.'

She nods. 'Yes.'

'Are they close in age – your son and your daughter?' I go on, wondering if I can get some more out of her – but she clams up again, taking Mia's hand and moving on a little faster, giving me the signal that she's closed the conversation down.

'Here's your wolf, Mia,' she says as we approach the enclosure.

Mia runs ahead of us and stares through the fencing. 'Where?'

'This type of wolf is quite shy,' says Robert, who's evidently read up on it. 'We have to wait very quietly and see if he comes out.'

'Oh.' Mia juts her lower lip. 'Come on, Wolfie!'

'Shh!' I remind her. We all wait in silence for a few minutes. I'm just about to suggest that we go and see something else and maybe come back later, when there's a movement in the bushes and the wolf pokes his head out. I actually have to put my hand over Mia's mouth to stop her squealing... and slowly, he comes right out into the enclosure for a moment before dashing back under cover.

'I seed him!' Mia squeals. 'I seed a wolf at last!' She looks around her, a frown deepening on her forehead. 'Where's the boy?'

'Which boy, Mia?' Robert asks her.

'The boy who cried wolf,' I explain in a whisper to him – and he manages not to laugh.

'Ah, well, I think he learned his lesson, and stopped crying wolf in the end,' he tells Mia with a straight face. 'So we don't see him any more.'

I smile at him. 'Well done, good explanation!' I hesitate for a moment. Helen's made it quite obvious she doesn't want to discuss her teaching career, but perhaps Robert will explain more. 'I understand you and Helen were both teachers. Are you sorry you changed jobs? You seem like a natural!'

For a moment I think he isn't going to answer. He sighs and shrugs, then looks down at me and admits, 'I do miss it sometimes, yes. But... well, it just wasn't working out, really – for me or for Helen.'

Why do I get the impression it was Helen in particular that it didn't work out for? But again, I'm sensing the subject is a bit off-limits, and anyway, Helen is suggesting that perhaps we should stop for lunch now.

'The café's just over there,' she says.

'I think it's a takeaway,' Robert corrects her. 'Look – there's quite a lot of outdoor seating free.'

'OK,' Helen says. 'Why don't you take the kids and find a table, Robert, and Jess and I can go and choose the food.' She smiles at me. 'You'll know what the kids would like, Jess.'

'Can I have a burger please, Mummy? In a bun?' Mia asks. 'Archie wants a burger too.'

We queue inside to order; Helen chooses chicken salads for herself and Robert, but I'm hungry and I'm not going to feel guilty about my pizza. I order a portion of chips too, to share with the kids. Archie will probably only eat half of his burger.

'My treat,' Helen insists, getting her purse out – but before she can argue, I've tapped my debit card and insisted that it's about time I paid for something. She protests all the way back to the table, but I'd made my mind up about this. After all, they bought the family ticket and she's already talking to Mia about the souvenir shop at the exit – which I know from similar experiences will be expensive. When we get back to the table, Mia's making a great show of needing the toilet – and before I can take her to find one, Helen grabs her hand and says she saw one inside the café.

'Come on, Mia. I'd like to go, too, so let's go together.'

Mia's quiet when they come back to the table, sitting with her head down, not looking at me. I look at Helen to see if there's any sign in her face of anything untoward happening. Has Helen had to reprimand her for something? Or has Mia, as usual, interpreted something Helen's said as a reprimand and is sulking about it? When the food's brought up, she eats even less of her burger than Archie eats of his, and only a couple of chips.

'Are you all right, Mia?' I ask her. 'Eat up, there won't be anything else until we get home.' But she just shakes her head. 'She's tired,' I tell Helen, but it's only an excuse, as I know the difference between a tired Mia and a grumpy one only too well! But I'm conscious of the way Helen's looking at the wasted food. Feeling guilty about it myself, I offer her and Robert the rest of the chips, and when they refuse, claiming their chicken salads have filled them up, I have to scoff the chips myself and end up feeling uncomfortable, with my jeans straining at the waist.

'You young people have bigger appetites than us,' Helen says, in the tone of voice that implies she and Robert are geriatrics. She turns to Mia. 'Now then, we've still got the lions and the tigers to see – or are you too tired for that?'

Mia shakes her head. 'No. I'm not tired.'

But the excitement definitely seems to have vanished from her demeanour. She doesn't show as much enthusiasm for the big cats as I'd expected – although Archie makes up for it, his eyes widening almost in disbelief at the size of the big male lion. He shuffles back in the seat of his buggy, covering his face with his hands as the lion strolls across the enclosure towards us.

'No!' he shouts, peering between his fingers. 'Go 'way!' – and we have to persuade him gently that the lion definitely can't get near him.

When we've finally seen all the animals we can cope with, we visit the souvenir shop on the way out. And I'm so busy arguing with Helen about the fact that she wants to buy the kids a toy each, that I don't even realise Mia has already gone to the shelf where the stuffed zoo animals are displayed and chosen a meerkat for herself (her new favourite, apparently, since seeing them today) and a red panda for Archie.

'No, something smaller, please, Mia,' I tell her – but Helen has played me at my own game and is already at the till with her card out and the two toys are being paid for.

* * *

'I can't thank you both enough,' I tell Helen and Robert on the train home. 'It's been a really lovely day.'

'We've both enjoyed it too,' they insist.

The kids are worn out. Archie's asleep in his buggy as we walk back from the bus stop – even though he's already had a sleep on the train. Mia's dragging her feet and complaining that she wants to sit down. So when we get home I make them a quick toasted sandwich – that'll have to do for today – and put them both in the bath to calm down the fractiousness before I read their bedtime stories.

'So at last, you've had your day at the zoo!' I say to Mia once Archie's snuggled down in his cot and she's under her covers, cuddled up with Ellie Elephant and the new favourite, Mr Meerkat. 'And wasn't it fun!'

'Yes,' she says sleepily. 'I liked the meerkats best.'

'And you finally saw a wolf!' I remind her. 'I liked all of it, did you?'

She nods and smiles, her eyes beginning to close.

'I liked *most* of it,' she says sleepily.

'Good.' I frown. I want to ask which part she didn't like, but she's half asleep, and anyway, it probably doesn't mean anything. It's probably just something silly like the burger not being exactly to her taste. She did seem a bit sulky at lunchtime – and it was after Helen had taken her to the loo. I wonder if I should ask Helen, tomorrow, whether anything happened. I sigh. I wish I didn't always have to second-guess what might have happened to upset Mia, where Helen's involved.

In the time I've sat there stroking Mia's hair and pondering all this, she's fallen fast asleep anyway – so I convince myself it couldn't have been anything too serious.

21

In the morning, Mia seems fine, cheerfully shovelling up her Rice Krispies and asking what we're going to do today, the last day of the holiday. I'm trying not to dwell on the comment she made last night, but I can't help it. My suspicions have been alerted again, and I'm still turning over in my mind the way her mood changed halfway through the day out; how she went quiet and seemed less excited. I'd have dismissed it as tiredness if she hadn't said, so pointedly last night, that she liked *most* of it. And now I'm torn between asking her exactly what she meant, or letting it lie while she seems perfectly happy.

I ponder over this for so long that the children are already well into a game of 'zoos' with their toy animals – well, Mia is, with Archie merely running around pretending to be a lion or a tiger and making a lot of noise – by the time I decide to gently probe a little.

'Wasn't it nice of Auntie Helen to buy you your meerkat and panda?' I say,

'Panda!' Archie agrees, grabbing it out of Mia's 'zoo' under the table and cuddling it.

'Yes,' Mia says curtly.

'I think that cheered you up, didn't it, after you were a bit sad at lunchtime. I suppose you didn't like your burger.'

She looks up at me in surprise. 'I did like my burger, I just didn't feel like eating it.'

'Oh, I see.' I'm trying to play this carefully, gently. 'Why was that? Did you have a tummy ache?'

'No!' she says, almost indignantly. 'I didn't. I had an upset-ache.'

'Oh, dear. What happened to make you upset, then, on such a nice day? Can you remember?'

'*Course* I remember!' She raises her eyes at me as if I'm being ridiculous. 'I was upset about Daddy.'

My heart gives a lurch. What? Why would she suddenly be upset about *Callum* while she was having an exciting day out? I hold out my arms to her and she drops her meerkat and comes for a cuddle.

'Why were you thinking about Daddy yesterday?' I ask her.

''Cos I seed him. At the zoo.'

I have to wait for a moment to let my breathing steady before I can ask her:

'Are you sure it was him? Not someone who looked a bit like him?'

'It *was* him. He smiled and waved at me.'

I stare at her for a moment. *Does* she still remember what he looks like? It's not as if I keep photos of him around the place! But I can't ignore this – especially as she did seem upset. But why would she be upset about seeing him? And if she really did see him, when did it happen? It could only have been when Helen took her back inside the café to use the toilet – otherwise I'd have surely noticed her looking at someone – I'd have surely seen him myself. She'd have told me – wouldn't she?

'Why didn't you tell me this yesterday, sweetie?' I ask her. 'Why didn't you say: *Look, there's Daddy*, when you saw him?'

"Cos you wasn't there,' she says straight away. 'But I told Auntie Helen, and she said it wasn't him. But it was, Mummy. I know it was him, 'cos he waved at me.'

She's on the point of tears in her frustration.

'OK,' I soothe her. She needs me to believe her, and I do, although I'm still hoping it was just a lookalike – perhaps the same lookalike I saw in the street, with the dog. But isn't it a bit of a coincidence that he was at the zoo? And he *waved* at her? However much Mia likes to make up stories, surely there was so much going on yesterday, enough excitement – she didn't need to fabricate the distraction of another pretend sighting of her father. 'Well, look, perhaps Daddy likes zoos too, lots of people do. Now...' I want to move on as quickly as possible. 'How about you take me on a tour of your zoo here? You can tell me all about each of the animals, their names and what they like to eat.'

'Yes!' she says, breaking out of my arms and pulling me down to crawl under the table. 'Right, so this is Ellie, she's an elephant and she eats trees with her trunk. And...'

Fortunately the distraction works – for Mia, but not for me. I'm steaming – not so much about Callum, who may or may not have been in the café at the zoo, on the same day as us. I hope not, because if he was, why? No, I'm cross about Helen. How dare she not tell me something so important, when I was right there, outside the café, at the time it happened? Even if she didn't believe it was him – and how would she know? – she should have told me about it. How many times have I asked her to tell me things like this?

After Mia's finished her guided tour of the toy zoo, I leave her and Archie playing with the animals on the floor and go to make myself a cup of tea while I try to calm down. Perhaps I'm being unfair. Perhaps Helen didn't want to talk about the incident yesterday in front of Mia. Perhaps she'll give me a call today to talk it over. She probably told Mia it wasn't Callum, even if she thought it might be, precisely because she knew I don't want him to see the children. What else could she have done?

But no – she knows I'd have wanted to be aware that he might have been there! She surely could have whispered something to me, alerted me about it, rather than let me carry on happily taking the children around the zoo where their *dangerous, violent* father might have been lurking.

I let the rest of the morning pass, but there's no phone call from Helen, and I'm getting more and more worked up, and I'm having to try harder and harder not to show it in front of the kids. Quite apart from my anger with Helen, it obviously still provokes a reaction in me, hearing my little daughter talking about Callum at all, and especially talking like she was happy to see him. I know it's irrational; she doesn't know, doesn't understand just how bad a father he is. But it hurts to think that she might be fantasising about him still being with us. I suppose this is what happens, when children don't see their fathers: they turn them into a kind of mythical figure and imagine their life being different if they were with them. Well, I just have to remind myself that she's only four; she can't possibly understand. I'm the adult, I'm the one who knows just how dangerous and manipulative he is. I have to keep hold of that fact and try not to take it personally.

I try to pull myself together while we're eating lunch. This is our holiday – the children's precious *mummy time* that we've all been looking forward to. I don't want it to be spoilt. But the more I think about everything that's been happening, the worse I feel. I managed, yesterday, to put to one side my real feelings about Helen and Robert arranging the trip to the zoo, but the truth is that I felt like an afterthought, hurt that Helen and Robert didn't initially include me. And I think again about how Mia's kept talking about being told off, and making up stories that make me slightly uneasy. How Helen and Robert have filled their flat with toys for my kids, and kept on about having the children overnight. How Helen seems to be able to make me feel like a bad mother, despite assuring me she doesn't think that at all. How I've started having doubts about the way I bring up the children, because she seems to disapprove of so much I do: the food I give them, the fact that I sometimes let them come into my bed, the dummy, the noise my friends and I made on just that one occasion...

I sometimes think she disapproves of me just because I'm a single mum, but of course, she never says so, she always says she thinks I'm doing a good job. I know I lost all my self-confidence because of Callum, so I do tend to take things personally and think everything's my own fault. And I always excuse everything Helen and Robert say and do because they've been there for me at exactly the time I needed someone – needed the help they've been willing, even eager, to provide. And it would have seemed so ungrateful, churlish, to refuse it. How else could I have managed to work all these extra hours? How could I have afforded a professional childminder? It's not as if they've done anything actually *wrong*. There's always been a reason for everything. So far. But now, I'm at a loss to know what reason Helen can possibly give me this time. And I'm going to have to find out. I suppose I'll have to wait until the kids are in bed this evening, and give Helen a call.

* * *

After lunch, Mia asks if we can go to the park and I agree; at least it will stop me sitting here thinking constantly about all my worries. It's a nice day and it's good to be outside in the sunshine, chatting to the children as we go through the usual round of swings, climbing frame, slide, back to swings, until they eventually tire of them all. We spend time watching the ducks, as usual, choosing names for them all, and we're nearly home when we bump into Helen and Robert on their way home from the Co-op.

'Ah, I wondered if we might see you today, as it's the last day of your holiday,' Helen says cheerfully. 'Want to come in for a cup of tea?'

Mia scowls. 'I want to watch TV.'

'You can watch it afterwards, Mia,' I say gently. 'Just a quick one, then, Helen, if that's OK. They're tired from the park.'

I might have used this as an excuse to go straight home, if it weren't for needing to talk to Helen. And once inside their flat, I don't waste any time. While she's boiling the kettle, I follow her into the kitchen.

'Mia's told me she thinks she saw Callum yesterday. In the café, when you took her to the loo.'

'Oh.' Helen gets mugs out of the cupboard, opens a new packet of tea bags. Is she taking her time so that she can think up an excuse? 'Yes, I meant to tell you about that.'

'Well, I wish you had done! I wish you'd told me right away, Helen – I've said before, it's pretty important that I know about these things.'

'Well, I know.' She turns to face me, looking worried. 'But I didn't want to upset Mia any more than she already was. It obviously wasn't really him, but—'

'How can you possibly know that?'

'Well, it would be such a coincidence, wouldn't it? Him being there, on the same day—'

'Yes, a coincidence, but not impossible! And Mia says he waved at her.'

She gives a little smile now and turns back to the kettle. 'Ah, well, as you've often told me, Mia does like to make up little stories, doesn't she. The person she pointed at wasn't waving. And he didn't look like he could be Mia's daddy. He looked too young. A teenager.'

'Well, appearances can be deceptive, can't they?' To be fair, I'd never have said Callum looked young for his age, but it wasn't for Helen to make the judgement, was it. I'm seething with frustration but trying my best to stay reasonable.

'Perhaps you should give me a photo of him, love,' she suggests calmly. 'So that I know who we're looking out for.'

'I haven't got any.' I cleared my phone of them all. I never wanted to look at his mean, smug face again. I sigh. 'Look, Helen, I don't want to argue about whether or not it was really Callum. But you *must* tell me, any time Mia says she thinks she's seen him – whether you believe her or not. It's really important, OK? If it *was* Callum, I'd have wanted to make sure we avoided bumping into him. And apart from anything else, I need to know what's upsetting Mia. I need to be able to talk to her about it.'

'I didn't realise she was upset. I'm sorry, Jess. I thought it was best to just brush it off and hope she forgot about it.'

'But I still needed to know!' I insist. 'You could have called me last night if you didn't want to say anything in front of her. Or this morning. Please, in future—'

'All right. Of course. I will tell you if it ever happens again. I'm sorry,' she says again. She's put the tea bags down and is looking upset now. Have I been too heavy-handed? No! It needed spelling out, firmly, didn't it, because she just doesn't seem to have grasped how much it matters.

'Well, I'm sorry too,' I concede. 'Sorry if I sound annoyed. But I just freak out if there's any suggestion of Callum being around the kids. I've told you: he's really bad news. OK?'

'OK.' She forces a smile. 'Lesson learned.'

The conversation is a little bit stilted as we drink our tea. But I'm glad I've made myself perfectly clear. I need to be more in control of this situation. Helen and Robert might be doing me a huge favour, but I'm still the children's mother. I need to make the rules.

22

Mia spends much of the final weekend of our holiday playing at zoos – and renewing her pleas for a pet. Seeing so many animals has just reinforced the unfairness of her lack of a baby animal of her own, in her mind. To make matters worse, apparently one of her friends at school has just been bought a kitten, and Mia suddenly seems to have become an expert in all things cat-related.

'Did you know, Mummy, baby kittens mustn't go outside or they'll get lost,' she tells me while I'm dishing up dinner.

'Yes, I'm sure that's true.'

'But did you know, Mummy, cats teach their baby kittens how to wash themselves? Did you know they wash by licking themselves all over? Like this!' She starts licking her hands and arms. 'They even lick their own bottoms!'

This is, of course, a matter for extreme hilarity, as Mia pretends to make the appropriate action and deliberately falls over in a heap, making Archie convulse with laughter.

'I'm glad we wash with water – aren't you?' I laugh with them.

'I want a kitten, Mummy,' she says, looking at me longingly. '*Please* can we have one, please, please, *please*?'

I sigh as, once again, I remind her it's not fair to keep cats or dogs in tiny upstairs flats, and that they cost a lot of money to feed, shaking my head at her suggestion that she would share her dinners with the potential kitten. We've been through all this so many times before and, to be honest, it's a shame. I would like the kids to have a pet. I'd like us to have a lot of things, but I'm not going to get myself into debt for them. The kitten will have to wait until the day I win the lottery. Or at least the day I buy a ticket!

* * *

Monday comes around quickly – too quickly – and I'm back at work. And I've only been in the shop for ten minutes when Tariq calls me into the office.

'Good holiday?' he asks – and then, without waiting for my reply: 'Now then, Jess, I wanted to talk to you about the extra work.'

'Extra work?' I ask, a shiver going down my spine. 'What extra work?'

'Well, the future events we're going to hold in the shop. Margaret and I both think you handled the spring event really well, so we'd like you to be very much involved on future occasions.'

'Oh, I see.' I must admit I feel pleased, flattered, that he and Margaret trust me to manage more events.

'But of course, we'll need you here on Saturdays whenever we have anything organised,' he adds. 'And of course, you'll be paid overtime – or you could take a day off in lieu during the week.'

'How often do you anticipate needing me on Saturdays?' I ask a little warily.

'Well, we'll have to see how successful the next few events are. So it'll be up to you, really, Mia – to make a success of them!'

He gives a little excited laugh, and I try to smile in response.

I want to say: *You know that's going to be difficult for me. You know I only see my children on Saturdays and Sundays. They're at school and nursery on weekdays – how is a day off in the week going to help?* But if I start whingeing about working more Saturdays now, without even taking time to think it through, it looks bad.

I take a deep breath and try my best to sound professional. 'Well, of course, Saturdays will depend on what childcare arrangements I can make.'

'Of course.' He smiles. 'I realise that. Obviously, you'll need to sort something out. But we're putting our faith in you to help the business grow.'

I don't know whether to feel pleased or worried about this. But what can I do? I just thank him, and hope it isn't going to be too regular an occurrence.

* * *

By the time I get back to Helen and Robert's to pick up the children, I've tried to put the question of extra Saturdays to the back of my mind. It might not happen too often.

'Have they been OK this afternoon?' I ask as soon as Helen opens her door.

'Of course. Come in,' she says. She's smiling, her eyes sparkling as if there's something, a secret or a surprise, that she's not telling me. But before she can say another word, Mia has bounded out of the living room, her face red with excitement.

'Guess what, Mummy!' she shrieks, jumping from one foot to the other. 'We've got a pet! His name's Beaky and he's ours but he's going to live here and we can see him and feed him any time we want—'

'All right, Mia, let Mummy get inside and get her coat off!' Helen says. 'Sorry, Jess – she's been so excited to tell you—'

'A pet?' I repeat, looking from her, to Mia, and back again, a feeling of dread immediately coming over me. Please don't say they've bought the kids a puppy or kitten that I've got to take back to the pet shop? 'What kind of pet?'

'Well, I'm afraid I wasn't up for getting a cat or a dog,' Helen says as I shrug off my coat and hang it up. 'But Robert and I talked it over, and decided a small pet that doesn't need too much work—'

'He's a bird!' Mia squawks. 'A budget-car.'

'Budgerigar!' Helen corrects her, laughing. '*Budgie* is easier to say, Mia.'

A budgie. They've got a budgie, as a pet for *my* children? They know I've told the kids they can't have a pet. They know how much Mia wanted one, and how firm I've had to be about it – how she's had to try to accept the disappointment. I really don't know how to feel about this. At the moment, to be honest, I feel like my authority has been undermined, even if they think they're being kind.

I follow them into the living room, where Robert has Archie in his arms, lifting him up to look at the small green and yellow bird sitting on a perch in a cage hanging in the corner.

I don't know what to say. The more I think about this, the less I like it. It feels like they're taking over, taking decisions out of my hands. Are they trying to *buy* my kids' affections?

'His name is Beaky,' Mia says again. 'Like my other bird.'

'The blackbird. I see,' I say.

'Come and see, Mummy, come and see him!' She grabs my hand and pulls me towards the cage. 'His cage has to be high up because he'll get scared if he's down low,' she says with the air of an expert in bird care. 'And me and Archie gived him some little bits of apple but he mustn't have too much. We're going to teach him to talk! Did you know, budgiegars can talk, Mummy? They can talk in actual words, like us, can you believe that?'

I try to smile, for Mia's sake, but inside I'm fuming. This is exactly why I've said *no pets*. I knew how excited Mia would be to have one, and I knew it would be impossible for me to look after one. So it feels like an act of one-upmanship for Helen and Robert to do this.

Mia's hugging herself, she's so thrilled about it all. Even Archie, although he's wriggling to get down from Robert's arms now, seems excited.

'Beaty!' he says joyfully, pointing at the cage. 'Beaty!'

'Yes, Archie, he's Beaky,' Robert agrees.

I turn round to face Helen again, struggling for words. I feel too cross about it to make a pretence of thanking them.

'Can we have a word, Helen?' I manage. 'In the kitchen?'

Her smile drops a little. 'Of course.' She leads me out of the kids' earshot and closes the door behind us. 'Is anything wrong?'

'Well, look, I presume having a budgie wasn't exactly top of your wish list. So... you and Robert have just done this to keep my kids happy?'

She grins. 'Oh, look, it's nice for us, too, to have a little bird to look after. And – well, I know how much Mia was longing for a pet, and now – since the zoo trip – she hasn't stopped talking about all the animals she likes. And of course, I realise it would be difficult for you, working every day like you do—'

'Yes, of course it would. That's why I've always said no to Mia about having a pet – any pet. Even if I could find the time to look after a bird, he'd be lonely when we're all out.'

And frankly, I didn't want one! And now Mia has learnt that

when Mummy says no, it doesn't matter because someone else can overrule her.

'Well, we've got all the time in the world,' Helen says, seeming completely unaware of my frustration. 'It will be lovely; we can try to teach him to say some new words, and it'll be a little bit of company for us, when the children aren't here.'

When the children aren't here.

I feel a little shiver. Helen's more or less admitting that they've got nothing else to do except sit in their flat waiting for the next opportunity to look after Mia and Archie – to have them here as often as possible. I've been trying to talk myself out of all the concerns I've had about Helen and Robert because I thought I was so lucky to have neighbours who loved looking after my kids. But was I being naïve? This has really got me wondering about how much they seem to want to intrude. To take over. To act like they're more involved in the children's lives than they really are... or should be.

But what can I say? I need them! And if I make a fuss, Helen might have a fit of pique at my ingratitude and decide they won't look after the children any more.

'Well, I suppose I just wish you'd talked to me about it first,' I say.

'Oh, Jess, I'm sorry.' Her face is a picture of distress. 'I hope you don't think we've gone against you or anything like that? Robert and I thought it was the perfect solution. We just want Mia and Archie to be happy.'

'OK. Well, thank you, then,' I say, aware that my tone is more than a little grudging. I open the kitchen door and go back to where the children are still happily talking to the bird.

'Say night-night to Beaky now, then,' I tell them, forcing a smile. 'He'll still be here tomorrow; you'll see him again then.'

And I'll still be feeling just as uneasy about it.

23

I feel grumpy and unsettled about the budgie for the rest of the evening, and take ages going to sleep, worrying about whether Helen and Robert are really trying to tempt my kids into spending more time with them – and if so, why? – or whether I'm getting too worked up about it. When I wake up the next morning, I have to admit to myself that of course, I know what's really wrong with me at the moment. I mean – apart from the worry about the budgie, the worry about Helen and Robert in general and the worry about Callum having possibly turned up at the zoo. To say nothing, of course, of all the worries about the rent, the bills and food prices that take up most of my waking hours. I know I'd have been coping with them all better if it wasn't for the date. This Friday, 21 April, is the anniversary of my mum's passing. It plays on my mind every year: not just the memory of that awful day itself, but the thought of my dad, and the guilt I feel even though I don't think our situation is my fault.

I do try not to dwell on it. I'm normally quite a rational person, and I tell myself it's only a date, it's no different from any other day. It's not as if I don't think about my mum on all the other days, because I do, every single day. And it's not like I go to the crematorium to lay flowers on the anniversary, or anything like that – she told me and my dad she didn't want us to. She was very clear about it.

'If you can't remember me without all those rituals, it's a bit of a shame, isn't it?' she said, laughing, even then. She was always laughing, my mum, always joking, right up till the last few days, when she stopped, and never started again. 'Remember me through our photos, through our favourite songs. Remember the things we liked doing together, the TV shows we liked watching, the games we played. Happy things. I don't want you making it worse for yourselves by thinking you owe me a duty, a *sad* duty. Please don't.'

So I've always tried to follow that. I keep photos of her by my bed; I talk to the children about her, sing the songs she liked, play Happy Families with Mia because it always made Mum laugh. I miss her *all* the time, not just on the twenty-first of April. She'd been dying slowly for months, over a year. Dad said her last day was a blessing, really, although I never knew whether he just said that to try to comfort me, because I wasn't there – I was at school. I suppose I never forgave school for that, and it took me a long while to forgive my dad for making me go.

So despite how hard I try not to make a big thing out of the date, the misery still creeps over me stealthily as it approaches, like a grey blanket smothering me in the night. I don't *want* to remember it: how I screamed at Dad when I got home from school to find out she'd passed away while I was in a maths lesson. How I ran out of the house and didn't come back until late in the evening – not caring that I'd added more anxiety to his terrible grief. How horribly I behaved. How it changed me forever.

And this year, it's worse, for two reasons. It's worse, in a peculiar way, because of Helen. It's all very well to look at her and think she's like my mum, but this week reminds me, more than ever, that she's *not*, and she can't ever replace her. And the other reason is, I've promised myself not to call my dad this year. Even when I was going through my most difficult, rebellious years, we always called to ask each other if we were OK on the anniversary. And even after he turned his back on me, I've still called him, despite the way he's responded. But this year, after he referred to my children as *brats*, I made up my mind he didn't deserve me – let alone them – any more. I'm not calling him this time.

But... what would Mum say, if she knew I wasn't even prepared to try?

'Be the bigger person, Jess,' she used to say, when I came home angry and upset because I'd fallen out with one of my friends. 'Be the *better* person. The argument might not have been your fault, but the making up could be your doing.'

So I haven't decided yet whether I'm going to put myself through it. And I'm still undecided as the next few days pass, until it's Thursday already, and tomorrow's the day of the anniversary.

* * *

'Beaky said hello, Mummy! I said it and he said it back!' Mia yells at me excitedly as soon as I collect the children from Helen's this evening.

'Beaty! Allo!' Archie joins in, jumping up and down on the spot on his chubby little legs.

'*Really*, Mia?' I look at Helen. 'Surely that's too soon for him to learn?'

'Ah, we specially asked for one that's already started talking,' she explains. 'And we've been talking to him to encourage him. We're trying to teach him *Goodbye* now.'

'Goodbye!' squawks Beaky at once, looking pleased with himself, and Mia almost collapses with excitement.

'See, Mummy! He talks to me!'

'He's talking to *all* of us, Mia. Auntie Helen's been encouraging him.'

'No, he's talking to me and Archie 'cos he's *our* budgiegar, not Auntie Helen's. Auntie Helen keeps saying he's ours.'

'Right.' I frown. Why would Helen make such a point of this? Surely the budgie is *their* pet – she and Robert bought him, and the cage and his food and everything. I hope she's not expecting me to pay for it all, because that would be the last straw for me!

Mia starts jumping about beneath the cage, calling out 'hello' and 'goodbye' constantly to the poor budgie, until Helen eventually tells her to stop or Beaky will get fed up with it and it'll put him off the idea of talking altogether.

'Yes, you might give him a headache. Let him have a rest now,' I agree.

Mia comes and sits down next to me, looking sulky.

'Can we go home now?' she says.

'Yes, come on, I think you're overtired.'

Back in our flat, I talk to her gently about her attitude.

'Well,' she says with a pout, 'Auntie Helen wouldn't let me talk to Beaky, and he's not her pet, he's ours.'

'Auntie Helen and Uncle Robert bought him, OK? And he's in their flat, and you were talking to him too loudly and upsetting him.'

'He *is* our pet,' she insists. 'Auntie Helen keeps on saying he is. She says we can go there as often as we want, to talk to him and feed him, and Uncle Robert's going to show me how to clean his cage out.'

'Well, that's nice of her, but he's still their budgie, Mia,' I insist. I feel like it's important she understands this. 'They paid for him – I didn't. If he was ours, we'd be keeping him here. And we can't.'

'But they bought him for us – for me and Archie!' She's starting to cry now, in her frustration. 'Auntie Helen *says* so. They're just keeping him in their flat for us. I have to go down there, at weekends as well, Mummy, because he's my budgiegar.'

I feel more and more rattled by this. As far as I'm concerned, it's Helen and Robert's bird. I don't want it to be ours – and particularly not Mia's and Archie's – that's ridiculous, they're far too young for the responsibility and I don't want it! Why is Helen so insistent on it being theirs? Why is she making such a point of telling Mia to go down and see the bird all the time – *weekends as well*?

Whatever Helen might say about it, it sounds to me like they've got this bird with the sole intention of luring my kids into their flat more often. Why? Because she thinks they need rescuing from their useless mother? That's more and more what it's beginning to feel like.

* * *

Friday passes slowly. I feel miserable and conflicted, both about Dad and about the situation with Helen. I've tried to move on from the confrontation with her about the possible sighting of Callum at the zoo, tried to get back to the previous relationship I've enjoyed with them, but now with this business of buying the kids a budgie behind my back, I really can't shake the feeling I have, a lot of the time, that there's something going on behind the scenes that I don't know about but don't like. As for Dad, I could have called him in my lunch break, but I didn't. I could call him this evening, or I could just stick to my guns and forget it – and that'd be that. It would close the door, forever. I'm so stressed about everything that, by the time the kids are both asleep, I decide to get one thing off my mind, at least, and give Dad a call. I don't think I'll be able to sleep if I don't try. The call goes to voice-mail, but I don't leave a message and I don't attempt to call again later. I feel slightly resentful that I've spent all week stressing about whether to call or not, and when I do, he's out. Well, at least I've tried. I've tried to be *the better person*, Mum. I can't do more than that, can I? Feeling completely drained, I turn on the TV and watch it for an hour or so without really caring what's on, before giving up and going to bed.

When I wake up on Saturday morning, I'm determined to move on, to stop worrying about everything else for now, and just stop caring about Dad. The kids are playing happily enough so I make a start on the housework. And then the drama begins.

* * *

I'm just hoovering the bedroom when my phone rings. I grab it quickly, wondering if Dad's seen the missed call and decided to call me back. But the caller is already speaking and sounds like an elderly lady – and quite distressed.

'Is that Jessica?' she says, her voice a bit faint and very shaky.

Nobody's called me by my full name since I was a child. I'm just about to ask who it is when she goes on:

'It's Pamela, dear. Next door to your dad. I found your number, it's on his—'

'Oh! Yes, hello, Pamela.' My stomach suddenly lurches violently, making me gasp and have to take a quick breath. 'What...? I mean, is everything OK? Is my dad—'

'I've just found him, dear. I knocked because I had a parcel delivered for him, you see, and I knew he was in, and his car was on the drive, but he didn't answer. I kept trying, but—'

'What do you mean, you *found* him?' I interrupt her. My breath's tight in my throat, adrenaline pumping so fast that I have to stand up and walk from the sofa to the TV and back repeatedly, my hands shaking, my legs trembling. 'Where? Is he... is he all right, Pamela?'

'I've got a key, you see?' she's going on, not seeming to have noticed the urgency in my voice. 'He gave me one, in case of emergencies, but I've never liked to use it, but I thought, when I kept knocking and ringing the bell and he still didn't... well, I thought I'll just open the door and put the parcel inside for him, but when I did, there he was, on the floor, so—'

'On the *floor*? Is he *all right*, Pamela?' I shout this time, and I hear the gasp of surprise at the other end of the phone.

'I don't know, dear. I've called 999. I'm waiting here for them, but I thought, *Pamela, you'd better call Jessica, she'll want to know*—'

'OK!' I gasp. 'I'm coming! Um – thank you. I'll be – I'll be there as soon as—'

'All right, dear. Drive carefully.'

I hang up. All I can think, very uncharitably in the circumstances, is *silly old moo. I don't even drive.* And this then brings the whole situation suddenly into proper focus. I'll have to call a taxi. I'll have to ask Helen or Robert to have the children. I need to do it – *now*. I have to go, *now*. And finally, the trembling and dithering stops and I'm full of purpose. And full of dread.

OK, so we never see each other. He's written me off, might not love me any more, but he's still my dad. And what would my mum think of me if I didn't rush to him now – if, despite everything, I couldn't be the *better person*? He didn't answer the phone last night. How long's he been lying there? Why's he been lying on the floor, possibly all night, possibly longer, and why doesn't Pamela know if he's all right? Why aren't the paramedics on the phone with her right now, talking her through performing CPR?

What the hell has he done?

24

———————

Helen can't understand me on the phone. I must be gabbling
incoherently. I take a breath.

'Sorry. It's... an emergency. My father. I... need to go.'

That's all I have to say. She says to bring Mia and Archie down
right away, they'll keep them both for as long as I need them to.

'How are you getting there?'

'I'll call a taxi.'

'No. Robert will take you in the van. I'll get him to go and pull
it round to the front of the flats.'

I pick Archie up, ignoring his protests, tell Mia to put her
shoes on in a tone of voice that must make her realise she'd better
not argue, and bundle them both straight down the stairs. Helen
meets me at the bottom.

'Sorry – I don't know how long...' I say, passing Archie over
to her. 'Sorry, kids – I'll be back as soon as I can...' I kiss them
both quickly, shakily, trying not to notice the anxiety in Mia's
eyes.

'Go, Jess – just go. Call me later.'

'OK. Thank you.'

Robert's already pulled his van up and jumps down to help me into the cab.

'Thank you so much for this, Robert, but I could have got a taxi,' I say as he pulls away.

'Don't be silly.' He gives me a quick glance. 'You've... obviously had a shock.'

'Well, I don't know what to think yet. My neighbour called me. There's an ambulance on its way.'

It's only a fifteen-minute drive to my dad's house, and by the time we arrive, the ambulance is already there. Robert pulls up behind it. For a split second I wonder what the neighbours in this smart avenue on the good side of town will be thinking if they look out of the window and see an ambulance and a white delivery van both pulled up outside one of their big detached houses.

Mum and Dad moved to this house when Dad got his promotion at the bank. I must have been about eleven. I haven't been back here since I moved in with Callum – when I found out I was pregnant. It feels like another world to me now: this leafy suburban street with the big expensive cars on the driveways and the houses with their security systems and Ring doorbells. A short time ago I thought I'd never be back again. *Never say never*, my mum used to say.

'Thanks, Robert,' I say, going to open the passenger door, but he stops me with a hand on my arm.

'Wait. You might need a lift to the hospital?'

I feel myself shudder. 'No. If... if they have to take him in, I'll go in the ambulance.'

'OK. Well, look, call me if you don't... or when you need a lift back...'

'No. Thank you for bringing me, Robert, but honestly, I'll get a taxi if I need to.'

'OK,' he says again. He looks at me anxiously. 'I hope... well, let us know. Whatever.'

* * *

Pamela's got Dad's front door open before I'm even out of the van.

'Hello, dear. The paramedics are here,' she says unnecessarily.

Dad's in an armchair in the lounge now. *Thank God*, I think, *he's not still on the floor. He's conscious.* His eyes are closed, he's very pale, but he's alive, conscious, breathing. I feel my own breaths slowing slightly.

'Dad,' I say.

I can't get near him. The paramedics are checking things; he's wired up to an ECG monitor, he has a pulse thing on his finger, a dressing on his head and one leg up on a chair.

He opens his eyes and stares at me as if he's seeing a ghost. He looks old.

'Jess,' he sighs.

One of the paramedics turns to me. 'You're his daughter?' he asks gently.

'Yes. What's happened? What's wrong with him?'

He takes me to one side and talks very quietly.

'He seems to have had a fall. He can't remember much. We've been checking everything in case something happened – perhaps a heart attack or a stroke – to make him collapse, but it doesn't look that way. He may... have had a drink or two. But we're going to take him into A&E, just to be on the safe side. As there's a head injury.'

'He fell and hit his head?'

'Last night, from what he says. We're assuming he knocked himself out. And that left knee's giving him pain too – he couldn't get up when he came round. He might have broken his kneecap, if he fell onto it hard.'

'He doesn't remember?'

'Apparently not.' The paramedic doesn't seem surprised. 'It could be a sign of concussion. Or it could just be the effects of the alcohol. He still has it on his breath,' he adds even more quietly.

I didn't think my dad was a drinker. But it was Mum's anniversary yesterday. He was on his own. I feel a flash of guilt, but swallow it back immediately, almost angrily. Whose fault was *that*?

'Will he... be all right?'

'We think he'll be fine, love. Might have a few bruises, the knee might take a while to heal. And as I said, the head injury needs to be watched for a while. We don't know exactly what time the accident happened, so—'

'Can I come with him in the ambulance?'

'Yes, of course. We'll be ready to take him in a few minutes. Want a cup of tea while you wait? You look a bit shaken.'

'I'm fine, thanks.'

They bring in a wheelchair, help Dad into it, cover him with a blanket, ask what he needs to take with him in case he's kept in. I go upstairs to find a bag, grab pyjamas and a toothbrush and the other things he might want. I don't know where he keeps anything, and I feel tears threatening, just at this realisation.

Pamela's leaving as I come back downstairs.

'Let me know how he gets on, dear,' she says.

I don't think she was ever particularly close to my parents, but at least she's been a good neighbour now that the occasion demanded.

'I will,' I promise. 'Thanks for your help.'

* * *

Thank goodness there's no delay when our ambulance arrives at the hospital. The paramedics hand over quickly to the doctor and nurse who receive us, telling them what they've been able to deduce about Dad's condition.

'OK,' the doctor says when the paramedics have said goodbye and left. He turns to me with a smile. 'Don't worry, we'll give your dad another check over now, but it sounds likely the head injury isn't severe. The scalp always bleeds copiously, even after a minor wound, so it often looks worse than it is. You say he's not on blood thinners?'

'I...' I look at Dad and back at the doctor. I feel so stupid having to say it, but: 'I don't know. Are you, Dad?'

'No,' he says. He can't meet my eyes. 'I'm not – I told the paramedics.'

'Just running over everything again,' the doctor explains calmly. 'It seems you lost consciousness briefly when you fell, but you knew where you were when you came round?'

'Yes. On my hall floor. I couldn't get up because the pain in my knee was excruciating. I... think I fell asleep eventually.' He gives a little cough of embarrassment. 'I'd had a few drinks.'

'OK,' says the doctor, unperturbed.

'I can't exactly remember how I fell,' Dad goes on. 'Perhaps I tripped over the doormat. I'd been out. I'm not sure what time I got in. I couldn't find my phone.'

I want to ask if he would have called me, if he'd had the phone, but the words stick in my throat. Of course he wouldn't have.

The doctor asks him some more questions, about whether he's got a headache now and whether he has any idea how long he was unconscious for. He does a few checks that the paramedics have already done, and I can see Dad trying to rein in his impatience.

'It's my knee that's bothering me the most,' he says.

'OK, we'll look at that now,' says the doctor.

Within minutes, he's arranged for Dad to have an X-ray of his kneecap, assured me that he probably won't need a brain scan but he will need another run-through of the checks in an hour's time.

'And if everything seems fine after that, depending on the X-ray results, he can be discharged but he'll need someone to be with him for the next twenty-four hours. Would you be able to do that?'

I freeze. I look at Dad, who's looked away from me again.

'I'll ask my neighbour,' he says eventually in a tight voice.

'No!'

I'm annoyed now. I've come out of my way, rushing to his side, abandoning my kids, and come with him to hospital, all despite the fact that I know what he thinks of me, that he looks down on me and doesn't want anything to do with me. You'd think he'd be grateful! You'd think he'd show some sort of appreciation, but no, he'd rather have his neighbour look after him. Well, I'm not having that.

'*I'm* going to look after you, Dad, whether you like it or not.'

God knows what the doctor must think of us, but his face remains impassive. I guess they see it all, here.

'Well, I'll leave you to discuss that,' he says, 'and I'll be back for another assessment in about an hour. They'll come for you for the X-ray.'

After he's gone, we remain in stony silence for a few minutes.

'I didn't expect you to come,' he says eventually. 'I didn't know Pam had called you.'

'Of course she called me – it's the normal thing to do, in most families.'

He nods. 'Yes. I suppose it is.'

'I tried to call you yesterday evening. The anniversary.'

'I went out. Couldn't face being at home on my own.'

'I suppose you went to a pub.'

'A bar.' He sighs. 'OK, I admit it, I drank myself senseless.'

'I hope you weren't driving, at least.'

'No. Walked. Got a taxi home. I presume that's where my phone is – it must have fallen out of my pocket.'

'Well, they'll call your land line if they find it.'

We both fall silent again. Then he looks up at me and I see his eyes are glinting with tears.

'I'm sorry,' he says very quietly. 'I'm... embarrassed. Mortified.'

Embarrassed about *me*? About giving up on me, insulting me and my children, not acting like a father? No, he's just embarrassed about getting drunk.

A little while later a porter comes to wheel him down for an X-ray, and I follow, still trying to rein in my emotions, keeping a picture of Mum in my head and imagining what she'd have expected of me. We're back in his A&E cubicle in a matter of minutes. Dad closes his eyes, and I wonder if he's actually asleep. I'm fidgeting in my chair, wondering about the children, imagining how cross Mia must be that I left in such a hurry. I didn't even give her any explanation about where or why I was going. I feel sick at the thought – how could I have put my worry about my dad, who doesn't care about me in the slightest, before my own children? I wonder if I should call Helen, to find out how they are, or if I should wait until I know more about how long I'll be here.

'You don't have to stay,' Dad says. Evidently he's not asleep after all. He's seen me looking at my watch. 'I'm perfectly OK on my own. As usual.'

I bite back my usual response about whose fault it is that he's on his own – because, perhaps fortunately, the doctor is approaching us now with a smile on his face.

'Good news,' he says. 'Your X-ray doesn't show any fractures, Mr Andrews. So as we suspected, your knee just took a really bad bashing on the floor. It's obviously very badly bruised and swollen. What happens is, the tissue inside the knee bleeds and swells and yes, that inflammation is actually really painful. You're going to struggle to walk for a while. I'd suggest, once we discharge you, you'll need to rest it with your foot up and apply ice to take the swelling down. We'll prescribe you some painkillers. But first of all...' He checks his watch. 'First of all, you've got another twenty-five minutes until we need to check you over again regarding your head. I'll be back then, and hopefully that'll be more good news.'

* * *

In the event, it *is* good news. The doctor gives Dad a leaflet about head injuries, which he stuffs in his pocket impatiently, and the prescription for painkillers, and tells him very sternly that being discharged doesn't mean everything is definitely going to remain OK, because sometimes things happen in the brain quite a while *after* a head injury, so he has to come back if there are any worrying symptoms. He lists these, even though they're on the leaflet too. He's obviously used to patients who stuff them in their pockets and don't read them.

'And he needs someone with him for the first twenty-four hours, at least,' he reminds me before leaving.

I wheel Dad along the corridor to the pharmacy to collect the painkillers and then outside into the fresh air. Luckily there are a couple of taxis waiting outside so we're back at Dad's house very quickly. I'm calling Helen while we're still in the taxi.

'How are the children?' I ask as soon as she picks up. 'Helen, I feel so awful about the way I left. Is Mia OK? I hope I didn't frighten her—'

'Jess, calm down, she's all right,' Helen soothes me. 'I've explained that there was something very urgent.' She lowers her voice. 'I... said it was a *friend* who needed you. I hope that was OK. I didn't know whether she knew about—'

'No,' I admit shakily. 'She doesn't.'

I glance at Dad, and don't go on. I've always pretended to Mia that her grandad lives too far away for us to see him.

'So how is he?' Helen asks.

'OK. Well, he's been discharged from the hospital but... he needs someone with him for twenty-four hours. I'm—'

'You don't have to,' Dad growls at me. I ignore him. He shouldn't be listening to my conversation.

'I'm going to be staying with him,' I go on. 'Shall I... some-how... collect the children and bring them over to—'

'Absolutely not!' she says firmly. 'Look, it's Sunday tomorrow, we're both free, we'll thoroughly enjoy having the children all day. We can take them to the park, play games, play with the budgie, whatever they want to do. I've got your key, so I'll go in and get fresh clothes and anything else they want. Don't worry about a thing. We'll all be perfectly fine.'

'Thank you both again. Please kiss the children from me, tell them I love them, and I'll be home' – I check my watch – 'tomorrow afternoon.'

'Whenever you can,' she says gently. 'I won't make them any promises, Jess. Just in case.'

Just in case.

The thought hasn't even occurred to me until now that the twenty-four hours might not be long enough; that, as the doctor warned us, something bad might happen before that time is up. I feel sick at the idea. What if I have to stay longer? What if I have to go back to the hospital with him? What if I can't get into work on Monday?

I feel a flash of guilt at the realisation that I'm more concerned with how this would affect me – the children, and my job – than with any anxiety about Dad's condition. But once again I dismiss that guilt as quickly as it comes. Why should I care? Why *do* I care? It irritates me that I do. But of course, I know the answer. I feel like I owe it to Mum. And that's all.

25

Dad insists on paying for the taxi and I don't argue. I help him out of it and up the step into his front door. He says he needs the loo, and luckily there's a downstairs one so I take him as far as the door and leave him to it, hearing him grunt with pain as he hobbles inside. It's late in the afternoon now and my stomach's rumbling – his must be too – so I wander into the kitchen and look for something for us to eat. The kitchen's exactly as I remember it, but looks shabby and neglected. There's hardly anything in the fridge. I put the kettle on, find tea bags, find some bread in the bread bin and put it in the toaster.

'Have you got anything else to eat?' I ask him irritably as he hobbles out of the loo.

'Only what's there,' he responds in the same tone. 'I'm not hungry.'

'Well, I am,' I shoot back. 'Looks like toast and jam, then.'

The jam has got mould on it. I scrape it off before spreading jam on four slices of toast. 'Eat this, whether you want it or not,' I tell him. 'Hold my arm, I'll help you into the living room. You should have taken the doctor's advice and borrowed some crutches for a week or so.'

'I don't want bloody crutches,' he mutters. 'I'm not a bloody invalid.'

I almost push him into the armchair, I'm so exasperated.

'Well, you'll have to manage somehow after I've gone home. I can't stay any longer than the twenty-four hours.'

'Didn't ask you to stay.'

I sit down in the chair next to him, pass him a plate of toast and take a bite of my own while I try to calm down.

'Is this how it's going to be?' I ask eventually. 'Constant bickering, even now, after we haven't spoken to each other, haven't seen each other for about five years? And before you say you didn't ask me to come, I'll tell you why I did. I came because Mum would have wanted me to, OK? She'd have asked me to *be the better person*. When Pamela called me, I thought you might have been dying. I thought you might already be dead. And I thought of Mum, and how she'd have felt if I just left you to die. I came, even though I don't think you deserve it, because Mum might be looking down and watching me, and I don't want to disappoint her, like I disappointed you. So just be bloody grateful, and stop complaining, all right?'

I stop, look round, and he's got his head in his hands. He's crying.

'Oh.' I put my plate down, swallow my mouthful of toast. I wasn't prepared for this. It's not just a question of a few tears trickling down his cheek; he's full-on sobbing, his shoulders shaking, looking for all the world like his heart's breaking. My default position should be to ignore it, to think it serves him right if he's upset, he deserves it, and more – but something about the sight of it – my big, domineering, stroppy father suddenly dissolved into this mess of weeping – makes me lose control of my own emotions, or you could say of my common sense. 'Oh, Dad! Please don't – I'm sorry...'

Before I know what I'm doing I'm beside him with my arms around him.

'Come on, you'll be all right, it was just a silly accident, you'll soon be OK again...'

'Don't,' he says, sounding like the words are choking him. 'Don't be sorry. It's nothing to do with the accident, I don't care about it, wouldn't have cared if I'd died. *I* should be sorry. You're right. Your mum would be disgusted with me. If she were still here to see what I've done – how I've refused to see you, to help you—'

'Well, I haven't exactly been the model daughter you were expecting,' I manage to say, if only to stop him crying. Am I crying myself? I think I am. For God's sake! I didn't want to be crying. I wanted to stay strong, I didn't want to fall for any of his sob stories, I've got enough of those of my own.

'I've just been so...' He gulps, wipes his eyes, swallows and tries again. 'I've been so damned unhappy.' His voice drops to almost a whisper. 'So very unhappy I've wondered what I'm carrying on for. I've considered *not* carrying on. What's the point of it all?'

'The point is,' I retort, wiping my own eyes now, my anger returning, 'that Mum lost *her* life when she would have wanted to go on living. She was happy. She loved life, right up to the end. She was lovely, and vibrant, and caring, and she shouldn't have been taken like that, in the prime of her life. You should be *grateful* you're still alive. I've been mourning Mum too, ever since she passed. I was only fourteen! I should have had a dad to comfort me, to reassure me and love me, but—'

'I couldn't!' he shouts. 'I was too damned *lost* without her, I couldn't be happy without her. And you went your own way, messing up your life—'

I shake my head and sit back down again. I don't fancy the toast any more.

'You should have had grief counselling, Dad. Perhaps we both should have. You still need it. You need treatment for depression, frankly.'

'Counselling!' he says dismissively. 'Depression! Huh. I've just got on with my life.'

'But you haven't, have you?' I'm surprised now to find I'm talking to him more gently, as if he were the child. As if I were sympathetic. 'You haven't been getting on with it, Dad. You're alone, so alone that on Mum's anniversary you have to get drunk, when we could have been together for it. You could have been with your *grandchildren*. You've done this to yourself. I was a heartbroken child, and you didn't help me. Yes, I went off the rails a bit. But I didn't do drugs, I didn't get into trouble with the police, I just messed up my school exams and got pregnant. I chose the wrong man because I was desperate for love, Dad – so desperate, I didn't realise he was... such a bad choice.'

He doesn't answer. He sits with his head down, nodding, as if in agreement. The toast falls off the plate, off his lap, and onto the carpet, but neither of us bother about it.

'I don't know why I couldn't let myself try,' he says eventually. 'I've wanted to.'

'Try what?'

'To... reconcile with you. Talk to you. See the grandchildren. It's been... as if I didn't even want to be happy. Like I've been punishing myself. My life has just been work, work, work, sleep, repeat. You're right. I'm so alone, I almost forget who I am. I'm like a robot.'

We lapse into silence again. I take the cold toast back to the kitchen and throw it in his food waste bin. There's nothing in there. What the hell's he been eating? I check the freezer. Hardly anything in it, even emptier than the fridge. At least there are ice cubes; I prise some out, put them in a plastic bag, wrap them in a tea-towel, and march back into the living room.

'Put this on your knee,' I tell him. 'Now, I'm ordering food. And I can't leave you to go to the shops, so I'll get a supermarket delivery. Enough to keep you going after I've gone home, too. What do you normally do for your meals? Your kitchen looks like nobody lives here.'

He shrugs. 'Takeaways. Restaurants sometimes. I get breakfast on the way to work. Eat at my desk.'

'I see.' I get my phone out, log onto my Aldi account and put Dad's address in. I'm halfway through making a list of groceries when I stop, embarrassed at myself. I can't actually do it. 'I... can't afford to pay for this,' I mutter.

'Of course not. I wouldn't expect you to. I don't know why you're bothering, but whatever you want, I'll pay.'

'Dad, I'm ordering enough for *you*. You're going to need to rest until you can walk properly with that knee.'

'I'll be going to work. I'll be fine to drive, the car's automatic. I can sit down all day at work. With my leg up, if necessary.' He actually manages a smile, but it looks more like a grimace. 'I can do what I like, I'm the boss.'

'Whatever.' I'm too tired, too hungry, to argue. 'I'm still going to order you some decent food. I'd have thought you'd have learned to look after yourself properly by now.'

'Yes. Your mum *would* be disappointed.'

Again, that fleeting half-smile. A fleeting glimpse of the man he used to be. Before.

* * *

By the time the shopping has arrived, it's quite late in the evening. I put it all away and cook us a quick meal: jacket potatoes with baked beans and cheese, with salad. Comfort food – I feel like we both need it – but healthy, too. I find myself wondering what Helen's giving the children to eat and hope it isn't broccoli.

We eat from trays on our laps. I'm absolutely ravenous and Dad clears his plate too. Afterwards, he asks me to put the TV on and we watch a film on Netflix, relatively companionably. I think back over the few short hours that have brought us back together – presumably temporarily, and not necessarily in a good way but at least with a little honesty.

I send a message to Helen, asking if the children have settled OK for the night and she replies that they're fine, they're asleep, I mustn't worry – but of course, I *am* worried. I presume she'll have taken them back to their own beds, and that she'll sleep in my bed for the night. I didn't ask; for once, I've got no choice but to trust her. But I'm counting the hours that I've got to stay here. They can't go fast enough.

'You need to sleep in the downstairs room,' I tell Dad when the film's finished and I've made us both a cup of tea. He sighs but nods in agreement.

It's the room that used to be a study, but that became Mum's bedroom when she got too weak to go upstairs. It's where she spent the last days and hours of her life. I've already looked, wondering if he's turned it back into a study, but no, it's still the same. The same bedding, the same bedside lamp, the same curtains. I don't know how he'll be able to bear sleeping in there, but I'm not having him falling over again trying to get upstairs.

'Would you like me to change the sheets?' I ask. I'm surprised at how gentle my voice sounds.

'No.' He suddenly looks embarrassed. 'They're clean. I... sleep in there occasionally.'

'Oh.' He's finally managed to surprise me. 'I see. OK. Well, I've put your toothbrush and towel and everything in the downstairs bathroom, so if I help you—'

'I'm all right.' He heaves himself to his feet, wincing at the pain. 'I've got to try to manage.' He limps, slowly, across to me and puts a hand on my shoulder. 'Thank you, Jess.' He finally looks straight into my eyes. 'I mean it. I appreciate it. Thank you.'

I stay sitting in my own chair as he hobbles out of the room, and I don't get up to go upstairs to one of the guest rooms until he's closed the door behind him and I've seen the light go off.

It wasn't a hug. I'd have felt uncomfortable with that. But that hand resting on my shoulder, that look in his eyes, meant something... a little something, perhaps, but could it be a start?

* * *

I wouldn't say our relationship has improved exactly, but at least Dad and I spend most of Sunday talking. I cook him a proper Sunday dinner, tidy up the kitchen for him, and he keeps telling me to leave it, that he's perfectly fine, even though he quite obviously doesn't look after himself properly. I've filled his fridge and freezer and stocked up his cupboards (he's transferred the cost to my bank account), so it's up to him now. And we talk.

At first it's difficult, both of us a bit cagey, a bit prickly. But eventually we get onto the difficult subjects. He asks me about the children.

'You mean the brats, who I bring up in squalor?' I shoot back, and he drops his head for a moment but doesn't apologise.

'How old are they now?' he asks.

'Mia's going to be five in June. And Archie's seventeen months.' I know my voice is automatically softening, talking about my kids, even talking about them to someone who's called them brats.

'What are they like?' he asks, and somehow I resist the urge to ask him why he cares, because – like any mother, I suppose – I can never resist talking about them.

'Mia's bright, clever, very imaginative. She likes to make up stories and she loves animals. She's sweet and loving but she can get cross, too. She's very protective of her little brother. Archie's still a baby, really. He's into everything now, toddling around, exploring things, and he can be so funny; he's learning new words every day but his facial expressions speak volumes! They both love books, like me. I've always encouraged that. We go to the library. Mia likes drawing and painting, too. She won a book token at my shop for her spring picture.'

'You work in a shop?' he says, looking surprised.

'The bookshop in the town centre. Chapters. I'm a sales assistant but...' I hesitate, but OK, I'll admit it, I want to impress him. 'But I've been working on our special events.'

He raises his eyebrows. 'I didn't realise you were working.'

'Of course I have to work. How did you think I was managing?'

'So what do you do with the children while you're at work?'

'Mia's at school and Archie's at nursery. And since my manager's wanted me to work longer hours, they spend time with my downstairs neighbours. They're with them now.'

'Your mother stayed at home to look after you until you started secondary school,' he says, making me take a sharp breath of exasperation.

'My mother had a husband earning a good salary in a bank,' I snap.

'And we waited until I was earning enough, before we considered having a child,' he goes on calmly.

'Well, there you go. I, however, messed up my life and ended up bringing the children up on my own. Sorry, Dad, some of us make mistakes. There it is.'

There's an uncomfortable silence for a while. Dad stares at his foot, which is resting on the stool, an ice pack on his knee. Then:

'Do you still see him? The father?'

'Callum? No, never, not if I can help it.' I'm not going to mention the times recently that he's appeared outside my flat. 'I'd be happy never to set eyes on him again.'

'It was that bad? The relationship? It couldn't be patched up for the sake of the children?'

I stare at him, incredulous.

'No, Dad, it couldn't. It was for the sake of the children that I left. I didn't do it for the fun of it – it wasn't easy. I was pregnant, and I had to go into a refuge until the council could find me a flat. I didn't know how I was going to survive, to be honest.' I swallow, look down at the floor. Why should I tell him? I never tell anyone. But – now I've started, I suddenly *want* him to know; want him to feel bad, if that's even possible. Bad that he's never asked, never cared, never even worried about me. 'Callum started hitting me when Mia was a baby,' I say, speaking quickly, before I can change my mind.

Dad gasps. Finally, some emotion, I think.

'It irritated him, having her in his flat, crying, keeping him awake – he took it out on me. He'd had no idea what the reality of life with a baby was like. Not that I did, either, to be honest, but I loved her from the moment she was born.'

'Why on earth did you have another child, then?'

'Because I was so young and stupid, I suppose,' I say with a sigh. 'I already knew I should leave Callum; I already knew he didn't love me, but I... guess I just needed someone. Anyone, even someone who treated me so badly. But when I realised I was pregnant again, I knew I really *had* to get out. He'd never been violent with Mia – only me – but with two children in the flat, I guessed it might only be a matter of time before he lost his temper with them too.'

'If I'd known all this—' Dad starts, looking distressed, but I stop him.

'Don't say you'd have taken me in. Just don't! I used to try calling you, Dad. You hung up on me, every time. Let's not go there.'

He closes his eyes, looking defeated. 'I was drinking,' he says quietly. 'I mean, a lot. As in...' He drops his voice to a whisper, looking embarrassed. 'I went to AA in the end.'

'And yet you're still drinking?'

'No. Only on your mum's anniversary. Occasions like that – I have a few, yes. I knew I had to get help, back then, or I'd have lost my job, but now I can handle a few, occasionally, without getting addicted again.'

'I'm not sure that's how it works. But that's up to you, at the end of the day.'

I feel miffed. We've gone back to talking about him, to him making his alcoholism the excuse for not giving a toss about his daughter and grandchildren. I take a breath and plough on with my story. I need him to know, now.

'So I packed up and left while Callum was out,' I say. 'The people from the refuge tried to talk me into getting a court injunction to stop him seeing the kids, but it would have meant telling the court about the abuse, going through it all in public... and I couldn't face it. But I have got sole custody – because he made it clear that he didn't want to see them anyway.'

I pause, thinking about the threats Callum made recently about talking to Social Services, and I feel the familiar shudder of fear. He *doesn't* want the children – I have to keep reminding myself of that. All he wants is to intimidate me – he enjoys it, and he knows how easy it is.

I shake my head and get on with the story.

'I found out later he already had a conviction for hitting a previous girlfriend. As well as other offences, all linked to his temper; causing affray, they call it, that sort of thing.'

'I'm surprised it took you that long to get out,' Dad says.

'I had nowhere to go!' I say, annoyed that he still doesn't seem to get it. 'Callum was housing me, feeding me. I couldn't work, I had nobody to look after Mia and no money of my own.' I pause, and add quietly, 'And I loved my kids. I don't think, now, of either of them being anything to do with Callum. They're *mine*. They're my life.'

Dad's gone completely quiet, and I fall silent too. I'm already regretting saying anything. Why did I? Why should he care? He's ignored my existence ever since I first got pregnant – the shame, for him, won't be diminished in any way by hearing what happened with Callum.

I get up and start to head for the kitchen to make tea, but as I pass his chair he catches hold of my wrist to stop me.

'I'm sorry,' he says, his voice coming out strange and broken. 'Jess, I'm sorry, I really am. I had no idea—'

'No. You had no idea, because you never asked. You never cared.'

'I was grieving. Your mother—'

'So was *I*, Dad. Why do you think I went with Callum in the first place? I was desperate for love! It was why I made such a catastrophic mess of things.'

He's still holding my wrist. I turn to look at him, and see he's actually struggling not to cry again.

'Not as much of a mess as I have, evidently,' he says.

* * *

I don't leave Dad until the twenty-four hours are up and I'm sure he's feeling fine, apart from his painful knee. I give him orders to take it easy – which I'm sure he won't – and to see the doctor about his depression – which I'm equally sure he won't.

On the way out, I call at Pamela's house next door to thank her again for calling me, reassure her that Dad seems to be OK and fill her in on what the doctor at A&E said. Pamela promises to keep an eye on him and call me if there's any change. I wonder what she thinks; she must, surely, wonder why she never normally sees me at the house, and why (presumably) Dad never talks about me.

I think there's a long way to go before I'd be able to say we we're reconciled, but there's a little bit of understanding and relenting between us that certainly wasn't there before. I'll call him after a couple of days to see how his knee is. He's actually agreed that he'll work from home this first week as it's still so painful. Maybe I'll pay him another visit... if he wants me to. And we'll have to see how it goes.

I'm trying, Mum. It's not easy, but I promise I'm trying.

26

I get home late on Sunday afternoon, collect the children from Helen and Robert and give them both the biggest hugs of their lives. Mia goes rigid in my arms, won't look at me, and refuses to speak to me.

'She'll come round,' Helen says quietly. 'She's missed you. She's punishing you, but she won't keep it up for long, trust me.'

Helen can probably see I feel like crying. It's been a tough couple of days, tough and emotional, and I'm exhausted. But I was so desperate to get back to Mia and Archie and it seems like only one of them is pleased to see me.

I bought a bunch of flowers and some chocolates for Helen and Robert – it felt like the least I could do. I do feel bad now for the thoughts I've been having about them. When it came to the crunch, I just dumped my kids on them and they stepped up immediately. I've tried to persuade them to let me pay them; they've had to feed the children since yesterday lunchtime. But they've refused.

'Thank you, you didn't need to buy us anything,' Robert says.

'But we don't want any money. It was an emergency. What sort of neighbours would we be if we can't help out in an emergency?'

'You're so kind. I hope they've behaved all right. Did they eat their dinner?'

'Yes.' Helen smiles. 'I asked Mia what she wanted, and Robert popped out to the shop and bought some sausages.'

I promise to tell them more about Dad another time. All I want to do now is get the children – and myself – home, and try to recover.

By bedtime, although Archie's being a bit clingy, constantly holding onto me and saying 'Mumma', at least he does seem glad I'm back, whereas Mia's still keeping up the silent treatment.

'I know you're upset with me,' I tell her as I tuck her into bed. 'Sweetheart, I'm so, so sorry I left in such a hurry without even saying a proper goodbye to you. But my... *friend*... had a nasty accident and needed me to go to hospital with them.'

She turns her face away from me.

'I missed you so much!' I try again. 'I'm so happy to be back.'

No response.

I sigh. I hope Helen's right; perhaps Mia will sleep off her resentment and be back to normal in the morning.

I give it one last try.

'Did you have a nice time with Auntie Helen and Uncle Robert?'

She sits up and gives me a furious look.

'No! I had a horrible time! We had *horrible* sausages and *horrible* mash and I had to sleep in Auntie Helen's bed!'

I look at her in surprise. 'What? I thought she was going to bring you back here to sleep, and stay in my bed for the night.'

'Well, she didn't.'

'But...' I hardly know where to start with this. 'If you slept in

Auntie Helen's bed, where did she sleep? Where did Uncle Robert—'

'No, not *their* bed, I mean the bed in their other room; it's a little bed.'

'You mean a single bed.' I've never looked in their spare bedroom, but I guess they would have a bed for a guest in there.

'A little bed, like my bed. But I didn't like it, Mummy, I wanted to come home! I cried and cried and I *told* Auntie Helen I wanted to come back home but she wouldn't let me, she said Archie would sleep better in their cot, but—'

'Their *cot*?' I repeat, staring at her. 'But they haven't got—'

'Yes, they have, they've got a cot in their bedroom; they put Archie in it to go to sleep when he has his naps. It's like his cot here. But Archie didn't like being in it all night, he kept waking up and crying and that made me cry even more. I don't want to go there at night-time any more, don't make me go again!'

She starts to cry, loud noisy sobs that shake her little body.

'Oh, darling, I'm so sorry.' I hold her close to me, but she's stiff and unrelenting in my arms. 'Everything's all right now. I'm back, and I promise I won't go away and leave you there again.'

'What if your friend falls over again, though?' she mutters.

'Well, I don't think that's going to happen.'

'Was there blood?'

Despite her anger and upset with me, she's still being such a typical four-year-old; anything to do with cuts or bleeding horrifies and fascinates her in equal measure, just as anything toilet-related has her both disgusted and convulsing with laughter at the same time. But I'm too stunned by what I've just heard, to be able to smile about it.

'Only a little bit,' I say. 'Now, how about we have a *proper* cuddle, before you snuggle down to sleep? You know how much I love you, don't you? You know I never would have wanted to leave you like that if I could help it. Do you forgive me?'

'Yes,' she says, finally relaxing into my arms. 'But don't do it again, all right? I was *very* sad, and so was Archie.'

* * *

I sit down in the lounge, feeling worried sick – and not only about the children's reaction to me being away. I knew Mia, especially, would have been upset. After all, this was the first time I've ever left them overnight. But it's this thing about a cot that's troubling me the most now. Since when did Helen and Robert have a cot in their flat? Mia said Archie sleeps in it whenever he has his naps there – but Helen told me right from the start that she puts him to sleep in the middle of their double bed. I know she's going to tell me, when I ask her about it, that it was yet another charity shop find, or a gift from Robert's friend with the kids who seem to grow out of everything so conveniently – but why has it never been mentioned? Why would they get a cot and keep it a secret? And a *little bed* – like Mia's, she said, in their spare room? Mia's isn't a full-size single bed, it's a low child's bed. I'd have overlooked this as Mia not knowing the difference, if it weren't for the cot. Now I can't think of anything else. They've got a child-sized bed and a cot. They've got cupboards and boxes full of toys. They've got their own toilet step and they've even got a budgie that they insist is Mia's and Archie's. What am I supposed to make of this? They don't just enjoy looking after my kids – they want them there all the time! Is the next thing I hear from Mia going to be that they've redecorated their spare bedroom in a zoo theme ready for her to move in permanently?

* * *

It's beginning to feel like half my life, these days, is spent in challenging Helen about things I'm worried about.

'Mia tells me she slept in your *little bed*,' I say as soon as she picks up the phone. 'And Archie slept in your *cot*.'

'Yes,' she says straight away, sounding surprised at my tone. 'I thought that would be better than carting them upstairs to your flat, making them even more upset because you weren't there—'

'I didn't know you had a little bed. Or a cot.'

'Oh – surely I've mentioned it?' she says. 'The bed's just a single bed, Jess – our guest bed – but it's only a three-foot one. You know how small our second bedrooms are in these flats! And it's quite low, so I thought it'd be fine for Mia. She's never been in it before and she wasn't very happy, of course, but I knew that was only because of missing you—'

'And the cot?' I snap before she can even finish.

'Archie's been having his naps in it for the last couple of months! It's safer than him being in our bed and possibly rolling off it. I'm sure I must have mentioned it! It was from that same friend who—'

'—who gave you all the toys. Well, how nice.'

I can hear the sarcasm in my voice. Helen's silent, and I suddenly run out of steam. What if I'm jumping to conclusions, and she really *isn't* doing any of these things to entice my kids into her flat at all? Perhaps the cot, and all the toys really were gifts? I rub my hand across my eyes. I'm driving myself mad with all this. I really wish I didn't have these suspicions and doubts about everything Helen says. If only I could find someone else to look after the kids, someone who's a registered childminder, who behaves like a professional and doesn't make me feel beholden to them! If only they weren't all completely booked up, I'd move the children to one of them right away, the way I feel now.

'I don't think you've mentioned having the cot before,' I say, a bit less aggressively. 'I was surprised.'

'Well, I'm sorry if I didn't tell you. I thought I did.'

She sounds unhappy. Well, I'm sorry if I've upset her, I suppose, but it still seems weird to me.

'All right,' I say. And grudgingly, I add, 'Sorry.'

'That's OK, Jess. You've had a horrible couple of days. You probably can't think straight.'

She's right. I can't. And the trouble is, when I do try to think straight, all I can come back to is this: it still feels like they're trying to lure my children down to their flat.

27

I've hardly slept for the last few nights, with the worry about Dad and then about Helen and the cot. I must look terrible at work because halfway through the week, Tariq takes me to one side and asks me whether I'm all right.

'Oh, yes, I'm OK thanks,' I say, feeling embarrassed. I can't tell him I'm still stressing over Helen and Robert looking after my kids, and possibly planning, even now, how they're trying to get custody of them by painting me as a bad mother. 'I'm just a bit tired. I had to spend the weekend taking my dad to the hospital and looking after him at home, and—'

Before I can get any further, Tariq starts to sympathise to such a degree that I realise he must presume Dad and I have a normal, close, father-daughter relationship and that I've been sick with anxiety about him – rather than just irritated, and slightly shocked to be back on some kind of speaking terms. Tariq's actually *so* sympathetic that he tells me I can take a long lunch break so I can go to check on Dad, and I decide to take advantage of this the following day.

'You didn't have to do this,' he says when I arrive. 'It must have been difficult for you.'

'No, my manager offered, so I accepted. But I can't stay long; it takes a while to get here and back on the bus.'

'I can imagine. I presume you don't drive.'

We know so little about each other's lives. I shake my head.

'Never learned. No point.'

'No. Running a car is an expensive business,' he says, nodding. 'Well, let me at least get you a cup of something and a sandwich—'

'No. Rest your knee. I'll do it.'

I want to check on his kitchen, to see if he's still got enough food and stuff in. To my surprise, there's fresh bread, more veg, and everything else seems to have been topped up.

'Has Pamela been shopping for you?' I ask when I carry in the coffees and sandwiches.

'No. I got another supermarket delivery,' he says. 'I don't really need it when I go into the office – I eat out, and—'

'Dad, you still do need it! You've got to eat at the weekends, and anyway, it's not good for you to always eat out. It must cost a bomb. You can surely cook a few basic meals?'

He shrugs. 'Of course I can. I had to learn, when your mum was ill.'

We both fall silent. I'm glad he's looking better, and looking after himself. I don't stay long, but as I'm leaving, he tries to give me a ten-pound note out of his wallet, telling me to get a taxi back to work.

'No!' I back away from the money. 'Thanks, but I'm fine. I've got time to catch the bus.'

'It would be easier to come at the weekend, wouldn't it? Maybe another time? Then you wouldn't have to rush off.'

'You want me to come again?'

He looks away. 'If you'd like to,' he says quietly.

'But I'd have to bring the children. I can't keep leaving them with my neighbours.'

There's a silence, and I have to bite my lip to stop myself from adding, 'The children, you know – the *brats*.'

I'm just about to head for the door when he calls after me, 'I'd like that, Jess. But only if you'd like it too.'

* * *

My friends are coming round this evening, and although I definitely won't be drinking and I'm going to keep the music down this time, I decide to pre-empt any possible problems by warning Helen and Robert in advance.

'I'll try to make sure it doesn't get noisy,' I say. 'And they won't be staying late, so—'

'Oh, Jess, why don't you just let the children stay overnight with us?' she says, and I feel myself flinch. She must be joking! I've only just about got Mia over the upset of staying with them last weekend. Why does she keep on about this? She seems far too desperate for an excuse to have them overnight.

'No, it's fine, thank you,' I tell her.

'Well, don't forget to send Mia down to help Robert clean out the budgie in the morning. She's so keen to learn how to do it.'

'OK.' It's true, I can't stop Mia talking about Beaky, and she does seem keen to learn everything about his care – much as the whole issue of them buying the budgie still rankles with me.

* * *

I find myself telling my friends, this evening, about Dad. They all fall silent with surprise as I describe how I rushed round to Dad's house and went with him in the ambulance.

'I thought you couldn't stand him!' Jules says.

'I never said that. I've just been... so let down by him,' I say. 'I kind of gave up on him.'

'He was horrible to you about your kids,' Lucy reminds me gently.

'I know. I thought I'd never forgive him for that,' I admit now. 'But now he says he'd like me to take them round to meet him.'

'*Really*?' Jules gasps. 'After calling them *brats*? I hope you told him to get stuffed?'

'Jules,' Lucy rebukes, as I look down at my feet, wondering whether I should have actually told them any of this after all, 'Jess's dad is the only family she's got – apart from the children, obviously. It has to be worth giving it a try, doesn't it?'

'Yes,' Miranda agrees. 'If he's sorry, and he's going to behave decently now, Jess, you might get some money out of him. He might leave you that big old house when he pops his clogs!'

'*Miranda!*' we all exclaim together, and the awkwardness vanishes as we all finally start to laugh.

'I don't want anything from him,' I say firmly once the hilarity has died down. 'It would just be nice for my kids to finally have a grandparent in their lives. But I don't know how I'm going to explain it to them. I told them he lives a long way away and that's why we don't see him.'

'So tell them he's moved back!' Jules says at once – and of course, it's so simple, so obvious, that I can't understand how I haven't thought of it before.

'I'll have to warn Dad that I'm telling them a little fib about it,' I say. 'He can pretend he's come back for work.'

'Don't worry too much about it all,' Lucy says. 'It might just be a one-off. Sorry to say it, but he might just be curious about them, and then go back to not being interested.' She pauses, giving me an apologetic look. 'I just don't want you to build up your hopes and then get hurt again.'

'I won't build up my hopes. I've spent too long not having any at all,' I remind her.

'Come on, pour out the wine, somebody,' Miranda says, looking round for the bottle she brought with her. 'Let's at least celebrate this father-and-daughter reunion, while it lasts, in case it crashes and burns by next week.'

'*Miranda!*' the others shout at her again, and before we know it they're pouring the wine, pouring me an alcohol-free drink and we're all raising our glasses and toasting *fathers and daughters*. They're my friends, I love them and I know they care about me, however little they can empathise.

* * *

I call Dad and arrange to go there on Sunday. Then I sit down with Mia and tell her I've got something important to share with her.

'Is it about chocolate?' she says excitedly. 'Or the seaside?'

I laugh out loud and hug her. 'No, sweetie. Something else. You know how I've told you that you've got a grandad, but he lives a long way away?'

'Yes,' she says. She pouts. 'It's not fair. My friend Phoebe's got *two* grandads *and* a grandma, *and*—' She pauses dramatically. 'And guess what else? A *great*-grandma. That's a mum of a grandma so she's very, very, very old.'

'Wow!' I say. 'But listen, this is what I need to tell you. Your grandad has moved back now. He lives quite near us, just on the other side of town, so—'

'My actual real grandad?' she squawks. 'Can I see him? Can I tell Phoebe?'

'Yes,' I say, smiling. 'We're going to see him tomorrow. But I want you to be very, very good, Mia, because your grandad has got a poorly knee, he hasn't been very well so he won't want any noise or naughtiness.'

I could kick myself for this slight exaggeration of the truth. But I really, really, want the children to make a good impression.

'I will be *very* good, Mummy,' Mia says solemnly. 'I promise. But you'd better tell Archie, because I can't promise *he'll* be good. You know what he's like.'

My mouth is twitching with a smile. Sometimes she talks just like a grown-up, and it sounds so funny coming from her.

'I will tell Archie, don't worry, but of course, he's too little to really understand. We'll just have to hope he'll be nice and quiet.'

Mia jumps up from the sofa and runs to get her drawing paper and crayons.

'I'm going to draw a picture for my grandad,' she says importantly. 'What do you think he'd like me to draw? Shall I draw Beaky? Does he know we've got a budgie-gar?'

'No, I haven't told him that yet, so you can be the one to tell him. And I'm sure he'd love a picture.'

'Will we go to see him every week now?' she asks me as she settles down to do her drawing. 'Phoebe sees her grandma every single week, *and* one of her grandads.'

'I don't know, Mia. He's... very busy.'

Oh, God. I hope I'm doing the right thing, here. What if he never wants to see the children again after tomorrow? What if he never wants to see *me* again? What if we just go straight back to where we were before?

'Is my grandad very old?' Mia asks next.

'No, not very,' I laugh. 'He's my daddy.'

'And your mummy went to heaven, so we can't see her.'

'That's right.'

I wasn't sure, when Mia first started asking me about her grandma, whether I was saying the right things or not. Was it still acceptable to refer to people going to heaven, or should I have taken a more factual and scientific approach? It felt too brutal, somehow – she was so young, and I was still too conscious of my own loss to face the inevitable questions about what happens to people when they die. I chickened out, I suppose. She'll learn in time.

'Shall I do a picture of my grandad too?' Mia says eagerly, pushing the half-finished drawing of Beaky aside. 'What does he look like?'

'Oh. Well, he's quite tall, and he wears glasses. His hair is dark, like mine but it's going a little bit grey at the sides, now.' That was a new thing I'd noticed. 'And he's very slim, and he wears smart clothes.'

'I can't do grey,' she says. 'He'll have to have black hair.'

Archie wakes up from his nap at this point and she jumps up, squealing with excitement again.

'Archie! Archie!' she shouts, running into the bedroom to see him. 'Guess what, we're going to see our grandad tomorrow, he's not very old but he's tall. He's got smart clothes and a bad knee, and we've got to be very good, so I'm warning you, no screaming, OK?'

'OK,' says Archie in his usual affable way, although I doubt he has any idea what she's talking about.

I'm glad she's so excited about the visit. As for me, I'm nervous, and at the same time, cross with myself for being nervous. If he doesn't like my kids it's his loss, not mine, I remind myself firmly. He's the one who's lonely. And he's the one who can change that, if he wants to.

It's Sunday afternoon and we're on the bus to my dad's place. Mia's excited about the journey, explaining importantly to Archie what I've already told her: that we're getting on two buses today – this one has an upstairs so it's called a double digger, and the other one is only a single digger.

'Digger,' Archie repeats, laughing. He's got a toy digger so I guess that's confused him completely!

'*Decker*, Mia,' I correct her.

'Decker digger?' she says, giving me a surprised look, and I can't help laughing. I hug her and find myself wondering how long this wonderful age of learning and discovery will last, before she starts teaching *me* things! Dad opens the door to us so quickly that I suspect he's been watching out of the window.

'Hello!' he says in the jovial tone of a proper grandad who enjoys seeing his darling grandchildren on a regular basis. 'Come on in, all of you. What do you do about the pushchair, Jess? Does it fold up?'

'Yes.' I bite back the '*of course*' hovering on my tongue. He probably hasn't had anything to do with a young child since I was little myself.

'Good, good. Well, now.' He stands back, ushering us all inside, looking ill at ease. 'Let's go through to the lounge, shall we? You must be Mia,' he adds as she follows him down the hall-way. 'And' – he looks round and smiles at Archie, who's holding tight to my hand – 'you must be—'

'He's Archie,' Mia informs him. 'He's only one, so he can't say much, but I've told him he's got to be very good.'

'Well, that's wonderful.' Dad gives her an awkward little pat on the head. 'You're obviously a very good big sister. Now, why don't you all sit down and I'll get you something to drink—'

'Just water please, for Mia,' I say quickly before she can give her orders, 'and I've brought Archie's sippy cup—'

'I wanted squash,' Mia whispers to me after Dad's gone out to the kitchen.

'Grandad probably hasn't got any,' I tell her firmly. 'And please, Mia, don't ask for biscuits. It's very rude to ask, OK?'

'Why?' she's saying, just as Dad comes back with a plate containing several different types of biscuit, and some little cakes that look like they've come from a patisserie rather than out of a packet from Asda. Mia's eyes are out on stalks now, and I have to stop Archie from immediately reaching out for one.

'You didn't need to do this,' I tell him.

'Why not?' He shrugs. 'Kettle's on, Jess. Here's the water for the children.'

The water's in a proper carafe. Mia's been given a grown-up glass, and I warn her quietly to be careful with it. To be fair, she's handling it lovingly, as if it's precious, but she can't take her eyes off the little cakes.

'They look like a princess's cakes,' she whispers to me, awe-struck.

Dad goes back to the kitchen and returns with plates – all the best china, of course, with gold rims. I remember them from when I lived here.

'Archie, you need to come and sit up here with me,' I decide, and position him on my lap, with Mia close beside us. 'Put the glass down when you're ready to hold a plate,' I tell her.

'I *know*, Mummy,' she says, raising her eyes at me. 'I've only got one pair of hands.'

Dad comes in just in time to hear this gem, and sees me laughing.

'That's what I always say to her,' I explain.

'Yes. That's what all parents say,' he agrees, smiling – and the ice is broken, a little, but I think I'll still be on edge until the cake eating is over.

'What would you like, Mia?' He offers her the plate.

She sighs, as if the choice is too much for her. 'A pink one, please.' And she takes it and puts it carefully on her own plate, staring at it as if it's almost too good to eat.

'Tockit,' says Archie, reaching for his favourite.

'Chocolate? That'd be my choice too!' Dad says cheerfully. 'What about you, Jess?'

'Oh, I think I'll just have a biscuit in a minute, thanks, Dad. I'm too busy watching these two at the moment. I don't want them to make a mess.'

'Ah, don't worry about that,' he says – but of course, I do worry. I'm not really happy until they've both finished their gooey cakes and I've wiped their fingers and they're finishing their drinks.

'I'm sorry, Grandad,' Mia says solemnly. 'I dripped a tiny drip of water on the carpet.'

He smiles at her. 'What's a tiny drip of water between friends, eh?'

'*Friends*?' she squawks. 'You're not my friend, you're my *grandad*!'

'Gaddad!' Archie joins in.

'We wanted a grandad for ages and ages,' Mia goes on. 'All my friends have got one and I wanted one too.'

Dad's taken off his glasses and is rubbing his eyes.

'Is your eyes sore, Grandad?' Mia asks innocently. 'My eyes get sore sometimes. Mostly if I been crying a lot. If Mummy tells me off. Or when I have to go to Auntie Helen's.'

Dad looks at me enquiringly.

'Helen and Robert are the downstairs neighbours that I told you about – who look after the children while I'm at work,' I explain, feeling myself sigh just at the mention of them.

'Ah, I see.' He nods at me. 'I was wondering whether it was some relative of—' He stops short, giving me a look, and I suddenly realise what he's getting at. I suppress a shudder at the very idea that I'd let any relative of Callum's look after my kids. Then it suddenly comes to me like such a flash of blinding light that I can't stop blinking. What if Helen and Robert *are* relatives of Callum? After all, how much do I actually know about them – apart from the fact that they've got a son and daughter, and never talk about them? Callum never knew his father, and he told me his mother – who was a drinker – threw him out when he started getting into trouble. But for all I know, he could have, say, an aunt and uncle who'd suddenly decided to move here from London, to try to keep an eye on their delinquent nephew... and take his side... trying to get his kids away from their mother. Moving into the flat below them, offering to help out, gradually taking over the children. It would explain why Helen shuts down any suggestion that any of us might have seen him around. As if she wants to keep it as her little secret.

I feel myself breathing heavily, see Dad glance at me in

concern, and try to get my panic under control. I'm being ridiculous. It's too far-fetched, too unlikely... isn't it? I give myself a little shake.

'Oh!' Mia exclaims suddenly, putting her glass down on the coffee table and running to get her little bag. 'I forgot! I done you some drawings, Grandad!'

'*Did!*' I try to correct her, but she's too intent on pulling the crumpled sheets of paper out of her bag.

'I done one of Beaky. He's my budgie-gar, he's the best budgie-gar in the world but he has to live with Auntie Helen and Uncle Robert otherwise he'd stop talking. And I done one of you, Grandad. Mummy told me what you look like but I couldn't do grey so you had to have black hair.'

Dad's trying to hide a smile now.

'Well, how lovely!' he says. 'Come and show them to me, would you, Mia? So this is Beaky? He really does look a very special budgerigar. Aren't you lucky? And...' The smile now takes over his face and he looks up at me and winks. 'This one is me? It's a good likeness, I think. I especially like the red shirt. And the black hair – excellent choice!'

I notice he's put an arm around her shoulders now and she seems not to mind.

'You can keep them if you want,' she says.

'Are you sure? That's very kind. I'll treasure them. They're very good.'

'I know.' She nods, and I laugh. 'I'm a good painter and drawer, aren't I, Mummy. I done lots of pictures—'

'*Did.*' I raise my eyes at Dad. 'I'm fighting a losing battle for her grammar, I'm afraid.'

'She's doing very well,' he says. 'She'll get there, don't worry.'

I have to swallow, hard. He's got no idea how much I've longed for a supportive parent to say those words to me. I want to tell him that I thought this day would never come, that even now, it feels surreal, that I'm still so afraid it'll suddenly all change, that I don't want to settle into it, believe it, start enjoying it. I'm holding myself back – but I can't hold my children back, even if I try. They're already deciding for themselves.

'I like having a grandad,' Mia says, leaning closer to him for a proper hug. 'Can I have a biscuit now, please?'

I start to reprimand her, but Dad's laughing.

'As you asked so nicely and said *please*, of course you may, Mia, if Mummy says it's all right.'

'Bikkit?' says Archie, immediately reaching for them, his eyes lighting up. I settle them both with a plate again and watch for crumbs.

'You're a happy little boy, aren't you, Archie?' Dad says.

'He's not always happy!' Mia says, spitting biscuit crumbs onto her plate. 'He screams very loud sometimes when his teeth are hurting or when Mummy says he doesn't get his own way. And sometimes at Auntie Helen's.'

'Ah, well,' Dad says. 'I suppose all babies scream sometimes, Mia.' He glances at me and says very quietly, 'I'm sorry you've had to rely on neighbours.'

He starts to talk to Mia again, asking her about her favourite biscuits, and I stare at him for a moment, just wondering. He's sorry I've had to rely on neighbours – to look after the children? I wonder... is he hinting that he could be looking after them, even if only occasionally? How could he, when he's still working, still running a bank? And anyway, would I *want* him to? No, it's too soon. I think back to the conversation with my friends, the way they warned me that this reconciliation might be short-lived. No, I'm just so anxious about Helen now, so worried about needing to find someone else, I'm clutching at straws.

Archie's finished his biscuit now, and I wipe his hands and

face and let him climb down and toddle over to look at Mia's drawings, which Dad's still holding.

'Beaty!' he says, pointing to the budgie picture.

'Yes, that's right, Archie: Beaky!' says Dad, smiling at him.

Archie grabs the other picture and points his chubby finger at it.

'Gaddad!' he says. He looks from the picture to Dad, pats Dad's hand and shouts joyfully, 'Gaddad!'

'Yes, Archie, I'm your grandad!' Dad seems to be having trouble with his eyes again, and I feel mine smarting too. I almost want to get my phone out and take a picture of him with the two children, to look at and cherish if this never happens again. But I don't. Because I want to believe it will; it will happen again because I think we both want it to. I think we both need to make sure of it.

'I'm sorry,' Dad says now. 'I haven't got any toys here, or anything for them to do.'

'That's OK. We won't stay too long.' I didn't risk bringing crayons, or even Lego, in case Archie started throwing things around. 'It's been exciting for the kids, they'll be getting tired, and it's school – and nursery – tomorrow. And we've got to catch the bus—'

'*Two* buses!' Mia corrects me importantly. 'One is a single digger...' She looks at me uncertainly. 'Digger-decker? And the other one is a digger-double.'

'Wow, that *is* exciting,' Dad says. 'But how would you feel about going home in my car today instead of on the two buses?'

'Oh, no, we can't,' I begin, but Mia's eyes are like saucers.

'*Car*?' she says, as if she's never heard of such a thing. To be fair, she's rarely, if ever, been in one! '*Can* we go in a car, Mummy?'

'You can't take us home, Dad. I haven't got car seats for the children. I've never needed them.'

'Oh.' His face drops. 'I didn't think of that. I'm sorry. Two buses, and on a Sunday... it's not easy.'

'We're used to it.'

'Yes, but now...' He hesitates on the word *now*, and our eyes meet, and I feel as if the world has suddenly tilted slightly. He doesn't go on, but he doesn't need to.

'We'd better get going,' I say again. 'It's been... really nice.'

'It's been very lovely,' Mia says in her best polite voice. 'And I hope you're all better now, Grandad.' She slips her hand into his. ''Cos Mummy said you was poorly.'

He squeezes her hand and nods, seeming to be unable to speak.

I feel much the same. And it's just as well that Mia chats constantly on the journey back, as it's not until we're on the second bus, and nearly home, that I can trust myself to speak without my voice wobbling.

Do I dare imagine that this is real, that it's going to last?

I don't know. But I hope so.

29

I feel like everything's changed since Dad's accident. Not just because of being back in touch with him and introducing the children to him, but also because of how differently I've started thinking about Helen and Robert now. The panic I felt when it occurred to me that perhaps they could be related to Callum has only abated slightly as I've tried to tell myself it's ridiculous, far-fetched, just me getting carried away by my own fears. But every evening now, I'm glued to Google on my phone, looking to see if any local childminders have suddenly got vacancies. None of them have, and anyway, their rates are even more than I expected.

It's got so bad that I'm worrying all day at work about what might be going on with Helen and Robert, and when I pick the kids up from them in the evenings I don't stop for a cup of tea, or give the kids time to finish their games or say goodbye to Beaky; I just want to get them home. Mia's picking up on my mood, and throwing tantrums because I'm reluctant to let her go downstairs to see the budgie on the days when Helen and Robert don't look after them. Helen's asking me almost every day if there's anything wrong, but I just shake my head. Even if there is something going on, she'll only deny it and give me such good excuses – as she's done all along, about everything – that I'll be talked into thinking I'm imagining it all, again. And I really don't think I am. Why is she so keen to have my kids, so often, never seeming to mind, always offering to do more, wanting to keep them overnight, getting all those toys for them, buying tickets for the zoo, even getting the budgie so that Mia would want to go down at week-ends to see him? Even my friends have thought it was all a bit weird, a bit over the top, but I've always defended Helen and Robert, said they seemed to be lonely and bored and explained how kind they are, how lucky I am to have them. I've defended Helen whenever Mia's got upset and said she tells her off, or nags her about vegetables, or takes Archie's dummy away – all these things might have raised alarm bells with me, if I hadn't needed Helen and Robert so much and *trusted* them so much. The truth is, I don't like it – any of it.

* * *

Dad calls me the next Saturday.

'Are you free today?' he says. 'Or tomorrow? I just wondered... it's only a suggestion... if you're not too busy...' He sounds almost nervous. How strange. 'I wondered if I could perhaps come round to see you and the children. Just for a little while – I won't stay long.'

It's so unexpected, I hardly know how to answer. After not seeing each other for five years, getting together three times in as many weeks seems almost bizarre. I look around the flat, taking in the pile of dirty washing on the kitchen floor, the breakfast things heaped on the work surface, the kids' toys and crayons scattered across the lounge floor, and the unmade beds I can see around the open bedroom doors.

'Well, to be honest, tomorrow would be better, Dad, if that's all right with you,' I say.

I feel awkward enough about him coming here, knowing that he once accused me of *living in squalor*, without giving him reason to suspect he was right. I need time to do a tidy-up and clean-up.

'Absolutely,' he says. 'It's far easier for me to come to you. Um... you'll have to give me the address...'

I think we're both acutely aware of the weirdness of this, of the fact that he doesn't even know where I live. If there'd been an emergency during the last few years, he wouldn't even have known where to find me; all he had was my phone number, and he never even called me, not once. I give him the address, explain where to park, and we agree he'll come tomorrow afternoon. I'm not sure how I feel about it; I don't even want to try to analyse my feelings, because they're too complex. Is it too much, too soon? Should I feel excited, or nervous? Should I tell the kids yet, or let it be a surprise when he turns up? For now, I'm just going to clean the flat, get some shopping, and act like it's a normal Saturday.

* * *

I don't tell the children about their grandad coming to visit until the Sunday afternoon. Mia, predictably, races around the flat in a whirlwind of excitement, trying to decide which toys she wants to show him first. Archie's repeating *Gaddad* over and over, trotting to the door every five minutes until my nerves feel shredded. I think we all feel relieved when the doorbell rings at exactly half past two.

'Hello. You found us all right, then?' I say, ridiculously, as if my father wouldn't even have a Sat Nav.

'Yes, no problem.' He sounds as uncomfortable as I feel –

equally aware, I'm sure, of the fact that this is the first time he's visited me since I left home.

'Well, come in.' I hold open the door and give a little self-deprecating laugh. 'Sorry, it's not very grand...'

He steps inside and gives me a smile. 'Jess, I haven't always lived in Barnwell Heights, you know. Your mum and I started our married life in a flat.'

I shrug. It's still hard to forgive the *squalor* thing. But before I can say anything, Mia has rushed at Dad with Ellie Elephant and Mr Meerkat in her arms, telling him their names and the fact that they're her *favouritist* toys – and at the same time, I've suddenly taken on board exactly what Dad's carrying. Two children's car seats, one in each hand, one bigger than the other.

He sees my eyes widen as he puts them down on the floor.

'I hope you don't mind,' he says, as Mia and Archie both stare at them, quite clearly wondering what they are. 'But it would make life a lot easier – if, as I hope, I'm going to be seeing you all sometimes now – however frequently or infrequently is up to you, of course...'

He comes to an awkward stop and just looks at me, waiting for an answer.

'But I haven't got a car,' I remind him.

'I know. They're for my car, obviously. But it's best if you keep them here. Then, if ever you get an opportunity to take the children out in anyone else's car—'

'I don't know anyone else with a car.'

He looks shocked. 'Oh. Well, maybe one day, if you learn to drive...'

I start to laugh, and he now looks even more uncomfortable.

'Dad,' I say. 'It's nice of you to get them. Thank you, I appreciate it. But I can't keep them here. Look how small this place is! I don't have any room to store anything *just in case* I might be able to use it one day.' I realise my reaction isn't what he'd hoped for, so I try to soften my tone and suggest more gently, 'Keep them at your place, if you don't mind? Then if you offer me a lift home again one day, I'll be able to accept.' I pause, and add, 'Did you check they're the right sizes?'

'Of course. I talked to the guy at the shop, explained the children's ages – he was very helpful. All right, I'll keep them at home. Now, then!' He seems to shake off the awkwardness and turns to Mia, who's almost beside herself now with impatience. 'Tell me all about these two very interesting animals. An elephant and a meerkat! Do they like each other?'

'Yes!' she says, nodding and adopting an air of importance. 'I know a lot about animals, Grandad, because we went to the zoo and *also* I've got a book. I'll show you my book. I wanted most of all to see the wolf, because of the wolf what blowed down the piggies' houses, and also because of the boy what cried. But in the end, I liked the meerkats best 'cos they was funny.'

'The boy who cried wolf,' I explain quietly to Dad as Mia rushes off to her room to find her zoo book. 'And they *were* funny, Mia. Not *was*. Come and sit down; I'll get the kettle on. Mia helped me make some little cakes. I won't give you one that she's nibbled the edges of!'

He laughs, and things start to feel easier between us. He takes a seat on the sofa and Archie toddles over to him, grabs Dad's knees and shouts *Gaddad* at him before falling back onto his bottom and giggling.

'The bruise on his arm looks worse than it is,' I say, as it's obvious he's noticed. 'It was my fault. He tripped over the Hoover; I'd left it in the way...'

Ever since the time he bumped his head on the cot while I was talking to Helen – and the fuss she made – I've been paranoid about every little bump and bruise either of the children get, wondering if she's going to report me to anyone. Thinking about this now, I tell Dad about that incident. But he just shrugs and smiles.

'That's nothing, Jess! He'll have a lot worse than that, trust me, as he grows up. I *dropped* you once, when you were a baby. It was only onto the carpet, from a chair, but I was so terrified I'd done you some permanent damage, I didn't know what to do first – pick you up and try to stop you screaming, or call an ambulance.'

'What *did* you do?'

'Yelled for your mum!' he admits. 'She checked you all over and said you weren't hurt at all, just frightened, and laughed at me for panicking. Kids are a lot less breakable than we think.'

I smile back at him. It's nice, hearing a story about Mum, about my childhood. I'm desperate for more, but I'll have to be patient.

'I think Helen thinks I'm a useless mother. She was horrified that I'd left Archie in his cot, but I was only just—'

I stop, remembering that Dad has evidently spent the last five years thinking I was a useless mother too. But he's looking at me, concern in his eyes.

'Does she criticise you?'

'Well, that's only part of it, to be honest.' I realise I'm desperate to confide all my worries to him. 'I'm starting to think they—'

But just as I'm about to blurt it out, Mia returns with her book and asks Dad to look at the pictures, which he does, obediently, commenting on some of the animals.

I go and make the tea, put the least nibbled or licked cupcakes on a plate and take them in with the children's drinks. I'm trembling – actually shaking – with the realisation that I nearly said it out loud, nearly actually voiced the fear that's been building in me, that I've been too afraid to put into words.

'Wow!' Dad says theatrically, pretending to look blown away by the sight of the home-made chocolate cupcakes. 'Who made these?'

But while Mia's prattling away about how she helped make the cakes, he's looking at me, the question still in his eyes. I shake my head. I can't. I can't talk about it in front of her. I probably shouldn't talk about it to Dad at all – after all, how well do I really know him? What exactly would I expect him to do, if I told him?

'Sorry,' I say instead, managing to give him a smile as Mia almost knocks the cakes off the plate as she skips around the room excitedly. 'She can be a bit full-on.'

'She's lovely,' he says quietly. He's looking at me earnestly, almost sadly. 'They both are, Jess. They're a credit to you.'

Once again, I'm tempted to remind him about calling them brats, but I don't. What's the point? Besides, I think it's obvious he's sorry. I don't want to ruin what might be our new chance here, by harping back to past wrongs. Even as I'm thinking this, I'm surprised at myself. Where has my resentment gone, my anger, my *hurt*? Why am I letting him off so easily?

'Mum would be pleased,' I suddenly blurt out – and I'm even more surprised by this than I am about not wanting to give him a hard time. 'She'd be glad we're... getting together.'

He nods. 'I know,' he says, softly. 'Thank you, Jess. And... well... sorry,' he whispers. 'For all of it.'

I shake my head. 'Let's not talk about it any more. Let's look forward, shall we?'

Thanks, Mum. I did this for you, you know. But I think, now... I'm really glad I did.

30

After the cakes are eaten and the tea has been drunk, Archie's rubbing his eyes and grizzling so I put him down for a late nap. Mia starts to talk to Dad about Beaky again, then suddenly stops as if struck by a brilliant idea.

'I know what, Mummy! I could take Grandad downstairs to see Beaky! Can I, Mummy? *Please!*'

'No, Mia, I don't think—'

Dad smiles at Mia. 'That wouldn't be right, Mia. Your auntie and uncle don't know me, and anyway they might not be home—'

'They *are* there, I've heard them downstairs, and I can tell them who you are!' she insists. '*Please* Grandad, come and meet Beaky, he's the bestest budgie-gar ever. I bet I can teach him to say *Grandad.*'

Dad looks at me doubtfully.

'*Please, Mummy*—' Mia starts again, and I hold up my hand to stop her.

'I'll call Auntie Helen, but if she's busy it's *no*, Mia, and no arguments, OK?'

'OK,' she says sulkily. 'Tell her Grandad wants to meet Beaky, though.'

Two minutes later, Mia's got her shoes on, I can hear Helen opening her door, and I stay at the top of our stairs, making the introductions.

'I won't join you,' I explain to Helen. 'Archie's asleep.'

I clear away the tea things while they're downstairs, wondering how it's going – what Helen thinks of Dad and, more to the point, what Dad thinks of her. They're gone about fifteen minutes and to my surprise, Dad comes back on his own.

'Robert wanted to show Mia something special, so Helen said she could stay for a few more minutes,' he explains. 'My God, Jess, I had to do a double-take when I saw Helen.'

'I know. Sorry, I should have warned you; she's a lot like Mum, isn't she?' I pause. 'Is that why you came back – did it upset you?'

'No. It's fine. It's just... to be honest, I wanted the chance to have a quick word with you, Jess – while we're on our own.'

'OK,' I say, feeling a bit wary now. 'What about?'

'Well, look, I don't want to interfere. I've got to admit, I've been really impressed to hear how well you've been managing on your own – the job, the kids, the childcare—'

'No, Dad, I'm *not* managing well!' I blurt out before I can stop myself. 'It's so hard, I'm constantly worrying about everything and I don't know what to do!'

'You started to say something earlier,' he says. 'About Helen or Robert criticising you. Is that what's worrying you?'

'Yes. Mostly Helen. She keeps making me feel inadequate, but that's not all, Dad. Mia gets upset about being left with them – not always, but often. She says Helen tells her off, but Helen always denies it. Mia only likes going there, now, because of the budgie, and I think that's why they bought it – to encourage the kids to go down more often. Helen *knew* I didn't want them to have a pet, I'd told her that! It felt like they were... purposely over-ruling me. Outdoing me – like they do with all the toys they keep getting, that they *say* are freebies. And...' I pause, shaking my head. 'This probably sounds silly...'

'No it doesn't. It doesn't, because you're obviously really worried.' He gives me a serious look. 'What else?'

'Well, they booked tickets to take the kids to the zoo during the school holiday, without even asking me, and, well, it sounds like a nice thing to do but I'd already told them I wanted to take the children there myself. I felt... sidelined. Like they...' I drop my voice. 'Like they wanted to take over.' Now I've started, I can't seem to stop. 'And now, I find out they've got a cot in their flat, for Archie, and a little bed for Mia. But they've never mentioned it to me, and Helen just brushes it off, saying it was another freebie, saying it just makes life easier and she thought I knew about it.' I stop and sigh. 'I expect you're thinking I should be grateful. And I *was*...'

'But now it all seems... just too much,' he suggests.

'Yes! Too much, as if... as if they want Mia and Archie to *live* there. Because I'm not a good enough mother for them. And that's not all, Dad. Mia says she's seen Callum, her dad – I don't even know if she'd recognise him but she insists it's him. She says she saw him in the street, with a dog, and recently, *I* even thought I saw him with a dog, too, but I don't know – I might have imag-ined it, I'm getting paranoid about him. The only reason he'd have a dog would be to tempt her to talk to him! And she thinks she saw him at the zoo, and only Helen was with her at the time and she completely denies it. I feel like I'm going mad, I don't know what to believe. Mia does tell lies, you know, she thinks it's just making up stories...'

'But you believe her,' Dad says.

'I don't know! I don't *want* to believe her – I don't want Callum anywhere near the children, Helen and Robert know that too. And would he really be at the zoo the same day as us? Is it too much of a coincidence? He's been round here a couple of times, too, hanging around, asking about the kids – it's really freaked me out.'

'Can you talk to the police?'

'It's not as if he's done anything illegal, he's just... just scaring me.'

'Do you think there's a connection? Between what Helen and Robert seem to be up to, and Callum appearing?'

'I don't know,' I admit miserably. 'I did have a panic the other day, wondering if they know Callum, if they're... somehow *in league* with him. But I'm stuck; I can't find another childminder. I've got to work the hours my boss wants, other-wise I'll be out of work, and I won't be able to pay the rent, and...'

I run out of breath and realise to my horror that I'm crying.

'I'm sorry,' I gasp. 'I didn't mean to say *any* of that, it just—'

He sits down next to me and takes hold of my hand.

'I'm glad you said it – all of it,' he says gently. 'And I'm so sorry you've had no one to talk to about these things. That's my fault, but look: I'm here now, and I want you to know you can talk to me whenever you want to – and I'll do what I can to help.'

'OK,' I say, wiping my eyes.

'So you've actually started looking for a different childmin-der?' he says. 'It'll probably cost a lot more than the neighbours.'

'I know, Dad, but anyway, they all seem to be fully booked. I thought Helen and Robert were the perfect option but now I'm really not happy about the kids going there.'

Dad's silent for a moment, thinking.

'Would you like me to have a word with them?'

'No!' I can't let him do that. They've only just met him, and anyway, I need to be the one to talk to them, if anyone does. 'Thank you for listening to me, though.'

I wipe my eyes. I feel strangely relieved to have told him. Even though I've mentioned some of these fears to Lucy and the other girls, I feel like telling Dad about it all has underlined everything even more, and made me even more sure about the need to look for a different option.

At that moment, the doorbell rings and Mia is on the doorstep, with Helen waving from the bottom of the stairs. Mia charges in through the door, clutching something in her hands which she throws down on the coffee table in front of Dad.

'Look, Grandad! Look what Uncle Robert did! It's a photo of me and Archie and Beaky! He tooked it on his phone last week and he got it printed and made big, and gived it to me! Mummy, can I stick it on my bedroom wall? Can I show Archie? Is he awake yet?'

Dad's trying to tell her how much he likes the picture, but Mia's already rushing into the bedroom to wake up poor Archie, whether he's ready or not, and just as Dad's trying to say, quietly while she's out of earshot, that he's glad I confided in him and that he's there to help, whatever I need, whatever I decide – Mia runs back into the room again and announces, almost as an afterthought:

'Also, Mummy, I sawed Daddy again. He was outside Auntie Helen's flat but she said to come away from the window and wouldn't let me wave to him.'

Dad and I exchange a look.

'Are you *sure* it was him?' Dad asks her – but I'm already halfway out of the door, running down the stairs, opening the outside door, looking around the side of Helen's flat. Nobody's there. I'm breathing heavily.

'Are you all right, Jess?' Robert's staring at me from his doorway as I come back inside.

'Mia says she saw Callum. Out of the window, while she was in with you,' I say.

'No.' He smiles. 'Well, she didn't say anything to us, and we didn't see—'

'She says Helen told her to come away from the window.'

He frowns. 'I don't think so. I was with Mia all the time, and I didn't hear anything being said about—'

'Right,' I say impatiently, shaking my head. 'Well, OK, maybe she's making it up again. Thanks, Robert.'

I trudge back upstairs, my heart still pounding. Would Robert lie to me? I know it's more likely that it's Mia telling the lie. But just the same, that sense of unease – no, *dread*, has come over me again at the thought of Callum being around here, knowing the kids are in their flat, looking through the windows...

'Either Mia's making it up again, or Robert's lying,' I mutter to Dad when he follows me into the kitchen to talk out of the children's earshot. 'And if it's him, then there's definitely no way I can let Helen and Robert keep looking after the kids.'

'Try not to panic,' he says. 'Look, if the only available childminders are too expensive, I'll pay, OK? And if you can't find anyone with vacancies, I'll... I'll... I'll damn well quit my job and do it myself!'

31

The summer half-term holiday is only a couple of weeks away and I'm panicking. I've been spending all my spare time – what little I have – desperately looking again for a new childminder. Meanwhile I feel anxious whenever the children are with Helen and Robert, trying not to constantly question Mia about whether everything is all right, whether she thinks she's seen her father again, for fear of making her even less happy to go there. I know Dad means well, and I know he's probably in a position to help me with the cost of a new childminder, although I feel uncomfortable about it, considering how recently we've got to know each other again – but he obviously wasn't serious about quitting his job! It's nice to know I have his support, though, and that he's taking my worries seriously. Fortunately Mia hasn't started to ask about half-term yet. She's far more interested in how the weeks are counting down until her fifth birthday.

* * *

But then everything suddenly comes to a head. At lunchtime on Saturday. I'm rushing back home with the kids after getting a bit of shopping in town and, as I go into the flats, I see a youngish woman with a suitcase, outside the door of Helen and Robert's flat, looking at her watch, and then staring down the road. She catches sight of me approaching the stairs to our flat and gives me a smile.

'Sorry to bother you,' she says. 'Are you their neighbour?' She nods at the door to Helen's flat. 'Mr and Mrs Fowler's?'

'Yes.' I smile back. 'Can I help?'

'Well, I wondered if you'd seen them this morning. It's just – they knew I was arriving today, but perhaps I'm a little earlier than they expected. They told me the access code to get into the block. But they seem to be out.'

'They were here earlier. Perhaps they've just popped out for something. Um...' I glance at her suitcase and put two and two together. She has a faint lilt of a Scots accent. She looks about the right age, and she's obviously come to stay; she must be the daughter that Helen told me about, who lives in Scotland. 'Would you like to wait upstairs for them – in my flat? Perhaps you could call them? I'm sure they won't be long, if they're expecting you.'

She nods and thanks me, and begins to follow me up the stairs, heaving her suitcase behind her as I heave Archie's buggy.

'I take it you're their daughter,' I comment cheerfully as I put my key in the lock. 'It's nice to meet you. I'm—'

But I don't get any further, because she's stopped, two steps below me, looking up at me in surprise.

'Their *daughter*?' she echoes. 'Oh. No. They... um, they haven't got any children. I'm their niece, Chloe. I take it you're Jess? I've heard all about you; they think the world of you and your little ones—'

She's going on, talking about how pleased she is when she

calls her auntie, to hear about their friendship with me and the kids, how it's given them a new lease of life, how she doesn't worry now about them being lonely... But I'm not really taking any of it in. I'm standing here outside my door with the key still in the lock, frozen, unable to open it, because all I can hear are those words reverberating in my head as if they're the only words I'm ever now going to be able to hear:

They haven't got any children.

They've lied to me. They told me they did. Why would they lie about it?

And I can only think of one reason: because they're trying to steal mine.

* * *

I have no idea what the niece must think of me. When I've finally managed to get my door open I somehow find myself inside, gesturing to her to sit down, ignoring the kids who are clamouring for drinks, for lunch, for the TV to be turned on, and for what feels like an age I just stand in the middle of the room staring at her, opening and shutting my mouth, wondering how the hell to say what I want to say, ask what I need to ask. I haven't even offered her a coffee or anything. She's looking at me a little anxiously.

'I'm sorry,' I manage to stutter out eventually. 'But... you're saying your aunt and uncle haven't got children? Grown-up children?'

She shakes her head. 'No.' She looks down at the floor. 'What did they tell you? I don't know if I should—'

'Yes, I think you should, please, if you don't mind,' I say bluntly.

But just at that moment there's the sound of the door downstairs opening.

'They're home,' Chloe says, quickly getting to her feet. 'It was nice to meet you, Jess, and thank you for... for inviting me in, but I'd better go back down now. Perhaps I'll see you around, I'm here for a week—'

'Yes. Perhaps. I mean please. Please do, if you... if you can, I'd like to know... to have a talk...'

She's already out of the door, pulling her case back down the stairs, and Helen's looking out of their door, exclaiming that Chloe's early, she's so sorry they were out, they went to get some fish and chips, she knows it's Chloe's favourite, come along inside, how was the journey, and – oh, thank you Jess for looking after her!

The door closes, and I'm left standing on my own doorstep, shaking with the shock of what I now know, what I now don't understand.

Why? Why lie to me? Why tell me they had a son and a daughter? Why *pretend*? Was it to make themselves come across as more trustworthy? To let me think that because they'd had kids of their own, they were safe to look after mine? To gradually spend more and more time with my babies, to spoil them with toys and treats while at the same time making me feel less capable as a parent? To keep urging me to leave the children with them at weekends, in the school holidays, overnight, buying them a pet bird to tempt them into going downstairs even more often?

Right up till now I've still been trying to tell myself it was ridiculous to imagine they were trying to steal my children from me, enticing them away, making me feel like they were better off with them. But now, all these doubts have come rushing back. Let's face it, I know what Helen thinks of me: a mother who has no quality time with her kids, who shouts at them and has noisy evenings with her friends and gives them bad food and dummies and lets them sleep in her bed and doesn't feed them broccoli. What's the plan? To wait till I've let one of them hurt themselves really badly, worse than the bruise from the cot, and then report me to Social Services as an unfit mother? Is Helen keeping a log, a diary, a list of all my failings? Are they planning to step forward as the loving 'auntie and uncle' who could foster my children and give them a better quality of life while I get put on some register of unfit parents and followed up by nosy people who visit me at home to find out if I'm improving?

Even while I'm telling myself to calm down, to stop being stupid, to stop having all these thoughts and concentrate on getting the children some lunch, I'm doing everything wrong because I'm so flustered. I've put butter on Archie's toast when he prefers it unbuttered, and I've cut Mia's toast into fingers when I know perfectly well she'll refuse to eat it because fingers are for babies. I've filled Archie's cup with squash after he asked me for milk, and I've made myself a coffee in one of the children's cups. And all the time, I'm trying to think what other reason there could be for this, some reason for their behaviour other than the worst-case scenario I'm suspecting. But what?

What the hell could make someone pretend they've got two children – a daughter living in Scotland and a son living in the US – if they haven't? The only possible explanation is the one I'm now obsessing over: they wanted me to trust them. And now I don't.

* * *

The children can obviously sense my mood. Mia asks to go down to see Beaky this afternoon as usual and I nearly bite her head off, telling her no. She runs off to her bedroom to cry and sulk, and I feel bad, but not bad enough to go and comfort her. I put Archie down for his nap and he's restless, spitting out his dummy over and over again and crying for it. I tell myself I was right all along – I'm a bad mother, a useless mother who upsets her own daughter and can't get her baby to sleep. The day is spoilt; I can't retrieve it, make it better in any way. I do some housework and let the kids watch rubbish on TV, and berate myself all over again. They'd better take the children away; anybody would do a better job of it than this – look at me, I'm hopeless.

By bedtime I've done my best to pull myself together. I give the kids their bath, sing to them, cuddle them, read to them, tell them I love them. I feel ridiculously like crying, as if I'm weak and run-down after a fever. When I'm sure they're both asleep, I call my dad.

'Perhaps they have their reasons,' he tries to soothe me after I've blurted out the whole story. 'Perhaps it's really sad for them – not having had kids. Perhaps they don't like talking about it so they just—'

'Just what? Make up a complete web of lies? Invent a daughter in Scotland and a son in America – why? Why not just say it's something they don't like talking about – I'd have understood that. But no, they let me believe they were experienced parents, so that they could gradually take over my kids, together with all my self-confidence. Not that I had a lot of that anyway, after Callum.'

He's silent for a moment.

'But you've built your self-confidence back up, now, haven't you, and I'd hate for this to change anything—'

'But, Dad, it *does* change everything! How can I let them look after the children now, knowing they've lied to me about something so important, something so *relevant*? How can I even face them now? I'll have to confront them about it, obviously.'

'You don't really think they're going to steal your children, do you?' he says, sounding more anxious now. 'Think about how many times they've been looking after them, while you were at work, and even while you were at the hospital with me and staying here the day afterwards. Be realistic. If they'd wanted to make off with the children, they'd have—'

'I'm not saying they'll *make off* with them. But they're definitely undermining me. Perhaps they're trying to push me into giving the children up voluntarily. And if Chloe tells them I know about their lies now, they might panic and... and do *anything*.'

'Sweetheart, I do understand how worried you've been getting about Helen and Robert, but try not to overdramatise this. Look, get some sleep and I'll see you tomorrow, OK? We can talk about it again then.'

I go to bed feeling frustrated. I thought Dad understood, but now I don't think he really gets how serious this is. *Am* I overdramatising it? Could there be a logical reason for lying about having children? If there is, I can't imagine what it could be.

* * *

I don't feel any better when I wake up. It's Sunday now, and I've asked Dad to come round, told him I've got to talk to him. I want to make him understand how worried I am.

I put the TV on for the children so that they won't hear us talking, and take Dad into the kitchen.

'I've been thinking about your whole situation with Helen and Robert,' he says. 'I don't think you should rush to put a stop to things straight away. But you obviously do need to talk to them about it – as soon as possible.'

'That's all very well, Dad, but Helen's supposed to be picking them up from school and nursery tomorrow. There's not much time to have this conversation, and her niece is staying with them

– it's going to be really awkward because it was her that told me—'

He holds up his hand to stop me.

'I know. I realise that. So you need to make other arrangements just for this week, OK? That'll give you time to think it all through a bit more, and have the conversation you need to have—'

'Other arrangements?' I retort. 'I haven't *got* any other arrangements.'

'Yes you have,' he says calmly, 'because I've sorted it already. I'll finish work early for the whole of this coming week, pick up the children for you and either take them home with me or – if you prefer and you've got a spare key – bring them back to your place until you get home.'

'You can't do that!' I exclaim. 'Your job!'

'Darling girl, I'm the boss. I can, and I will. I only had to shift one meeting to earlier in the day. Trust me, I put in enough hours that I don't get paid for.'

'Well, on Wednesdays and Fridays it's later anyway – Mia goes to after-school club so Archie stays later at the nursery. But I'll have to tell the school and the nursery, and they'll want a photo of you and your phone number; it's such a hassle, I don't think—'

'That's not a hassle,' he says, laughing. 'I'll sort it out. Don't worry. They won't mind, will they – the children?'

'Mind? I think they'll be over the moon. You're their number one favourite person at the moment!'

'Good. And you can tell Helen and Robert – just use the excuse that, as they've got their niece staying, you thought it was only fair to make other arrangements.'

'OK. Yes, that makes sense, doesn't it. Thank you, Dad.'

'It'll give you some breathing space, to decide how to

approach the subject with them. Then, we'll see where we stand, for the following week.'

'Oh! But – that'll be the half-term holiday! They were going to have the children all day, every day.' I put my head in my hands. This is going to be awful. How am I going to extricate myself from this relationship?

Dad takes my hands away from my face and holds them for a moment.

'Don't panic. Until you've talked all this over, you don't know how things will pan out. But – worst-case scenario – if you really can't let them keep having the kids, it's no problem, I'll take the week off work. As long as you trust *me* to have them?'

I look at him closely to see if he's taking the piss. He's not. He looks deadly serious.

'After all,' he says softly, 'I've hardly been the perfect grandfather up till now. There's no reason, really, that you should trust me now that I've... come crawling back, expecting to be forgiven.'

'I *have* forgiven you,' I reply equally quietly. 'And I do trust you. I don't know why. I suppose it's just kind of instinctive.'

We look at each other seriously for a moment – a moment that's suddenly interrupted by a yell from the living room and – when I rush to see what's happened, Mia is crouching over Archie, stroking his head as he lies on the floor crying.

'He falled over and hit his head on his car,' she says. 'I don't think there's blood, though, Mummy.'

'Aw, poor baby.' I pick Archie up and sit him on my lap, wiping his tears away. 'Oh dear – another lump on your head?' I meet Dad's eyes and he smiles and shakes his head.

'All children have little knocks and bumps,' he says, 'whatever *anyone else* might think.'

I nod at him. He's right; it's not always my fault. Archie's a toddler; this is what they do. I'm *not* a bad mother just because he has a little accident.

'Why don't you come and sit down and talk to Grandad, both of you?' I suggest, and then add, watching both their faces carefully, 'Would you like Grandad to pick you up from school and nursery this week, for a change?'

'Instead of Auntie Helen?' Mia says at once, her face brightening.

'Yes. Will that be nice?'

'Yay!' shouts Mia. She throws herself into Dad's arms. 'I will be very happy, Grandad. And so will Archie.'

I don't know how this is all going to end up. But for now I'm just so grateful. Grateful that Dad's in a position to help, grateful that he's come back into my life, so unexpectedly, at exactly the time that I needed someone, and that the children seem to have taken to him so immediately and so well. That's all I can think about for now. Until I've had the conversation I need to have with Helen and Robert.

32

The children are so tired after their day with their grandad that it's not difficult at all to get them to bed early. And once they're both asleep I pick up my phone and take a deep breath before calling Helen.

'Oh, hello Jess!' she says cheerfully. 'Are you all OK? We haven't seen you all weekend – didn't Mia want to come down and help with Beaky?'

'Dad's been here today,' I tell her. 'And I know you've got your niece staying, so we didn't want to disturb you.'

'Don't be silly, you'd still be welcome,' she begins, but I stop her.

'No. It's not right. I don't suppose you see Chloe often, so we'll stay out of your way while she's here. Dad's going to pick the children up this week.'

'Oh.' There's a silence that lasts just a fraction too long. 'You didn't have to ask your dad to do that. I'd still have been happy to meet the children as usual. Chloe would have come with me.'

'I appreciate that, but honestly, Dad's happy to do it – luckily it's easy enough for him to finish work early. And if Chloe's staying for the following week, it's half-term, and Dad would be able to have the kids then, too, if—'

'Oh, no, that's not necessary.' She sounds slightly panicked now. I wonder whether Chloe's mentioned our conversation about their pretence – their lies. 'Chloe's only here for this week. We'll be on our own again next week and we're so looking forward to having the children – we've started talking about what we might do together—'

'OK, well, we can decide that nearer the time,' I say.

Do I sound as sharp, as brisk, as I think I do? I can't help it. I really want to have the discussion about the lies right now, get it out of the way, so that I know where I stand... but at the same time, I'm dreading it. Once I find out the truth, it might mean I can never trust them again. How can I trust people who lie about something as important as having children of their own?

'All right, then.' Helen sounds hurt. I suppose she thinks that now I'm back on good terms with my dad, I don't need them any more. I have a momentary flash of regret. I used to think they were so good to us. But I've had so many doubts... and now it looks like I might have been right all along.

They haven't got any kids. They want mine.

* * *

Dad brings the children back here this week, on all three days that Mia's not at after-school club. It's easier than driving them to his place and back again, and they're both absolutely thrilled about it. He doesn't spoil them by buying them new toys or treats, but he's kind and patient with them; he seems to cope fine with Archie's grizzling because of his sore mouth, and I don't hear Mia complaining once about *being told off*, or being lectured about eating vegetables or anything else.

'I like Grandad looking after us,' she says towards the end of the week. 'It's much nicer than going to Auntie Helen's.'

I ask her why, but she just shrugs and clams up. Again, I wonder what she's keeping from me, and I feel more worried and suspicious than ever.

'I've booked next week off,' Dad says when I call him on the Friday evening. 'If you don't need me, that's fine, but if you do, I'm free, OK?'

'Thank you.' I sigh. 'I need to talk to Helen and Robert tomorrow.' I've psyched myself up for it now, but I still feel shaky and anxious. Chloe's due to leave in the morning. I've seen her in passing a couple of times while she's been here, but I deliberately haven't stopped to talk. It's all too uncomfortable; I suspect she probably feels the same.

'You won't want the children with you when you have that conversation,' Dad says. 'Why don't I take them out somewhere for a little while tomorrow?'

'Oh, Dad, you've already done enough,' I protest, but he says, seriously, in response:

'No, Jess, I haven't. I haven't done enough, anywhere near enough, and if I can just make a feeble attempt to make up for it now, then please let me – to ease my conscience a little.' He pauses and adds, 'And because I really enjoy their company!'

'Well, OK.' I give in. 'Shall I call you when I know what time I'm going to go and talk to them?'

'Good idea. It's supposed to be a lovely day tomorrow. Get their sun cream and sun hats ready and I'll take them to the park.'

'Thank you.'

* * *

I call Helen in the evening. Again, she sounds really happy to hear from me.

'We've missed having the children this week, Jess,' she says wistfully. 'Do you want to bring them down and join us for coffee tomorrow? Chloe's got to leave soon after breakfast, sadly.'

'Actually, Helen, I'd like to see you and Robert on my own tomorrow. Dad's going to take the kids to the park so that we can talk.'

'Oh.' She sounds as anxious as I feel. 'Well, all right, of course. I hope it's nothing serious?'

So it seems Chloe hasn't said anything.

'I'll explain tomorrow,' I say. 'What's a good time?'

We agree on eleven o'clock, and I message Dad to tell him. I feel edgy, jumpy, and I can't concentrate on the TV this evening or focus on doing anything. I keep trying to work out exactly how I'm going to broach the subject with them, but end up deciding I'll just have to jump straight in as soon as I get there.

* * *

'Jess!' Helen greets me with a hug and a big smile, which I find difficult to return. 'Lovely to see you. Have the children been all right with your dad this week? You didn't need to—'

'It's been fine,' I say abruptly. Then I remember my manners and add that I hope they've had a nice week with their niece.

Helen goes to make the coffee while I wait in the lounge, only half-listening to Robert as he tells a funny story about Beaky apparently taking a shine to Chloe and sitting on her shoulder while she moved around the flat.

'Here you are,' Helen says, putting a steaming mug down in front of me. 'And chocolate biscuits. What a pity the children aren't here – they're digestives, Mia's favourites!'

'Helen,' I interrupt, because if I don't say it now, it's just going to get harder and harder. 'Both of you. I need to ask you something. Why did you tell me you had children – two grown-up children – and you haven't?'

It comes out quite aggressively. Both their mouths have dropped open in shock.

'Chloe told me,' I go on quickly. 'Because I thought – when I met her – that she was your daughter. You said your daughter lives in Scotland. But you haven't got a daughter at all, have you – or a son in America. *Why* lie about it? I don't understand.'

Robert coughs, looks at Helen, distress in his eyes, and back at me. Helen closes her eyes and drops her head, as if she's not going to take any further part in the conversation. But Robert's voice, when he finally speaks, is kind of croaky, as if he's got a sore throat.

'We did have,' he says very quietly.

'Sorry?'

'I said, we did have them. We had a daughter, Grace, who'd gone to live with her cousin in Scotland. She was working at the hotel Chloe's parents – my brother and sister-in-law – run up there. And we had a son, Tom, who was studying microbiology at a university in the States.'

'You *did* have...?' I repeat, my heart suddenly filled with horror. Oh my God. What nightmare scenario have I unwittingly uncovered here? I stare at Helen, wanting to know, but at the same time not wanting to know. Wishing I'd never asked. But before any of us can say any more, she gets to her feet and walks slowly out of the room, her head still hanging, and shuts herself in the bedroom.

'I'm sorry...' I stutter, staring at Robert, but he shakes his head.

'No. It's my fault. I should have told you. Helen... couldn't, you see. She still finds it so hard to accept that they've gone – our children – passed away, both of them. She shouldn't have mentioned them at all – that would have been better. But...'

'Oh, Robert, I'm so sorry.' My eyes have filled with tears. 'How awful – both your children? How long ago did they pass away?'

'Christmas three years ago. They'd come home for the holidays. Grace hired a car, drove down from Edinburgh, picked up her brother from the airport the following day – we were living in London then – and...' He closes his eyes and runs a hand through his hair. 'And it was foggy, freezing fog. There was an accident. A terrible accident...'

'I'm *so* sorry,' I say again. I feel completely at a loss now. Robert's taken off his glasses and is wiping his eyes; without thinking any more about it, I get up and go to sit beside him, giving him a hug. 'I should have been more tactful. It didn't occur to me it could be—'

'Why would it? It's not your fault. You must have been upset to think we'd lied to you. We wanted a new start, you see. We had to leave our jobs – we couldn't function properly, we were both too... traumatised, I suppose you'd call it. And eventually we wanted to move somewhere completely different, start over, try to make a new life for ourselves. Somewhere where nobody knew what had happened.'

'I understand.'

'And, well, meeting you – the pleasure of helping you with your children – it's been so good for Helen. She's actually been *almost* happy again. We love them, Jess – we love you, too. I'm sorry we didn't tell you the truth, but—'

'It doesn't matter. I'm just sorry I was so... insensitive... about it. I couldn't understand why Helen would lie to me. I was upset, but now I understand, and, oh, God, Robert, I wouldn't have wanted to hurt Helen like this. Will she be all right?'

'Yes.' He manages a ghost of a smile. 'She still sometimes has a bad day, when the memories come flooding back. We both do. But since we've been here, helping you with the kids, getting to know you all – it's made such a massive difference to both our lives.' He pauses, before rushing on, 'I realise your dad's back in your life now, back in the children's lives, and we're happy for you, we really are. But... please don't deprive us completely of their company, will you? We still want to help, and I'm sure your dad won't be able to completely take over.'

'Of course. I'll tell Dad you're still OK to look after the children next week, then, or – maybe if he wants to do a couple of days...?'

'And we do the rest? That would be perfect, Jess. Thank you.'

He's thanking me for letting them look after my children. I'm absolutely thrown by the whole conversation, of course – already berating myself for not even considering the possibility that Helen and Robert *did* have the two children they'd told me about... but just not any more. Losing both your children – I shudder as I turn my thoughts away from the whole idea of it.

'Can I... should I... go and say sorry to Helen?' I ask. My coffee's gone cold but I can't face it now and he doesn't comment on it.

'Let me do that for you,' he says gently. 'She probably feels terribly guilty about lying to you. But it wouldn't have felt like a lie, at the time – you see? Please don't worry. I can understand why you were upset. Helen will talk to you tomorrow, I'm sure, when she's had a chance to recover herself. Why don't you bring the kids down tomorrow afternoon to see Beaky, and you and Helen can discuss how we'll share the holiday week with your dad.'

'OK.'

I get up to go; it doesn't feel right to stay any longer and I'm sure Robert wants to go and comfort Helen. But it takes me the rest of the time until Dad brings the kids back from the park – hot, excited, and sticky from ice-cream – to pull myself together, stop blaming myself, and accept that I really couldn't have known there was such a horribly sad reason for what Helen told me.

'I'm glad you're able to trust them again,' Dad says when we've managed to have a whispered conversation about it while the children aren't listening. 'So you're OK with them still having the kids now?'

'Yes, I think so. Robert said perhaps they could share the half-term with you, if that's OK with you?'

'Of course, love. I'll do whatever you want.'

'Thanks, Dad.' I pause. 'Robert says they really love the children. And me.'

'That shouldn't make you feel obligated to them,' he warns me softly, 'if you're still uncomfortable with the way they treat Mia and Archie.'

I'd nearly forgotten I was uncomfortable with any of it – I'm just so relieved to find out it wasn't all part of a plot.

I sigh. 'Perhaps I've just misinterpreted everything. Perhaps Helen hasn't really been criticising me at all – it's just that she's a bit old-fashioned in a lot of ways. And she was a teacher, so she's probably a bit strict at times.'

'Well, let's see if, between us, we can make this work so that everyone's happy – but most importantly, the kids are.'

I hug him, breathing in his dad smell that I'd almost forgotten about but am already now so used to again.

'How awful it must be for them,' I say, feeling tears spring to my eyes again. 'Losing their children like that.'

'It's always awful to lose a child,' he mutters. 'Even when it's your own damned stupid idiot fault. But I've been lucky; I was privileged to find you again.'

33

'Uncle Robert asked if you and Archie would like to go down and see Beaky this morning,' I tell Mia over breakfast on the Sunday.

'Oh good. He probably needs my help cleaning out the cage,' she says importantly.

'Probably,' I agree with a smile. 'And I'll come down too and have a chat with Auntie Helen, OK?'

'Yes. And Archie can just... play.'

That decided, we get ourselves ready and head downstairs. As soon as we're inside, I give Helen a hug and whisper how sorry I am that I upset her yesterday.

'My fault,' she whispers back. 'I should have told you, Jess. I wish I had, but it's just... so hard. Come in, all of you. Robert's waiting for you to help him with Beaky, children! Come into the kitchen, Jess. Let's get the kettle on. Robert says you'd like us to share the holiday childminding with your dad – is that all right? We were a bit worried you wouldn't want us to have them any more, after... what you found out. I was so relieved to hear you've forgiven me, Jess, for not telling you the truth. I'd hate to lose you as a friend – and lose the children – after what I went through—'

'It's fine, Helen,' I tell her. 'But I'd like Dad to be involved with sharing the childcare anyway, and it means you don't have to have the kids for the whole week.'

'Well, of course I'm glad for you, and your father – glad you've been reunited,' she says, trying to look as pleased as she's pretending to be.

* * *

I know the truth is that Helen's probably disappointed, probably would have preferred to have the kids to herself every day. But personally, I'm relieved. I must admit I still feel anxious during the days Helen and Robert look after the children during the holiday, taking them out for a picnic and to a local summer fete. Mia pulls a face when I tell her they're going to them rather than their grandad for those first few days, but bounces out of bed on the mornings that Dad's having them. Why? Is it just – as Dad suggests – that he's still a novelty? Or that she just loves having a grandad after so long without one?

On Dad's days at the end of the week, he takes the children out in the car – which they both love – one day to a park a little way away that has a paddling pool, and the next day to a petting farm. This, in particular, has Mia jumping around with excitement when I get home, as she describes the various animals they were able to stroke and feed.

'Do you know what, Mummy, there was horses there but they was little ones what's called mini-ture. And mini-ture goats! And sheeps, and pigs, and wallababies what look like kangyroos...'

Archie immediately begins to hop around the room in an imitation of the wallabies, which is quite realistic until he gets dizzy and falls over.

'Calm down, both of you!' I say, laughing. But of course, it's lovely to see how much they've enjoyed their day with their grandad.

* * *

Mia's fifth birthday is straight after the end of half-term this year, falling conveniently on a Saturday. Her three closest friends from school will be coming round this afternoon for tea, cake and probably a complete meltdown of over-excitement. I've bought her a Lego Friends pet shop – I just hope it doesn't kick off all the complaints about not being allowed a dog or a cat again – and a book, which I tell her is from Archie. She unwraps them both really quickly, squeals with delight and starts taking pieces of Lego out of the box straight away.

'Be careful – Archie's going to pick them up and put them in his mouth,' I warn her, and she raises her eyes.

'Isn't it a pain, Mummy, having a little one in the family,' she says, but takes her Lego to sit up at the kitchen table with good grace. Perhaps she's really going to be grown-up now she's five!

* * *

I've promised we'd pop down to see Helen and Robert this morning, so that they can see the birthday girl. Helen looks almost as excited as Mia when she opens the door.

'Happy birthday, darling!' she exclaims, wrapping Mia in her arms. 'Now, close your eyes, and Uncle Robert's going to bring you your present.'

There's a rustling of paper and a thump as something fairly heavy is put down in front of Mia.

'OK, you can open your eyes now, poppet,' Robert says. 'Sorry about the way it's wrapped – it was a difficult shape—'

But I can see what it is already. So, I think, can Mia. She pulls off the first sheet of paper, her eyes wide with excitement, while I stare, horrified. What the hell have they done?

'Do you like it, Mia? It's your favourite colour!' says Helen, all smiles.

A bike, a pink bike. I just look back at Helen and Robert, wondering how the hell I'm going to say this, how to phrase it so it won't upset them. But then I think again. *Why*? Why buy such an expensive present – and why do it without even checking with me, without asking whether it's appropriate? A jigsaw puzzle or a cuddly toy or a game would have been lovely. This bike is new, it's expensive – they're surely not going to try to pretend it's a hand-me-down or a charity shop find, this time? Are they just trying to outdo me – *again*?

I've got to tell them quickly, because Mia's already grinning from ear to ear, excitement mounting as she holds the handlebars of the little bike and starts jabbering about how much she's wanted a real bike...

'Wait a moment, Mia.' I turn to Helen and Robert, doing my best to hide my irritation. 'Look, I'm sorry to say this, to disappoint you, but I'm sure I've already told you: Mia's grandad's bought her a bike. He hasn't even given it to her yet.' *And now his surprise is completely ruined.* 'It's very similar to this. You should have checked with me – I hope you'll be able to take it back.'

'Oh,' says Helen. 'I don't remember you telling us, Jess.'

'Oh dear,' says Robert.

Their faces have both fallen. I feel a flash of sympathy, even though it's their own fault, but mostly I'm just annoyed. Mia's looking from them to me and back again, her face a picture of confusion and doubt.

'Grandad's got me a bike too?' she says. 'Is it pink?'

'Yes, sweetie. He'll be bringing it round later.'

'Oh. I can't really have two bikes, can I, Mummy?' she says anxiously. 'Shall we give one of them to one of my friends?'

'No, Mia. We can't take this one.'

Helen and Robert look at each other, their eyes wide with anxiety.

'Um... maybe your dad could take his one back to the shop, Jess?' Helen says.

I stare at her in disbelief. '*No*, Helen, you'll have to take this one back! Dad's been looking forward to seeing Mia's face when he gives her her first bike. *And now you've spoilt it for him,*' I add, half under my breath.

'But we can't...' Helen begins, looking flustered.

Robert touches her arm, frowning. 'We'll have to, Helen,' he says quietly. 'We'll... sort something out.'

I sigh with exasperation. Of course they'll have to sort something out! I look at the bike again. Perhaps they've got it cheaply from eBay or whatever and can't return it. It doesn't look second-hand – it's shiny and new-looking – but frankly it's their problem, anyway. I'm more concerned with how upset Mia's looking now. She's confused and worried and she knows I'm not pleased.

'It's all right, sweetheart,' I tell her. 'It's just... a mistake.'

'We'll buy you something else instead, Mia,' Robert says, seeming to recover himself a little. 'We're sorry, Jess. You're right, we should have checked. And all this time we've had it hidden in the spare bedroom, under a duvet at the side of the wardrobe!'

'Yes, we'll buy you something else,' Helen agrees. But she's still looking at Robert, panic in her eyes.

'Well, honestly, there's no need,' I say.

'Yes, there is,' Robert insists. 'Mia, can you give us some ideas of what you'd like, so we don't make another mistake?'

'Well.' Mia brightens up immediately. 'I'd really like a magic painting set like my friend Faiza has got. And some more beads. And some silver shoes like my friend Phoebe's got. And—'

'All right, Mia – just one thing, thank you,' I say.

Helen and Robert are managing a smile now, but I can sense the awkwardness, I can feel it in the air, and there's something strange about it – something I don't understand. They both looked... shifty, uncomfortable, somehow. I could almost imagine they've obtained this bike in some nefarious way, and now don't know how they're going to get rid of it. Perhaps I'm just imagining it. But whatever – they should have known better.

* * *

Mia talks of nothing else but the bike we've had to refuse, for the rest of the morning. She's quite obviously uncertain about it all, one minute looking sad about not being able to keep it, the next remembering that she now knows she's getting one from her grandad. I message Dad to warn him that her reaction won't be quite what we'd hoped – and why. *Not to worry*, he messages me back. But I do, I feel bad for him. It's the first birthday present he's ever bought her and it feels a bit spoilt.

He comes round at lunchtime, smiling, shaking his head at me as I try to whisper my regret again.

'Happy birthday, beautiful!' he says, reaching out to kiss Mia. 'This is for you – as I think you know! I haven't tried to wrap it up, but I've tied pink ribbons all over it.' He lifts the bike in from outside. 'I hope you like it.'

'It's pink like the other one!' she says, her excitement back straight away.

Dad laughs. 'Well, isn't that funny! Everybody must know you like pink.'

'Can I keep this one, Mummy?' she asks me. 'Can I actually ride it? I've never rid a bike before.'

'Yes, of course you can. You'll soon get the hang of it. Look, it's got stabilisers so you won't fall over. We can take them off when you're bigger.'

The little pink bike has a basket on the front and a little seat for a doll – or Ellie Elephant – behind the saddle.

'Is it all right, Mia? Do you like it?' Dad goes on, as Mia's fallen silent, probably still a bit unsure whether anyone's going to change their mind about her having this bike too.

'I love it, thank you, Grandad! Can I ride it now?'

We carry the bike downstairs and go out onto the path, where Mia practises wobbling along while Dad runs behind her, and I take some photos.

'Bike!' says Archie, hiding behind my legs as Mia swerves out of his way at the last minute. 'Mia bike!'

'Yes, Archie!' I laugh. The sun's out, the air feels warm and pleasant and I find myself shaking off my irritation from this morning and enjoying a wave of happiness. I look at Dad, and wonder what happened to the sad, grieving, bitter man he'd been until so recently. He's sparkling with as much enjoyment of the day as Mia is. As I am. Life seems good, suddenly, and again I find myself hoping Mum can somehow see how things are turning out. How we are, now. How we're making it work.

'Come on, Mia – we need to have lunch and get you changed into your best dress before your friends come,' I remind her after a while. 'There'll be lots more time to practise on the bike during the summer.'

Dad's bought some accessories: a safety handle that fits to the back of the bike so I can hang on to it if we take it out while Mia's learning to ride, and an immobilising lock so we can keep it on the landing at the top of the stairs.

'I'm really sorry about the surprise being spoilt,' I say again quietly to Dad while Mia's gone to put her dress on.

'Ah, it's fine. She seems really happy anyway,' he says. 'Don't worry, Jess. It's Helen and Robert's problem, isn't it. Nice gesture, though.'

I suppose he's right – it was. But I wish I didn't feel so perturbed about why they looked so very uncomfortable about it.

34

Mia's exhausted by the time her friends have left. She loved her little tea party; it's probably the first time she could remember the previous year's birthday, and knew better what to expect – added to the fact that each of these three friends have now had their own fifth birthdays and she's been invited to their parties.

It's not until she's in her pyjamas, sleepy and cuddly and ready for her story, that the incident of the bike at Helen and Robert's comes up again. I think, up until now, she's been far too focused on sausages, ice-cream, birthday cake and games, but I guessed she would eventually want to talk about it some more.

'I didn't need *two* bikes, did I, Mummy?' she says, frowning.

'No. But Auntie Helen and Uncle Robert didn't realise Grandad was buying you one. So they thought it would be a lovely present.'

'But it wasn't them what bought it.'

I look at her in surprise. I'm not sure if she knows what she's saying – she's so tired, half asleep already, with Ellie Elephant and Mr Meerkat in her arms and her new storybook lying on the bed, ready for me to read to her.

'Yes, it was,' I say. 'But it doesn't matter, now, Mia—'

'No, but it *wasn't* them. 'Cos I know who it was really from. 'Cos I saw him, bringing it, but they didn't know I was looking. And it was a long time ago so I forgot. I didn't know it was for me.'

She's more awake now and she sounds anxious, even guilty about it. I'm not sure she's making any sense, though.

'Who, Mia?' I ask her gently. 'Who did you see bringing it?'

She turns her face away. 'I'm not allowed to say.'

OK, I'm worried now. This is odd – she definitely looks guilty, and... almost scared.

'Who told you you're not allowed to say?' I press her – and of course, the answer is obvious.

'Auntie Helen.' She still won't meet my eyes. 'She says I'm not allowed to say it, not ever.'

'Not even to me?' I stroke her face, turn it towards mine. 'I'm your mummy, Mia. You can tell me anything, all right? I'm not going to be cross, even if Auntie Helen said you shouldn't tell me.' I pause, still stroking her face, her hair, her shoulders, trying to make her feel safe. 'We shouldn't have secrets, you and me,' I go on softly. 'Tell me. Who was it who brought the bike to their flat? Was it a delivery person – like when I get things from Amazon?'

She shakes her head, her eyes wide with anxiety now.

'Who, then?'

'Can I whisper it?' she says.

'If you prefer.'

She sits up, leans towards me and puts her soft little mouth right next to my ear. And in an instant, I know. I think I've suspected it already, but now, with her warm breath tickling me and her little arms tight around my neck, I don't even need her to say the words. I've guessed.

'It was Daddy.'

* * *

I'm shaking as I sit down on the sofa later. I tried to stay calm in front of Mia, and while I was reading her story. I asked her if she was really, really sure it was her daddy who'd brought the bike, and she nodded earnestly and began to tell me again, about the other times she's claimed to have seen him.

Of course, I know only too well by now how Mia makes up stories. I know she'd enjoy a little fantasy about her daddy buying her a bike, leaving it with Helen and Robert as a surprise. But deep inside me, I know there's truth in it. I think Callum's somehow been getting involved with Helen and Robert; he's worked out who's been looking after the kids and he's been hanging around outside their flat. Has he actually been to their flat while Mia and Archie were there? If Mia's telling the truth, he has, and she's seen him. I feel a cold sweat coming over me just at the thought of it. I'm still trying to keep reminding myself I can't always believe what she says... but that look in her eyes tonight, the way she was afraid to tell me, the insistence that she'd been sworn to secrecy. I don't think she could actually act that out so well.

The horror of what all this means is overwhelming. Just as I've moved on after the worry of Helen lying about having children, I'm now faced once again with not being able to trust them any more – for an even worse reason, if it's true. How can I trust them? They *know* – I told them from the very beginning – that I don't want Callum anywhere near the kids. Has he been intimidating Helen and Robert, forcing them to let him see the children? How much has my poor little daughter been bottling up, how much has Helen frightened her into keeping quiet? And why?

I call Dad; I've just got to tell somebody. I can hear the fear and frustration in my own voice. Can I really trust Helen and Robert after all? Will I ever get Callum out of my life? Will I have to *move* to get away from him?

'Right,' he says finally, when I pause for breath. 'You're obviously going to have to talk to Helen and Robert again. Perhaps if you tell them you're worried that you'll to have to move, they'll see how serious you are. But this could all just be Mia—'

'Making up stories. I know. I've been pretty sure, whenever she's mentioned seeing Callum before, that it was just her imagination, but now I'm really beginning to wonder if it's been true, every time.' I pause, thinking. 'Mia says it was *ages ago* that she saw him bringing the bike. She'd forgotten about it.'

'Perhaps she saw him from the window. Perhaps Helen did at least keep him from going into the flat.'

'But she still let him leave a present – a hugely expensive present! – for Mia. And she didn't tell me!'

'Yes, it seems so.' He pauses. 'Do you want me to be with you when you talk to them?'

I shake my head. 'No. There's no need. But...' It feels like an exact repeat of the previous occasion. I sigh. How is this going to end? 'Could you possibly take the kids for a little while again tomorrow?'

'Of course. I'll come round in the morning. And don't worry. If it all falls apart this time – if you can't use Helen and Robert any more to look after the kids, I'll do it. Short term or long term. Whatever you need.'

I don't know how to thank him enough. But then I remember the years when he turned his back on me, and I know he must feel that, whatever he does for me now, it can never be enough. I don't need to say anything. He's got to live with his regrets, just as I live with mine, but it's not the past that matters. It's what we do now that counts.

35

Helen looks worried. I'd almost say nervous. Has she guessed? Is it obvious, what I want to talk to her about? Robert's not here, but I can't wait for him to come back, I need to grasp the nettle, right now. I follow Helen into the kitchen, where she's insisted, irritatingly, on making a cup of coffee before we start to talk. 'I need to ask you something,' I begin, while she's fussing with mugs and milk and teaspoons. 'I'll come straight to the point.'

But before I can get any further, her phone starts ringing. I want to tell her to ignore it, this is more important, but she swings around, looking for the phone, dropping the packet of coffee as she does so.

'Shall I get your phone for you?' I suggest, sighing, as she goes to the cupboard for a dustpan, gets down on her knees and starts to sweep up the coffee. The phone's already cut off and started ringing again, driving me mad with its incessant silly tune. Perhaps I can just turn it off without her noticing.

'Thank you, love. It's probably just Robert. He's only gone to—'

I'm not bothering to listen. I grab the phone from next to the sofa. It's still ringing. She's got no security on it and no cover, so as soon as I pick it up I can see the caller ID. And it's not Robert. It's Callum.

My legs go so weak, I actually have to sit down. I don't care what Helen thinks or what she says about it – I'm going to answer this call.

'What took you so long?' he says as soon as I hit reply. 'I've got a problem I need your help with.'

I haven't even had a chance to speak yet. I'm not sure that I could if I tried – my voice will shake.

'Is it Robert?' Helen's calling from the kitchen. I ignore her.

'Did you hear me?' Callum says. He's shouting. He sounds desperate. 'I'm in trouble, right? I need a lawyer. You've got money, haven't you? I need someone to get me out of this mess. They've arrested me. Another stupid woman accusing me of stuff...' He pauses; I can picture him trying to calm down, making himself sound more reasonable. More believable. 'The silly woman's saying all kinds of stuff, saying I beat her up and *raped* her, for God's sake! It's a misunderstanding, obviously, OK? But I need the money, I need it today – if I can't get a good lawyer, they won't believe a word I say. Look, if I get banged up, I won't be able to help out any more. There won't be any more presents for the kids, they won't get their dad back in their lives—'

'They're not getting you back in their lives, whatever, Callum!' I yell. I'm yelling so hard my throat hurts. Helen appears in the kitchen doorway, her face draining of colour. 'Yes, it's me – bad luck,' I carry on shouting into her phone, ignoring Callum's spluttering angry response. 'I'm so glad I took this call. I knew something was going on. Well, you're not getting any help from anyone around here; you can get banged up for the rest of your life for all I care, so—'

Helen's grabbed the phone from me, but Callum's already

hung up. For a few seconds we stand facing each other, both breathing heavily. I can feel my heart racing. I don't know whether to shout at her or just collapse in tears.

'He's been arrested,' I say eventually, as if I even need to. I'm croaking from all the yelling. I feel sick. 'What the fucking hell's been going on, Helen? Why's he calling you? Why's he in your contacts?'

'Arrested?' she repeats faintly, feeling behind her for the sofa, sitting down abruptly beside me. 'What for?'

'Well, it seems another girl's reported him for beating her up. And raping her.'

She gasps. 'Oh no—'

'Oh *yes*, Helen, and you can bet your life it's true. It's not the first time.' I raise my voice again. 'So tell me, what's been going on? He's been coming round, hasn't he? You've let him come here, let him see the children, despite everything I told you. That bike – you didn't buy it at all, did you? It was from him. Mia told me – she saw him bringing it. She wasn't lying, was she, about the other times she's seen him, either.'

Helen's looking down, now, guiltily, avoiding my eyes.

'How could you *do* that?' I demand angrily. 'How could you tell Mia to lie to me?' I remember my previous suspicions. 'Did you know Callum already? Have you known him all this time – what exactly is he to you? A nephew or a cousin or something? Did you move here *knowing* I lived upstairs, with his children? Is that it – you're on his side, you've been *helping* him worm his way into seeing my kids, trying to get them taken away from me—'

'No, Jess!' Helen's got tears in her eyes now. 'No, absolutely not, we'd never met him before in our lives, until...'

'Until what?'

She gives a little sob. I wait, not caring if she cries or not, not getting taken in by it, refusing to be softened. There's the sound of a door slamming and suddenly, Robert's putting his head round the door, calling out a cheerful, *Hello!* – and then a shocked silence. He comes to stand in front of us both, looking from one of us to the other, his eyes wide with distress.

'What's happened?' he says, sitting down next to Helen, putting a comforting arm around her.

'I've found out,' I say abruptly. 'I know. About Callum, about him coming here, when you'd both promised me you'd never let him see the children—'

'We didn't *let* him see them, Jess,' Robert says quietly. 'We wouldn't go against your wishes. Any time Mia saw him, it was an accident. He just happened to be here. But—'

'He *happened* to be here?' I retort. 'So you admit he's been coming here – regularly, by the sound of it.' I stare at him for a moment and then look back at Helen. 'And you expect me to believe you've only just met him? Who *are* you, really? Friends of his, God forbid? Not that I thought he had any.'

'No,' Robert insists. 'Honestly, Jess, we'd never met him, and we never let him come in, until he turned up here one day—'

'And you called the police, did you, like you promised me you would?'

Robert sighs, as if I'm being deliberately difficult.

'Look, that first time I saw him – when you'd been arguing with him outside here – I admit I wasn't sure about him at all,' he says. 'But then, when he knocked on the door one day and introduced himself properly and started to talk about the children, well, he seemed so distressed about the situation—'

'Yes, I bet he did,' I say between my teeth. 'That's Callum all over, putting on an act, lying through his teeth—'

Robert looks at Helen and shakes his head.

'It wasn't like that, Jess. He didn't ask to see the children, although he did tell us how much he missed them – and, well, we saw there was another side to him.'

I can't believe this. I can't believe these are the same two people I liked so much, who I trusted with my children! I *knew* there was something not right. Why didn't I trust my instincts?

'But we didn't let him come in when the children were here,' Helen says now. 'And if we saw him outside when they were here, I told Mia to stay away from the window, and I went out to warn him to leave. That was the deal.'

'The *deal*? Helen, you don't do *deals* with people like Callum—'

'He wanted to see the children, of course he did – he's their father!' She looks down and adds quietly, 'It hurts us, Jess, when we hear of people being separated from their children – after losing ours, the way we did. That's why we're so happy to see you and your dad reunited.'

I nod, a little impatiently. I get it – I know their story now, I do feel for them, but for God's sake! Some people *don't* deserve to be in their kids' lives!

'But he respected what you'd decided about Mia and Archie, Jess,' she goes on earnestly. 'He's been decent about it.'

I snort with derision at this, but she ignores me and goes on:

'He told us how much he was hoping you'd eventually let him be a part of their lives. But if he happened to see them by chance—'

'Chance? Really? Mia said she saw him walking a dog – and I think I did, too. I don't believe he's even got one – he wouldn't be able to look after it. He probably borrowed it to tempt Mia into talking to him.' I'm thinking aloud now. 'And she saw him at the zoo – when you were with her, Helen – it really was him, wasn't it?'

'He bought us the tickets, Jess,' Robert admits. 'He wanted the kids to have a treat.'

'What? The tickets were from him? And you knew? I bet you knew he was going to be there, watching the children, sneakily, like... like something out of a horror film! You must all have been gutted when I decided to come along too that day!' I shake my head at him. 'He didn't want the kids to have a treat. He doesn't care about them! Can't you see? He was just manipulating you.'

'We told Mia not to tell you she saw him at the zoo. And the other times. We kept reminding her it would upset you,' says Helen, 'but she's only little, she found it hard—'

'Of course she found it hard to keep lying to me! What a horrible thing to tell her to do!'

So this is what it's all been about: all Mia's talk of Helen telling her off. She wasn't telling her off, she was trying to drum the rules into her; trying to protect her lying bastard of a father!

'Oh my God. He totally took you in, didn't he?' I go on, sitting back in the chair, shaking my head. 'You fell for it. This is what he *does*, for God's sake! He manipulates people. He pretends to be charming and reasonable—'

'He really does seem to love the children, Jess,' Robert says, a pleading tone to his voice now. 'He brought toys for them, and the cot—'

'I knew it! I *knew* it was strange, the way you kept acquiring all these toys. And getting a cot! I couldn't quite believe they were all second-hand from your friend – I knew you were lying to me...'

'We did get them toys from the charity shop at first, it wasn't a lie... but then Callum started—' he begins, but I cut him short.

'Do you know, I was actually worried sick when I found out you'd got Archie a cot? I thought you were preparing to keep the kids here – to take them away from me, report me as an unfit mother or something—'

'*What?*' gasps Helen, her eyes wide with distress. 'Never, Jess! We'd never—'

'Well what the hell was I supposed to think?' I'm shouting now in my frustration with them. 'I'd never have thought you'd go against everything I told you, and let Callum—'

'We trusted him,' she admits quietly. 'We thought you were overreacting. Being over-protective of the children – not that we blame you for that...'

The absurdity of it is too much. I close my eyes, sighing, shaking my head.

'Well, whatever you thought, you were wrong, and it wasn't your place to make those judgements. Callum *doesn't* love the children. He has no interest in them whatsoever. Whatever he was doing, it was all about him: getting you on his side, getting back at me for daring to live a good life without him.'

'But he takes full responsibility for the break-up,' Robert insists. 'He admits he was working too hard, didn't pay you and the children enough attention, but now—'

'*Now?*' I've had enough of this. I raise my voice. 'Shall I *tell* you what he's done now, Robert? He's been accused of raping and beating up another girlfriend. It's not the first time: he did the same to me. And after I left him I found out that he'd been violent to at least one other girl before me. And don't you dare tell me it's not true, that it's just an accusation, someone trying to spite him – because I *know* it's true. I know, because I lived through it – I know exactly how violent he can be. Oh, I was lucky enough to survive and get away, but I had plenty of bruises to show for it, and some broken ribs that I never even went to hospital about. But that's nothing compared with the damage he did to me *up here*.' I point to my head. 'He treated me like garbage, and I ended up feeling like garbage. I was scared of him, but scared to leave him because I had nowhere else to go and I thought...' I swallow, determined not to cry, determined to make them understand. 'I thought it was my own fault; my own fault for getting pregnant, and then for wanting another baby even though I knew he didn't want one, didn't want either of them. My fault for being with him in the first place, for throwing everything away, for letting down my parents – my mum would have been so disappointed in me! Don't you see? This is what he does. He treats people like shit, and at the same time, to outsiders, he acts like Prince Charming. The best thing I ever did was to finally get away from him, get my kids away from him, get sole custody of them and hope never to set eyes on him again. So thank you very much for letting him back into our lives. I don't know how he found out where I live, but he'd have given up trying to see the kids if you'd called the police, like I asked you to. He doesn't want to see his children; he doesn't give a damn about any of us. He wants to hurt me, that's all. He just can't bear to let me win. He can't bear it that I'm OK, that I've got on with my life, and that I'm not scared of him any more.'

Even as I say this – *I'm not scared of him any more* – I feel astounded at myself. Is that actually true? Yes! I might feel a lot of things about Callum – none of them good – but I've stopped being scared, because I've done it: I *have* won. I'm doing OK, whereas he... he'll always just be scum.

Helen and Robert have both gone silent, their faces white with shock.

'Do you get it, now?' I ask quietly, suddenly feeling so tired I can hardly get another word out.

'Why didn't you tell us?' Helen pleads. She looks close to tears. I start to feel sorry for her. I know exactly how easy it can be to get taken in by Callum. Look what happened to me! I actually believed he loved me. 'If we'd known...'

'I tried to tell you. I thought it would be enough that I'd said, insisted, he wasn't allowed to see the kids. It never occurred to me that he'd try to get to them through *you*, by trying to win you round, putting on his act, playing the victim. I can't believe you've been so naïve, but then – so was I, when I first met him. I should have spelt it out to you, just how badly he treated me, just how much of a thug and a bully he is. But... it's not easy to talk about.'

'No.' Robert looks crestfallen. Helen's nodding, slowly.

Of course. They know exactly how it feels to have a personal history that's difficult to talk about. I shouldn't have directed my anger at them. It's not their fault they've been lied to and manipulated.

'I just feel hurt that you've kept all this a secret from me,' I explain. 'I mean, I get that you weren't letting him come round while the kids were here – but if I'd known he was coming at all, I could have warned you, explained what I've told you now. How did he even find out the kids were with you?'

'He said it was the day we found the baby blackbird,' Robert says. 'He must have been watching; he said he saw me taking Mia inside with me.'

'Oh yes. He was still hanging around outside when I got home that day,' I remember. 'He threatened to report me to Social Services for *neglecting his children*.'

I'm almost spitting the words out in disgust. Helen looks like she's about to cry.

'He made us believe him, Jess,' she says miserably. 'He said not to tell you because you'd be upset, that you'd say he was inter-fering, but that all he wanted to do was bring toys and presents and have an influence on his kids' lives.'

'Have an *influence*? How?'

'Well, he was interested in what was going on in their lives. What they liked doing, what they liked to play with, and eat, and so on.'

What they liked to eat. I see.

'And did he express opinions? About what they should do, what they should eat, whether Archie should have a dummy, whether they should come into my bed at night or be woken up by me and my noisy friends... whether I was a bad mother, to put it bluntly?'

Her cheeks colour. 'If you put it like that, then yes, I suppose he did. We took it as being *caring*, Jess.'

'*Caring!*' I say with a snort. 'He doesn't care about anyone other than himself. And the irony is, he was trying to make *me* seem like an unfit parent. And feel like one!' I look at both their faces. They're so distressed, and look so guilty, but there's something else there too: confusion. I understand. It's probably going to take them a while to completely accept the truth and come to terms with it; it took me much longer, even though I lived through his abuse. Well, thank God, at least Callum won't be coming anywhere near any of us now, whether they like it or not. He'll be remanded – it's a serious offence he's been accused of. And he'll be convicted. I just know it.

'We're so sorry, Jess,' Helen says now, with tears in her eyes. 'You know how much we love you and the children. It's... just horrifying... to think we've been taken in.'

'I know.'

'If you don't trust us to look after the children any more,' she goes on now, 'would you at least let us *see* them occasionally?'

I take a moment to reply. To be honest, I'm still angry. I don't blame them so much for being taken in – Callum could do that to anybody – but for going against what I'd told them. But I look at their distressed faces. They've lost their own children – that grief will never go away. And I do believe they love my kids, despite all this. 'Of course I'll let you see them,' I say. 'And if you still feel you want to look after them, that you can get over this... setback... and start again, then of course, I'm grateful to you both. I do trust you.'

And finally, I know it's true: I do trust them, because all the doubts I had, all the worries about the things Helen, especially, was saying to me, all the concerns I had about the stories Mia was coming home with, I now know were because of Callum. *Everything* is his fault: all the misunderstandings, all the misconceptions, everything Helen and Robert got wrong or falsely assumed, was down to him, not them. They're good people. They weren't trying to steal my kids or paint me as a bad mother, they were manipulated, pretty much *groomed,* into believing Callum wanted the best for his children, when what he really wanted to do was punish me. I don't think he's capable of feeling anything but hate for anyone.

* * *

I've pulled myself together by the time Dad comes back from the park with the children.

'I just feel sad,' I tell him once Archie's having a nap and Mia's busy with Play-Doh at the kitchen table, and Dad and I have been able to have a long, quiet talk together. 'So sad, to think of those basically decent people being hoodwinked into believing all of Callum's crap.'

'Well, hopefully he'll be out of your hair now for a good long while, now that someone's had the courage to report him.' He pauses and gives me a very direct look. 'You know you should, too, don't you?'

He's right, we both know it, but... I shake my head. I don't think I can do it.

'I know it'd be hard. But the more witnesses that come forward now, the stronger the case against him. You could be helping to save more women from going through what you did. It could be good for you. Cathartic.'

Could it? I ask myself after Dad's left. Now I've decided I'm not scared of Callum any more, could speaking out actually make me feel better? I don't know, but perhaps I mustn't rule it out. For the sake of the next woman he meets after he's finally let out of jail this time, perhaps it's time I faced up to the challenge I refused to contemplate before. I need to remind myself that he can't hurt me any more. Not me. I've moved on. I'm a survivor.

36

The change in Mia is gradual but noticeable. She's coming back from Helen and Robert's place more cheerful, not complaining so much about having to go there, not giving me those awkward looks that told me there was something going on. There are no more reports of being 'told off' or of being lectured about 'veggiebles', and definitely no mentions of her father. A couple of weeks later I ask her if she'll be happy about spending time with them during the summer holidays, which are fast approaching.

'I'd rather be with you,' she admits. 'Sometimes I miss you and I feel sad.'

'I know, sweetheart. I miss you both, too. I'm sorry I can't be with you all through the holidays, I really am. But I've got two weeks of the holiday off! We can look forward to that, can't we. And for two weeks of it you'll be going to the holiday club, and Archie will go to nursery – and Auntie Helen will meet you for the afternoons. And the other two weeks you'll be with Grandad.'

'Yay!' she shouts. 'We like Grandad looking after us, don't we, Archie!'

'Gaddad!' Archie repeats in his usual agreeable way.

'And you're all right about the holiday club? And Auntie Helen?' I press gently.

'Yes, Mummy. I'm five now, I'm a big girl, I don't make a fuss. I'll look after Archie.'

I smile. My placid baby son is far from needing Mia to hold his hand, but if it makes her feel better to play the role of the comforting big sister, that's a win all round!

* * *

What I *haven't* told them yet is that for one of the weeks I'm off work, we're going on holiday. It was Dad's idea, and Dad's paying, of course. He made it sound like I'd be doing him a favour by accepting, and originally he wanted to take us abroad somewhere, but I told him the kids are too little to appreciate that, and it would be frankly too much hassle. Instead, we're going to Cornwall. Dad will drive us all down there, and he's booked us into a lovely hotel right by the beach, where there are lots of facilities for families, and places to visit. I hope he's not going to find it all too hectic and end up regretting it, but he insists he's looking forward to it, talking about it like an excited schoolboy, a light back in his eyes that had died the day my mum did.

* * *

The next event at the bookshop – a summer-themed one – goes even better than the Easter one. The shop is crowded out for both sessions. My friends turn up for the morning one, having secretly agreed to surprise me, and they all tell me afterwards how impressed they are with what I've organised.

'You're really good at this stuff, Jess!' squawks Miranda afterwards, and I try not to be offended by the surprise in her voice.

They've all queued up to buy the new summer novel whose author has been speaking this morning. 'You should look into doing event management full-time,' she adds. 'You could earn a lot more than you do here.'

'I don't think so,' I say. 'I'm happy here. For now, anyway. It works for me. And it works for the children. That's all that matters.'

Helen and Robert bring Mia and Archie along for the afternoon session, and Dad comes too. The children's authors I've booked to talk this afternoon are both brilliant, reading from their books to an enthusiastic audience; one of them even acts out parts of his story as he's reading, swapping his hat every time a different character's talking. It's hilarious and the children convulse with laughter. Mia pleads to be bought a copy of the book afterwards, and Archie asks the author for one of his hats! Later, Tariq shows me coverage of the event on local news media, and I must admit I'm chuffed to see pictures of myself with the authors, and posing with Margaret, Tariq and Emma.

'Taking on this event work has been good for you,' Dad says later when I show him the articles and the photos. 'Good for your self-confidence, I think, and you obviously enjoy it.' He pauses, then adds, 'But I've been wondering if you've ever considered doing what you always wanted – teaching. You could still do it, you know. You have it in you. I've seen it – the way you are with the children. You have a natural urge to educate, to bring out the best in them.'

'That's just because they're mine.' I turn to him and shake my head. 'Of course I can't do it, Dad. I don't have any qualifications for a start, and how exactly would I be able to go to uni now?'

To be honest, I can't deny I think about it sometimes. But I know it's just a daydream.

'Besides, teaching is a really tough job these days,' I add.

'As tough as what you're doing now? Working full-time, juggling the childcare? I don't think so. You'd never have to worry about school holidays again, for a start. And as a mature student, you'd only need GCSEs in English, maths and science – you got those, didn't you.'

'Somehow.' I shrug. 'But it's not going to happen, Dad. It's too late. I've got a job, I can pay the rent, that's all that matters now.'

'But it might not *always* be all that matters,' he says softly. 'Don't rule it out, Jess. You're not on your own now – you've got me. I've been considering taking early retirement for a long while; I'm fortunate, I can afford to, but I always worried that I'd be bored. I wouldn't be, though, if I were to be spending time with my grandchildren.'

I turn and gape at him. 'Now you're being unrealistic. I'm grateful for the help you're giving me now, but there's no way that's going to happen. I can't go to uni – quite apart from anything else, I'd never be able to afford it!'

'But I could,' he says.

'That's ridiculous. I'm not going to be a teacher, I'm quite happy doing what I'm doing.'

'If you say so,' he says gently, with a smile. 'But it's a serious proposal, Jess, so just… promise you'll consider it.'

'OK.' I laugh and agree. 'Perhaps I'll think it over while I'm lying on the beach in Cornwall.'

* * *

And so, for now, everything continues in the way I'd planned, the way that the children and I are comfortable with, and that I can cope with – just about, anyway. Mia's enjoying the holiday club better this time. Archie's as easy-going as ever about being left at nursery. Helen and Robert are, let's face it, the perfect childminders, who quite clearly dote on both children and I know they'll regret, for the rest of their lives, the mistake they made with Callum. Dad is living his dream; he's working less hours, 'winding down to an early retirement', as he puts it, and throwing himself into grandparenthood with gusto. He looks ten years younger, and Mia and Archie adore him.

I know my life's still not perfect. I still find it hard work – and stressful – working full-time while the children are so young, even with the help I'm now so grateful for. I'd love to spend more time with them. Archie will be two in November, and his baby days will soon be a distant memory. Mia already gives me cause, occasionally, to imagine what she'll be like as a teenager – when she sighs and raises her eyes at me, or begs for a new T-shirt or a particular toy because one of her friends has got it – and Dad often warns me about how fast they'll grow up.

So, yes, there are decisions I have to make.

Should I continue in a job that's so far worked well for me, and now gives me some added responsibility and satisfaction, to say nothing of a little extra pay? Or should I take Dad up on his offer to fund me through a teaching degree?

But there's one thing I have definitely decided: I'm going to make a statement to the police about Callum. I've always thought that if I had to go to court, I'd have trouble facing him. I worried that I might go to pieces, damage the fragile recovery I've made so far and have nightmares just from looking at him.

But now, I feel stronger. I'm ready. In fact, I think it could be a great feeling to look into his eyes and speak out about what he did to me. It will be a matter of pride to have helped convict him, perhaps even helped to stop him hurting someone else.

I'm not that troubled teenager any more, the hurt and grieving adolescent who rushed into a relationship with the first man who showed an interest in me, rushed into living with him, rushed into having my children. I know better now; I'm a grown-up, and most importantly, I'm a mother. My decisions will impact Mia and Archie, the most important people in my life. I'll never forget that.

I might not be the best mum in the world – because as my dad says, every parent makes mistakes, has regrets, thinks they should have done things differently. Sometimes I get cross, I get impatient, I'm too tired to give the children all the attention they deserve. I take the easy options, don't insist on them eating broccoli and I probably let them watch too much TV. No, I'm not perfect.

But they know how much I love them, and I do the best I can. And I think... I'm *sure*, now, that that makes me, if not a really *great* mother... at least good enough. *I hope you'd have been proud of me, Mum. I like to think you would.*

ACKNOWLEDGEMENTS

Thanks to Emily Yau and everyone at Boldwood Books, for all the hard work that goes on behind the scenes. We authors are just one part of a busy and talented team.

ABOUT THE AUTHOR

Sheila Norton is the author of contemporary, feel-good fiction set in Devon. In 2022 she won the RNA's Best Christmas Novel for her twenty-third book *Winter at Cliff's End Cottage*.

Sign up to Sheila Norton's mailing list here for news, competitions and updates on future books.

Visit Sheila Norton's Website: www.sheilanorton.com

Follow Sheila Norton on social media:

 x.com/NortonSheilaann
facebook.com/SheilaNortonAuthor

Boldwood

Boldwood Books is an award-winning fiction publishing company seeking out the best stories from around the world.

Find out more at www.boldwoodbooks.com

Join our reader community for brilliant books, competitions and offers!

Follow us
@BoldwoodBooks
@TheBoldBookClub

Sign up to our weekly deals newsletter

https://bit.ly/BoldwoodBNewsletter

Milton Keynes UK
Ingram Content Group UK Ltd.
UKHW040916070224
437358UK00004B/146

9 781785 136610